Praise for Alan Govenar

"Govenar turns the reader into a hitchhiker in this beautiful, often trippy, and intimate exploration of the search for meaning when innocence is lost. Amidst the complex backdrop of the 1970s, an eighteen-year-old pseudo-hippie sets out to find answers without knowing the questions. His search for love, identity, purity, restoration, and his voice in the overwhelming and infinite universe, takes the reader on a fast-paced journey across North America. It is raw and haunting and will stay with the reader long after the final page is read."

—HANNES BARNARD, AUTHOR OF *HALLEY'S COMET*

"Haunting, heartbreaking, and always life-affirming, *The Early Years of Rhythm & Blues* is a triumph of the spirit and a celebration of the soul."

—NEW YORK TIMES

"There may be no regional genre of music more prone to tooting its own horn than Texas blues, and with good reason. Alan Govenar's new book, *Texas Blues* . . . is the finest, most comprehensive roundup yet."

—AUSTIN CHRONICLE

"In this compact, vivid hybrid, Govenar transforms his taped and transcribed interviews with dancer Norma Miller into her account of life as a globetraveling Lindy Hopper in the 1930s and '40s . . . Govenar captures both Miller's remarkable experiences (including incidents of racism on the road) and her sparkling evocation of American music and dance when swing was king."

—KIRKUS REVIEWS

"Govenar deftly teases out . . . a dialogue about race, justice, and class in America."

—HUFFINGTON POST ON *TEXAS IN PARIS*

Other Books by Alan Govenar

The Early Years of Rhythm and Blues
Stoney Knows How: Life as a Sideshow Tattoo Artist
Meeting the Blues: The Rise of the Texas Sound
Portraits of Community: African American Photography in Texas
Stompin' at the Savoy: The Norma Miller Story
Extraordinary Ordinary People:
Five American Masters of Traditional Arts
Texas Blues: The Rise of a Contemporary Sound
Osceola: Memories of a Sharecropper's Daughter
Lightnin' Hopkins: His Life and Blues
Texas in Paris
Boccaccio in the Berkshires
Deep Ellum and Central Track
See That My Grave is Kept Clean

Come Round Right

A novel

Alan Govenar

DEEP VELLUM PUBLISHING
DALLAS, TEXAS

Deep Vellum Publishing
3000 Commerce Street, Dallas, Texas 75226
deepvellum.org · @deepvellum

Deep Vellum is a 501c3 nonprofit literary arts organization founded in 2013 with the mission to bring the world into conversation through literature.

Copyright © 2025 Alan Govenar.

First U.S. edition, 2025
All rights reserved.

Support for this publication has been provided in part by grants from the National Endowment for the Arts, the Texas Commission on the Arts, the City of Dallas Office of Arts and Culture, the Communities Foundation of Texas, and the Addy Foundation.

LIBRARY OF CONGRESS CATALOGING-IN-PUBLICATION DATA:

Names: Govenar, Alan B., 1952- author.
Title: Come round right / a novel by Alan Govenar.
Description: Dallas, Texas : Deep Vellum Publishing, 2025.
Identifiers: LCCN 2024042602 (print) | LCCN 2024042603 (ebook) | ISBN 9781646053742 (hardback) | ISBN 9781646053872 (epub)
Subjects: LCGFT: Novels. Classification: LCC PS3557.O918 C66 2025 (print) | LCC PS3557.O918 (ebook) | DDC 813/.54--dc23/eng/20240924
LC record available at https://lccn.loc.gov/2024042602
LC ebook record available at https://lccn.loc.gov/2024042603

Cover art and design by Daniel Benneworth-Gray
Interior layout and typesetting by Andrea Garcia Flores

PRINTED IN THE UNITED STATES OF AMERICA

Based on true events, names and identifying details have been changed and rewoven into fiction. This book gives voice to parts of me that I have kept private for more than fifty years, bringing to life feelings I have learned to live with, feelings that have shaped who I have become.

RIDE #14
MARCH 21, 1971
8:07 A.M.

FACING THE TRAFFIC ON THE 11TH AVENUE entry ramp to I-71 South, my duffle bag slung over my shoulder, I thrust my thumb into the cold morning air.

The Nashville skyline is calling me.

With a truth to tell.

A twangy sound with a heavy percussive beat.

Bob Dylan's "Like a Rolling Stone" mixed with Walt Whitman's "Song of the Open Road."

The Nashville skyline. Three hundred and seventy-nine miles away.

The lodestone for me.

A magnet. Pulling me closer each step of the way.

The freeway is teasing me. Seeing my past in the faces of strangers in the car windows speeding past me.

Thunderstorms rumble in the distance.

I take a deep breath.

It's the first day of spring.

Hoping for someone to make eye contact with me, Aaron. Aaron Berg. Eighteen years old. A hippie with frizzy hair and a scar on my chin. A scruffy pea coat I bought in a second-hand store. Washed-out bell bottoms. A Woodstock patch sewn on one back pocket and a peace sign embroidered on the other.

I rub my palms together. I'm freezing inside.

A car slows down and stops on the gravel shoulder about fifteen feet in front of me. The rear passenger door creaks open, and a puppy darts out of the car to poop. A little girl, maybe four years old, is close behind, but slips. I drop my duffle bag and scoop her up, her hands clutching my neck, my left arm holding her tightly, as I catch the puppy with my right hand.

The girl's mother hurries toward me.

I'm out of breath. I lower the girl and the puppy onto the back seat of the car as gracefully as I can but almost topple over.

"You're the nicest man ever," the girl giggles.

I feel like a clown.

Her mother looks at my duffle bag, and then at me, grateful for my help. I can tell she disapproves of hitchhiking, but she seems to understand I'm in need. She says she'll give me a ride and motions for me to sit next to her in the front passenger seat.

"My name's Angie."

"I'm Aaron," I reply, glancing at her mint green eyes.

I don't know what to say. Just like I never knew what to say to girls like her in high school. She has a blond ponytail and starched blue and white striped blouse, with a pointy nose and narrow chin bobbing up and down as she talks.

"I'm not going very far," she says in a cheery voice, and then raises the index finger of her right hand up to her lips. "Shh . . . shh . . . . I love the way Jenny breathes when she's sleeping. I don't even have to look. I can tell."

"Yeah." I nod. "Cute."

I sink into my seat, withdrawing, musing about the healing powers of the lodestone. Deep down I know I can be more than who I am right now. I just need to get there.

Scouring the landscape, I'm lost in my thoughts.

We drive for about twenty-five miles, and she drops me off near an on-ramp to the freeway that looks just like the one I started from. I thank her, and she drives away, her tires squealing as she speeds off the gravel shoulder onto the blacktop.

RIDE #15
MARCH 21, 1971
9:45 A.M.

EVERYTHING I WANT TO FORGET POPS IN and out of my head. It's as if I'm stuck in a pinball machine in an arcade I've never seen before, my memories ricocheting off the bumpers but never scoring any points.

The clouds overhead thicken.

I have this gnawing feeling in my gut. If I had only done this... then that... then what?

Finally, a car stops. A dinged-up white Oldsmobile. The passenger door opens slowly. The driver is a gray-haired woman, with heavy bags under her eyes, sizing me up before she waves me in with a little grin.

The interior of the car smells like air freshener, a mix of cinnamon and cloves, sort of like a Christmas cookie.

"I'm a talker," she says. "But not a chatterbox. I'm okay with quiet. It's the companionship that matters. That's what I like about hitchhikers. They want to reach out, see the world and meet people, trust people. Believe me, we need more of that."

"Yeah, that's for sure."

"I can just tell you're on a mission. I can see it in your eyes. Where you headed?"

"Nashville." I smile.

"Well, you got a long way to go." She chuckles. "I can only take you about fifty miles. Then I have to scoot off on my own to see my daughter and my newest grandbaby. Why, he has the biggest dimples I've ever seen."

I focus on the road ahead and she stops talking, giving me room to space out. But as much as I want my mind to go blank, it won't.

"To be honest," she says, "I don't know much about hippies, and I was kind of thinking I might learn something from you. Some people are just poseurs, you know, pretending to be someone they're not, and I pray you're not one of them."

"Don't worry. I'm not."

"Then why are you acting so pouty?"

"Pouty? In my heart . . . I . . . uh . . . have a lot of love to give."

"Then show it!" she exclaims, pulling one of her hands off the steering wheel and waving it in front of my face.

"I'm trying. Believe me. It's just that these days . . . I'm having a hard time . . . I mean, it has nothing to do with you."

She purses her lips, acknowledging me in a way that makes me feel worse, but seems to make her feel better, and she leaves me alone, freeing me to gaze out the window. The landscape glides by, the sun flickering through the trees, reminding me of the flipbooks I loved to make when I was a kid.

"It's okay," she says. "Whatever you're going through, it will pass. If you ask for forgiveness, you will receive it."

My mother used to say those same words. It didn't matter what I was doing, she could always find something that was wrong, whether I didn't tuck my shirt in right or wasn't washing my face with acne soap. She made me feel so self-conscious that I kept mostly to myself. If the kids in my class rushed to be first in the lunch line, I hung back. And when they grabbed a table in the middle of the cafeteria, I watched from afar and found my own seat in a different area of the room, usually with kids I didn't know. I liked watching what was going on but didn't feel the need to participate. Sometimes I felt as if I was an extra in the movie of my life.

Then I met Adriana, and she took my hand, leading me through the fog to places I could never have found on my own.

Adriana always had a direction in mind; I didn't. I longed for one, wishing I had some goal or end that might guide me and give me purpose, hoping it was just one more ride away.

SEPTEMBER 18, 1970
3:15 P.M.

WHEN I SAW ADRIANA FOR THE FIRST TIME, I was in the lobby of my dorm, wiggling the key out of the lock of my mailbox. Grumbling. "How could I be so stupid?"

And she ambled up to me with a swagger. "You're right. You do look stupid."

My jaw dropped and she giggled. "I don't want to hurt your feelings, but . . . " Then she flashed a peace sign, spreading the index and middle finger of her hand and waved it in front of me in a circular motion, beckoning me to come closer so she could show off the goodies that were neatly wrapped inside the box she was carrying. One by one, she pulled them out. "Prosciutto," she said proudly. "Soppressata di Calabria, pickled eggplant, grain mustard, peppered crostini, and almond biscotti. Want to picnic?"

"Sure!" I smiled. I was done with classes for the day, and apparently, she was too. I couldn't believe it. A girl like her interested in me.

We walked outside and sat on the stone wall surrounding the shady commons near the dorm. And she pivoted around, gazing up at the sky, and placed her picnic box onto the grass.

"Wow . . . this is so cool."

"Me, or the food?" Adriana joked.

"Both."

Adriana pulled a thermos from her knapsack and offered me a swig of red wine.

"Where'd you get that? How old are you, anyway?"

"Eighteen . . . just like you, I bet."

"Well, yeah, but you got to be twenty-one to buy wine."

"That's true," she said coyly. "But I have an ID. A very special one. A driver's license that a friend made for me last summer in New York. Let's say I have connections, you know, to people who can do things others can't."

"Connections?"

Adriana rolled her eyes. "Okay," she admitted. "There's a guy who works for my father and, well, I guess making me happy is part of his job."

"Huh? Sounds complicated."

"Not for my father," she said, then changed the subject back to the wine. "This Italian red is amazing. You can smell the aromas and taste the flavors of olives, rosemary, Mediterranean herbs, with a hint of eucalyptus. I could go on and on. It's a Frappato from a vineyard near Ragusa, a hilltop city in southeast Sicily, close to where my father's family lived for centuries, that is, until everyone moved to New York, you know, for business."

I raised my eyebrows. Acting silly. "Business?"

"In my father's family, every first son was named Cosimo Romano. And my father was number six."

"Importing wine?"

"Well, sort of." Adriana grinned.

"The only wine in my house was Manischewitz." I smiled. "A Berg family tradition. Concord grape. For Passover."

Adriana grimaced.

"That's right." I laughed. "Sweet and sticky."

"Well, I grew up on the best, little sips when I was a kid, a glass after I was confirmed in the Catholic church."

An early autumn birdsong swirled around in my brain. Was it a buzz from the wine, or was it just Adriana? I'd never met anyone like her.

After a few more swigs of wine, Adriana slid her arm around my waist, pulling me gently to her side, and I leaned into her. Her face relaxed, and as I watched, she seemed to space out, taking my hand into hers, inviting me into her own little universe.

I placed my hand on her thigh, scooting closer, and realized that she had a brace on her leg. Adriana didn't say anything about it. Finally, when she stood up, she straightened her leg nonchalantly and the brace snapped into place. I saw there was an ankle strap and metal stirrup attached to her shoe, but I was so drawn into her deep blue eyes that it didn't matter. She carried herself with a poise and grace that focused my attention away from her weak leg. She talked with her hands, rolling her wrists, and gesturing with her fingers, punctuating what she said and imbuing her face with a bright glow.

Adriana seemed so comfortable with who she was, even though she was different in a way that might make others insecure. Me, I'd always done whatever I could to fit in. It was like I was constantly trying to learn the dance that everyone else had always known. It was a riddle, a puzzle for which I could never seem to find the missing piece.

"What are you thinking about?" Adriana asked. "You're acting so moody. It's like you're with me, but you're not. Please, be here now!"

"I'm sorry."

"You better be. You're never going to find salami like this in Columbus."

"I'm sure of that."

Adriana wasn't satisfied. She gave me a hug and rested her face on my chest, and when she sensed my goosebumps, she laughed. Then she brushed back my kinky, lopsided hair with her palm and stroked my patchy boy's beard with her fingertips.

"You're adorable."

"Back at you," I said, smoothing my hand around her shoulder.

Adriana was beaming, and so was I.

As the day darkened around us, Adriana pulled a joint from a little pouch she had tied to the calf band of her leg brace, and when she leaned over and lit it up, I was ecstatic, but a little jittery. Somehow, the mix of anticipation and paranoia made the rush from the pot even more delicious. I had smoked grass a couple of times before, but never like this.

It was 1970, the fall after the May killing of four unarmed Kent State students by the National Guard at a Vietnam War protest. Even though Ohio State was more than a hundred miles away, National Guardsmen patrolled the campus every day.

Adriana took a long toke on the joint. "There's probably a soldier with a gun over there, hiding in the bushes across from us, spying on us, ready to attack when given the command."

"I'm ready." I laughed. "I had lots of guns when I was a kid."

"Is that so?"

"Yeah, plastic ones. Toys. My father was a cop."

"Really?"

"Well, not exactly. He got a job as a security guard in a hardware store right out of high school. He never carried a gun . . . well . . . that I knew about. But just his badge alone, that he kept in his top desk drawer, made me think he did."

"The men in my family were GI Joes—World War Two, the Korean War, Vietnam," Adriana said with a mix of pride and resolve. "I could go on and on."

I stared into the darkness under the trees and struggled to convince myself that there was no way we were going to get busted. I took the joint from Adriana and pulled in a big hit, holding it in before letting it escape very slowly from my lungs.

The jolt from the pot shook me up, and I was having trouble focusing.

"Something wrong?" Adriana asked. "You look like you've seen a ghost."

"Uh . . . no. I'm okay. I just need to pee."

"Oh, oh, oh," Adriana said with a silly smirk, looking at the bulge in my pants. "It must be hard to hold it in."

I could feel myself blushing.

"Oh, oh, oh . . ." Adriana smiled.

And at that moment, the sound of her voice carried me away. I drifted off. It was like she was singing but it wasn't her I was hearing. It was Sister Ethel. An old woman I met when I was a kid. She had a voice like that. It was like she was standing there in front of me. I stepped backwards, a little woozy, and said, "I'll be right back."

"Something wrong?" Adriana asked.

"No. No. I . . . uh . . . just got to go pee," I said under my breath and staggered off.

"Don't go too far." Adriana giggled. "You might get lost."

I was a Cub Scout when I met Sister Ethel. I was on my way home after a camping trip with my troop. And the bus got a flat tire in New Gloucester, Maine in the middle of a place called the Shaker Village.

It was early Sunday morning, and we had to wait for road service. The den mothers figured it was best for us to get off the bus. The air was crystal clear, the sun streaking across the farmland in front of us. A group of five or six Shakers approached us. They were all dressed in old-fashioned clothes that looked they were leftover costumes from a Hollywood movie.

I'd never heard of Shakers and giggled. "They're goofy."

"Who cares?" another Cub Scout said.

"Well, I do," an old Shaker woman said. "My name's Sister Ethel." Then she positioned herself between us and the den mothers. Everyone shut up.

"Good day, good day," she said with a smile, focusing on me. "We're not goofy."

I was embarrassed, thinking Sister Ethel was such a weird name. I was about to laugh, but I could feel her eyes studying me.

"We are all Shakers here," she began. "We believe above all that God is love."

Her face glowed in the morning light, and she motioned for me and then everyone else to follow her into a building that she called the Meeting House.

"We welcome you to join us in worship."

None of us knew what we were supposed to do. Two of the den mothers huddled together, and one finally stepped forward and said, "Thank you, Sister Ethel. Yes. A learning experience for all the Scouts, and for me."

A few of the kids groaned. Me, I just followed along.

A man with bushy grey hair greeted us. "What a glorious day!"

One by one we took our seats on a long wooden bench, and when the service began, I felt trapped, caged in by a religion I knew nothing about.

The man at the pulpit lifted a Bible from the table at his side and said, "We know you boys are Jewish. And some of you might feel strange being here, but for us, there are no strangers in God's house."

Sister Ethel stood up and sang "Oh, oh, oh," and the lyrics of her song carried me to a place I'd never been before. The melody was simple and the line "To turn, turn will be our delight" brightened me up. And when she was done singing, she walked over to me and said, "Bless you."

I nodded, and she handed me an LP in an off-white jacket with pale blue letters that read: "Praise Be, Sister Ethel Sings Shaker Hymns."

"Thank you," I said softly, and she smiled. "You are a very special boy, I can tell, even if you don't know it yet. God's will, God's way."

The rest of the day was better than expected. The Shakers even helped change the bus tire and sent us on our way with pimento cheese sandwiches, dried apples, and bottles of water.

When I got home, I was so charged up, I couldn't wait to tell my parents everything that had happened. But when I gushed about Sister Ethel's amazing voice, my mother tensed up. My father acted more understanding but didn't say much other than "that's interesting." I trudged off toward my bedroom and my mother followed me, telling me in a stern voice, "Stay away from those people. Shakers are a cult. They never marry, and they don't make babies. So one day, they're going to die off."

I was confused. I didn't really understand what she meant.

Once in my room, I kicked off my shoes and sat on the edge of my bed. I took my new LP out of my knapsack and began to hum Sister Ethel's song, "To turn, turn will be our delight." And from that day on, I never talked about Sister Ethel to my parents again, or anyone else. I hid that record between the mattress and box spring of my bed. It was my secret, and I only took it out when no one was around, listening to it on the record player in our den and trying to sing along.

I could see Adriana in the distance. It looked like she was getting ready to leave.

"Wait up!"

"What for?" She was miffed.

I hurried toward her, and apologized for taking so long, and after my third "I'm sorry," her face relaxed.

I wanted to tell her about Sister Ethel, but it was too much too soon. Just thinking about saying Sister Ethel's name aloud made me feel a little strange—a Jewish kid obsessing over a Shaker hymn.

"Do you have a UTI?" Adriana asked in a snarky voice. "Or does it always take you ten minutes to pee?"

"Not usually," I said timidly.

Adriana sighed. "That's a relief."

I started humming, hoping to change the vibe.

And Adriana loosened up. "I love to hum. Once upon a time, I sang in the choir at church."

"You did?"

"Yes . . . but let's not talk about that," Adriana said, and she gazed at me, and me at her, grooving on every second of our time together. Then I started giggling, and it wasn't long before Adriana joined in. All of a sudden, we were in synch without even trying.

From that moment on, I couldn't stay away from her. We started seeing each other every couple of days—after class, before class, any time of day and night. I never knew exactly what to expect, but whatever happened seemed just right. Every conversation seemed to flow, picking up where we'd left off, whether we were talking about Janis Joplin, The Supremes, or the protest rants of Abbie Hoffman, sitting in a burger joint, or cuddling on a couch in the dorm lobby. Then, one day, Adriana whispered into my ear, "I'm falling in love with you," and touched a place inside me that I never knew existed.

"Me, too," I said, and she cupped my cheeks in her hands, and eased her lips onto mine. We were dancing, and my feet never touched the ground.

RIDE #1
OCTOBER 2, 1970

WHEN ADRIANA SAID SHE WANTED TO GO to Buckeye Lake, it sounded so right. Her eyes widened and she looked like an angel. She couldn't stand still. No matter how little space she had, she found a way to move around, shifting from foot to foot, swirling her arms in the air and exaggerating every gesture. "We can hitchhike. It'll be easy."

"Indeed." I smiled. "I started hitchhiking in 1967—the Summer of Love. I was fifteen years old, and I'd heard about a Love-In on Boston Common, and there was no way my parents were going to let me go. I was a loner, so I just took off, but I didn't make it there. I got stopped by a policeman in Swampscott, who threatened to bring me to juvenile hall if I didn't turn around and walk home. Well, needless to say, I did what he said, but it didn't stop me. By the time I was a junior in high school, the roadways were filled with hitchhikers. It was like I had to stand in line just to give it a whirl."

Adriana rolled her eyes, and as I rambled on about my hitchhiking treks into Boston, I knew she was going to one-up me.

"Well," she said. "My best hitchhiking trip was to Woodstock, with my boyfriend. It was tough, but we plodded along like everyone else. The roads were lined with people just like us. It didn't matter how old you were or where you came from. We were all on the same mission."

I was jealous. "I had friends who went, but my parents wouldn't let me go."

Adriana poked me in the side and laughed, telling me how she had made her mother think she was going to spend the weekend at her girlfriend's parents' place in the Catskills.

"Woodstock changed my life, Aaron. Peace and love. I believed it. And I still do. For the first time in my life, I was with people who didn't just see me as a crippled kid with a leg brace. Not that my boyfriend saw me that way. But sometimes, even he acted a little strange when we were in public together."

"What do you mean?"

"It's hard to pinpoint one thing exactly. It's just the way I felt inside. And when we broke up, I was sure he was stalking me. I'd see him in places he never went to, but somehow, he knew that I did."

Adriana could tell I wanted to change the subject but wasn't quite ready to let me off the hook. "The way you're acting, Aaron, makes me wonder."

"Wonder?"

"Yes, wonder. I don't want to repeat the mistakes I've made before."

"How's that?"

"It's easier than you think, Aaron."

"I suppose..."

"I always wanted to be normal. But ultimately, I had to accept that normal doesn't exist."

"Yeah ... What matters, I think, is who we are right now, and hopefully that's enough."

"Maybe," Adriana smirked. "But on some level, we don't really have a choice. We've got to embrace what we have and not dwell on the rest. You know, love the one you're with ... oops, sorry, song lyric."

"Crosby, Stills, Nash & Young. Yeah!"

I moved closer to her. There was something about her that was drawing me in, and I was so ready.

"Oh, Aaron, I can't believe I actually met you."

Adriana's boobs stretched the seams of her red turtleneck sweater as she swooped her arms around me. She never wore a bra. She said it was because of her Italian roots. "My grandma told me she was born in a vineyard and during the first few weeks of her life, she took naps in a basket full of white grapes."

I wasn't sure what to say. In my mind, Adriana didn't look Italian at all. She had a Snow-White complexion and iron-straight blond hair that reminded me of Joni Mitchell.

Adriana grabbed my hand and headed toward the front door. The sky was hazy, and the air had the woody smell of autumn. Dusty leaves swirled in a light breeze across the asphalt in front of us. Adriana danced backwards, weaving her hands around me. It was like I was standing in the middle of a merry-go-round, and all the carousel animals had Adriana's face. When we reached the freeway, I stuck out my thumb and Adriana mimicked my every move. She loved teasing me, but in the most endearing ways: shadowing me, hugging me from behind, tickling me in the side.

It wasn't long before a Ford Bronco stopped. The driver rolled down the window to ask where we were going, and when I told him, he reached over and opened the back door.

Adriana scooted onto the seat, releasing the lock on her brace, and then lifted her weak leg quickly onto the floorboard. I sat in the front. The radio was blaring a strange mix of bluegrass, gospel, and country pop.

The driver said his name was Yancy, but he didn't say much else. He just focused on the road ahead without ever seeming to pay much attention to us. His profile was chiseled and a little severe, but when he sang along with the radio, the crow's feet around his eyes loosened up. I couldn't understand why Yancy had decided to pick up a couple of hippie college kids. Adriana bopped around on the back seat as we drove along, giving every sign of grooving to Yancy's music.

Finally, Yancy spoke up. "I'm so glad I stopped. I needed, well, you know, a little break from being by myself. I mean, you know, sometimes I feel like I'm living a country and western song, lonely and heartsick. Stuck in a place I'd rather not be."

Adriana leaned forward and placed her hand gently on Yancy's shoulder. "I can identify with that, and I don't even like country music." Yancy glanced at me, as if he was looking for permission to talk to Adriana. I was out of my element. I wanted to say, "It's not up to me," but didn't.

"My girlfriend left me for someone I thought was my friend, and I'm just boiling up inside."

"What happened?" Adriana asked.

Yancy scowled. "Don't get me started."

Adriana didn't respond, sensing that she was making both Yancy and me uncomfortable.

"I just don't want to be punished for my feelings," Yancy muttered.

I nodded. "Been there, done that."

"I thought you never had a girlfriend in high school," Adriana blurted out.

"I didn't," I said under my breath. "But . . . well . . . because I didn't think any of the girls I was attracted to would ever go out with me."

"Now, you're talking my language." Yancy laughed.

"Boys are so dumb; I can't believe it." Adriana giggled.

Yancy turned the volume up on the radio, and nothing more was said. I watched the mile markers on the side of the road, confused, replaying the innuendos of Adriana's voice in a recording that sounded different each time I heard it.

After a while, Yancy slowed down. "This is my exit."

I was impatient, but Adriana placed her hand again on Yancy's shoulder, whispering, "Thank you," and he replied, "God bless."

When we got out of the car, I looked at Adriana, and she smiled. "You gotta love Yancy. Man, he was a trip."

"Did I say something I shouldn't have?"

"If anything, Aaron, you didn't say enough."

"What?"

Adriana acted as if there was nothing wrong. And that was enough. It was kind of strange, but I didn't want to second-guess what Yancy, or Adriana for that matter, was really thinking.

"All good?" Adriana asked.

"As good as it gets."

"You look worried," she said. "Something wrong?"

"Well..."

"C'mon, Aaron. If you don't tell me, I'm going to shut down."

I couldn't tell who was more insecure. Me or her. So I brushed it off and muttered, "I really am in love with you."

"Back at you," Adriana giggled. "But remember, when you think of me, I'll always be fine, fine as red wine in the summertime."

And I said in a shaky voice, "I don't know that I've ever had red wine in the summertime."

Adriana reached over and interlocked her fingers into mine and cooed, "Poor baby," bussing my cheek with a silly kiss. "You're going to love it."

RIDE #2
OCTOBER 2, 1970

I RAISED MY THUMB INTO THE AIR, and after about ten minutes a beat-up Pontiac Catalina pulled over. The man and the woman in the front seat were dressed in saffron-colored robes.

"Welcome," the woman said, watching Adriana adjust her brace. "Where you headed?"

I cleared my throat. "Buckeye Lake,"

And she nodded. "Wonderful. We can take you to the South entrance."

Once we were settled, the couple started chanting, "Hare Krishna, Hare Krishna, Krishna Krishna, Hare Hare, Hare Rama, Hare Rama, Rama Rama, Hare Hare," and didn't stop until Adriana asked to be let out near one of the hiking trails.

Part of me was elated, glad to be at our destination, but the rest of me wanted to hear more of their chanting—the mantras resonating within me, connecting me to the times I hitchhiked into Harvard Square. Hare Krishna kids usually clustered together outside the MTA station, chanting, playing small hand cymbals and other exotic instruments. It was hypnotic and reminded me of the way I felt when I first heard Sister Ethel singing Shaker hymns. I was in harmony with my life, if only for a few minutes.

Adriana pushed open the car door.

"Peace be with you," the man said, and the woman handed Adriana a copy of the Bhagavad-Gita.

Adriana tried to be polite, but when we left the car, she pinched her fingers together and scoffed, "Cosa pensano di fare!"

"What?"

"It's Italian. It's a nice, maybe not so nice, way of saying, 'What do you think you're doing?' I don't know what to make of that religion, but one thing's for sure: it's not for me."

I shrugged. "Personally, I kind of admire their . . . uh . . . devotion."

Adriana gave me a sidelong look.

"I mean it," I said softly.

Adriana shook her head, as if I was so wrong and she was right. She walked ahead of me into a small meadow just east of the hiking trail, spreading out the Indian blanket she had brought with her in a beach bag. I hurried to catch up, and when I sat down next to her, she nestled up to me. I repositioned myself, careful not to bump into her braced leg.

Adriana sensed my nervousness and said, "Get over it, Aaron. I've worn a brace ever since I started to walk and can do just about anything anyone else can and maybe more."

"That's for sure. I just don't want to hurt you, you know, by accident."

"I get it. But remember, I'm okay with it. I learned a long time ago that this is my cross to bear. Look, my weak leg, my paralyzed leg, the doctors said, was caused by a birth defect. It wasn't my mother's fault, and it isn't mine. This is who I am. Love it or leave it."

Just listening to Adriana made me think more about all the stuff I'd carried inside since I was a kid, stuff that made me wonder who I truly was and who I really wanted to be.

Adriana sat with her arms wrapped around her knees, leaning against me. The clouds streaked across the horizon, mottling the light across the wild grass in front of us. I gazed up at the sky looking for answers, and the crows in the buckeye trees seemed to echo what was going on in my head.

Adriana took my hands into hers. "Look into my eyes and tell me what you see."

I was speechless.

She laughed. "It's not that difficult! I'll go first."

She stared into my eyes, a smile tweaking the corners of her lips. "In your eyes, I see chocolate, maybe a little hazelnut."

I could barely focus on what she was saying. I was so turned on by the patchouli oil she used as perfume.

"When you smile, Aaron, there's a hint of cognac."

"Well, for me," I murmured, "your eyes are like sapphires . . . rare and oh, so exquisite."

Adriana nuzzled my earlobe and then lay back on the blanket. I stretched out beside her, and we watched the huge cumulus clouds blowing across the skyscape spread out above us.

"Aaron, tell me, have you ever met anyone like me?"

"Never. I can hardly believe you're actually real."

Adriana inched herself closer to me as if she wanted me to kiss her, but instead turned onto her side. I spooned up next to her.

Adriana purred, "Let's listen to our breathing."

Then she turned over and cradled me in her arms. In the pulsing of her fingers, I sensed that no matter how strong she said she was, a part of her was still vulnerable.

I closed my eyes, but just as I was losing track of time, Adriana sprang up and giggled. "Let's thumb wrestle."

I reached for her hand, and we fumbled around, thrusting our thumbs up and down and around. Adriana's thumb was shorter than mine but difficult to trap.

"Are you double-jointed?" I asked, frustrated that I couldn't pin her thumb down.

Adriana snickered, pressing her thumbnail into the fleshy part of mine, flipping her hand slightly to the side to catch me by surprise.

I jerked her thumb back, and she almost lost her balance, but lunged herself into my lap, nearly knocking me over. We laughed so hard that I got hiccups. Adriana held her breath, and I did the same, and after a few minutes, the hiccups subsided.

"You are such a goof," Adriana cackled, and I blushed.

Adriana straightened up, and our lips touched ever so lightly.

A part of me felt off-balance, but I knew that something important was happening between us.

"Time to go, silly boy," she said playfully and stood up, pretending that she was flying. She spread her arms out to the side and said in a lilting voice, "Gliding like an eagle."

RIDE #3
OCTOBER 2, 1970

WE MADE IT BACK TO THE HIGHWAY and had no trouble getting a lift. A scrawny-looking guy with a long ponytail in a rusted-out Chevy Malibu slowed to a stop. He peered out the window with bloodshot eyes and said, "Been up partying all night. But believe me. I'm fine. Mighty fine."

There was a floppy-eared basset hound curled up at his side.

"He's just an old coot, like me," the guy laughed. "Better watch it, he might yawn, or even worse, fart."

Adriana and I squeezed into the back seat, and before he jammed his foot on the accelerator, he lit a narrow stick of incense and propped it up in the ashtray. Then he popped an eight-track tape into the player bolted under the dashboard. The sounds of the Fifth Dimension singing about the Age of Aquarius filled the car, and the guy rambled on about how he was the most hopeful person on earth. But his voice was so raspy that we wished we had earplugs.

After about twenty-five miles, he dropped off us at the entrance to his exit ramp, and when we got out of the car, we were both a little trippy, wondering what we had just been breathing in.

"Incense plus," Adriana giggled, and I swung my head back and forth.

Adriana jabbed me in the side, and within minutes of sticking my thumb out, another car stopped. Inside was a middle-aged Black woman named Blanche, who didn't say much, but hummed spirituals, heartfelt and resonant, the rest of the way to Columbus. Adriana sat in the front seat, and I stretched out behind her.

Blanche's voice was so sonorous that I drifted off into another world, somewhere between waking and sleeping. And when Blanche pulled off the freeway to let us out, I didn't want to leave. I told her I loved her singing, and she just looked at me with her big brown eyes glowing.

"That so?" she asked humbly in a southern accent, and then said, "That's very kind."

At the dorm, Adriana invited me up to her room and offered me her special blend of cinnamon and clove sun tea that she had made the previous day.

I stumbled backward, acting as if I was intoxicated.

Adriana joked, "You really are a nerd. That's what I love about you."

And I melted. Even though we lived in a co-ed dorm, I had never been on one of the girls' floors. Just being in Adriana's room made me feel like a voyeur. There were lace panties in a heap on one of the desks, a makeup kit opened on another, an eyebrow pencil on the floor, a lipstick tube uncapped, and books splayed out with highlighters stuck in their spines.

Adriana turned and faced me with a look that asked me to come closer. I stepped toward her, and she put her arms around me and kissed me with a passion that made me dizzy. Her tongue was electric in my mouth. I so wanted to please her. She ran her fingers through my hair and said in a seductive voice, "Is this your first time?"

"Yes...yes," I whispered, hoping I wasn't going to disappoint her.

Adriana interlocked her fingers with mine, and said, "Just relax... just relax. You're doing fine."

Adriana's eyes led me to her bed and eased me backward onto the mattress, propping herself on top of me, unbuckling my belt and unbuttoning my jeans in a flurry of movement that turned me on in ways I never thought possible. She slipped off her clothes, then loosened the straps on her brace and took it off, lowering it carefully onto the floor beside the bed. I looked at Adriana in awe as she pivoted around so gracefully, and then gazed at the empty brace without her leg inside, marveling at the effort that she made every day to wear it. I turned onto my side and extended my arms, stretching my fingers around Adriana's waist in a tender embrace, pulling her gently toward me.

Adriana eased forward. The shapes and sensations of her legs on mine excited me, and as I touched her skin, my body tingled. The toes on Adriana's left foot twitched ever so slightly, and her knee rolled to the side as she placed her hand lightly on my belly and drew intricate patterns on my skin with her fingertips. Her thighs were milky white and flushed pink as I massaged them.

Adriana tickled my ear with her tongue, and we toppled over as she guided me between her thighs and her lips engaged mine. Our bodies merged together in an intensifying rhythm. My heart was beating fast, and my skin felt aglow.

Adriana thrust her hips forward, rocking me deep inside her, uttering sounds that defied words, sounds flooding me with emotions I never knew existed within me. Her hands tightened around my forearms, and my body surged up and down, up and down, up and down.

Adriana's breathing calmed and her body relaxed. I felt so completely in love. Adriana rested her face on my chest. But as she rolled over onto her side, I saw tears in the corners of her eyes.

"Are you okay?"

Adriana turned toward me. "I'm more than okay, Aaron . . . so much more than I could have ever imagined. I have never felt this kind of love."

I could barely catch my breath: "Me too. Me too."

Adriana pecked my ear with her lips.

I closed my eyes, and she snuggled closer, her skin so warm and smooth. I floated off into a dreamy landscape of swirling clouds and muted colors. I felt Adriana watching me. When I looked up, she was starry-eyed, riffing on how she wanted to start planning our next trip.

"To Niagara Falls!" she exclaimed.
"Niagara Falls? Wow! Really?"
Adriana sat up. "Yes!"
"I'm ready. When do you want to go?"
"Sometime soon." Adriana giggled. "Very soon."

When she talked about Niagara Falls, she could barely contain herself. And the more she rambled on about it, the date she wanted to leave kept getting closer. After reading in the Old Farmer's Almanac that Buffalo usually had its first snow by October 25, she pleaded with me to leave on November 1—All Saint's Day—convincing me that stars and the planets would be in exactly the right place.

RIDE #4

NOVEMBER 1, 1970

ON THE MORNING WE LEFT FOR NIAGARA FALLS, Adriana woke me up early. I was so sound asleep that I thought the phone ringing was just in my head.

"What? Uh... I was in the middle of a dream," I said, pulling the receiver closer to my ear, stumbling through my words. "Adriana. Oh, Adriana, you were there in never-never land, and I was spinning around, and you were waving an American flag in my face. Crazy, huh?"

Adriana was impatient. "Tell me later... okay?"

"Yeah ... sure."

"Aaron, I have to tell you something. I got this amazing vibe in the shower this morning. It was like I was channeling. As if someone was speaking to me in an unearthly voice, insisting that we leave the dorm at exactly one o'clock this afternoon. I know all this sounds spacey. But please, believe me."

I was stunned. "All right, but... I just hope we have enough time to get where we need to be. We have a six o'clock check-in at a youth hostel in Ashtabula that I heard about from one of the kids of my floor, and I called. And hey, I booked us a place to stay."

Adriana gushed, "That's great! Really. But please, get a grip. I know what I'm doing. I only want to do what's best for you and me."

We'd only budgeted fifty bucks for the whole trip, and I didn't want to spend most of it on a motel room on the first night. But sure enough, when we finally got to the highway and Adriana put her thumb in the air, the first car stopped: a businessman in a suit and tie on his way to visit his mother in Euclid, not far from Ashtabula.

I could hardly believe that Adriana's premonition was so right. Not only was he going exactly where we were headed, he was driving a new BMW. Walking toward the car, Adriana strutted along, proud of herself.

The driver looked to be about twenty-five, with short black hair and a neatly trimmed moustache. Probably under the influence of Adriana's vibe, he said that she reminded him of a girl he knew when he was a kid. But then, he rambled on about himself as he drove down the highway, bragging that he worked in the sales and marketing division of a Fortune 500 company.

Glancing at Adriana in the back seat, I caught her eye roll. I shrugged. It didn't matter to me that the guy was so full of himself. I'd never been in a BMW, and everything about it wowed me—the control panel, the stereo, the steering wheel, even the carpet.

But if the driver was pleased that I liked his car, he gave no sign. If anything, my enthusiasm seemed to annoy him. He turned up the radio. It was tuned to a Top 40 station and the music drowned out any chance of further conversation.

I turned around to look at Adriana, and she poked her index finger into her mouth, as if to say if she had to listen to any more of this awful music, she was going to puke. We both snickered, and the driver's eyes flashed toward Adriana, in the rearview mirror, then at me. Still, he didn't say anything.

When we got to the Ashtabula exit, the driver pulled off the freeway, telling us he knew where the hostel was and that he wanted to drop us off at the front door because he remembered how much it sucked to be a freshman in college.

I thanked him for helping us out, and he smirked. "Stay well. That is, if you can."

Adriana intertwined her fingers with mine. "What I love best about hitchhiking is that you don't have to live the lives of the people who give you rides."

"That's what you think," I joked. "But that's not necessarily so."

Adriana tightened her grasp on my hand.

"Don't you think you were a little harsh," I said timidly. "I mean, he did drop us off exactly where we wanted to go."

Adriana sighed. "Enough. I may act tough, but I'm a pussycat inside. Believe me."

"Ha!" I smiled. "With big fangs."

Adriana poked me in the side, and playfully pulled me toward her.

At the entrance of the youth hostel, a balding middle-aged man with a big gut greeted us at the front door. He extended his hand and grasped mine with a firm shake. "I'm Gus, well, actually Augustus, but in school kids called me Max. And I never really understood why."

Adriana and I introduced ourselves, without saying much more than our names, and Gus recited the house rules in a formal voice and then asked if we were married. We shook our heads no, and he told us we had to sleep in separate rooms. "God's will, God's way," he said in solemn voice that reminded me of Sister Ethel, explaining that the youth hostel was an outreach mission of a local Catholic church. I didn't really care so much, but Adriana was freaked out and pulled me away from Gus, stammering that she wanted to look for another place to stay. It reminded her of the convent where she went to school as a kid and was paddled by the nuns if she stepped out of line.

Adriana was more mercurial than I'd realized, and as much I wanted to be sympathetic about her past and her bad memories, this hostel was only five bucks for the night, ten for both of us. Adriana and I stared at each other in a kind of stalemate, and finally she gave in.

Gus showed us to our respective rooms, in opposite wings of the building. We expected to see some other people, but it soon became clear that we were the only ones staying the night. Gus offered us dinner, but Adriana insisted she wasn't hungry and trudged off to her room.

I followed Gus into the kitchen, and we sat together at a small table. Gus said grace, and while we ate, Gus and I swapped small talk about the weather and the forecast for the upcoming days.

"Hitchhiking to Niagara Falls might not be such a good idea at this time of year," Gus muttered.

"But that's the point. To see the Falls with no one else around."

"Do you trust in the Lord?" Gus asked, knitting his brow, clearly concerned about our well-being.

I swallowed hard.

"Do you believe in Jesus?"

"I ... uh ... was raised Jewish ... and ... uh ... I know Jesus was a Jew."

"Indeed," Gus said solemnly, lifting his Bible from a side table. "'If you declare with your mouth, Jesus is Lord, and believe in your heart that God raised him from the dead, you will be saved.' Romans 10:9."

I didn't know how to respond. So, I just kept my eyes focused on the food he had prepared for me—meatloaf, mashed potatoes, and green beans.

"Delicious," I said, and Gus smiled. "Amen."

We both stopped talking, and the silence in the room seemed to make us more at ease with each other.

When we were done eating, I asked if I could take something to Adriana, and Gus nodded. He pulled a paper plate out of a cabinet and loaded it with food, placing it on a tray with a napkin, silverware, and a glass of water. But when I knocked on Adriana's door, she didn't want to open it. I left the tray outside and told her the food was tasty, but she didn't answer. A couple of hours later, I tried again. The food tray was still there, and the meatloaf was stinky. So, I picked up the tray and carried it to the kitchen.

Once I got back to my room, I saw the duffle bag with all our stuff. Adriana thought it was easier for us to pack together and then take turns carrying the duffle bag. Gus must have brought it to my room, and when I looked inside, Adriana's toiletries, clothes, and underwear were still there. I was pooped and figured that if she wanted anything, she'd come and get it. I undressed and crawled under the covers, but it took me hours to fall asleep. I felt guilty for not bringing Adriana's things to her. The mattress was hard, and the pillows felt like they were filled with scraps of foam rubber.

I could hear Adriana chiding me in my sleep. "Hope you enjoyed your meatloaf."

I kept saying to myself, "I tried to bring you some. I did. I did." And finally, I conked out.

In the morning, Adriana was short with me. "It wasn't the first meal I went without. And no doubt, it won't be the last."

"Well, I brought you a tray and knocked on the door. But you never answered."

"I must have been in the shower. You could have tried again."

Adriana's presence was commanding, and I just slid along, as if I was wearing hockey skates on autopilot over an iced-over pond.

Gus called out to us. He was making bacon and eggs. Adriana seemed a bit more relaxed, and despite her distrust of anything Catholic, she was hungry and wasn't going to turn down the food. But she barely looked in my direction. Gus winked at me as he handed Adriana a plate, but when he served me, he left off the bacon, because, I guessed, he wanted to show his respect to me as a Jew by not serving me something not kosher. Little did he know the smell of the bacon made my mouth water, but I didn't want to disappoint him, so I just ate my eggs with a couple of pieces of toasted white bread that he slathered with butter and marmalade.

After breakfast, I followed Adriana to her room.

"I'm sorry," I said. "I should have brought you your toothbrush."

"Some fresh panties this morning would have been nice. Fortunately, I don't drip."

"What?"

"You know what I'm talking about. I can wear my panties for two days in a row without any problem."

I was perspiring. "I really am sorry."

"It's all right, Aaron. I forgive you."

"Thanks," I said, stepping closer, and she pecked my lips with a quick kiss.

As we headed for the front door, Gus asked, "Need a ride to the freeway? It's a long way to Niagara Falls. And I only want to help. You know, I hear they have a little wedding chapel overlooking the Falls."

"Not for us," Adriana sneered, and Gus replied, "Know what I like about you, missy? You got spunk, and all joking aside, that's a good thing. God bless."

We followed Gus to his Dodge van, and he gave us a ride to the on-ramp of the freeway, tuning the radio to a Christian station that played what he called the contemporary devotional sound—electric guitar, bass, drums, organ, and lots of lyrics about being reborn. Adriana was on edge, fidgeting and tapping her fingers on the back of my seat. I was amused. For me, it was like I was a tourist in a foreign country where I didn't speak the language.

RIDE #5

NOVEMBER 2, 1970

IT WAS A LITTLE PAST 8:30 A.M. WHEN WE CAUGHT A RIDE in a hippie van headed in the direction of Niagara Falls. Adriana and I couldn't have been happier. We settled into the back seat and the driver turned toward us and grinned. "Howdy."

"Howdy." I chuckled.

"C'mon in. I'm Johnny, from Waco, and this here's Princess Jane, from Mineral Wells, deep in the heart of Texas."

Adriana introduced herself in a squeaky voice, and I did the same. Johnny and Jane looked at us like we were nuts, but I could tell they were pleased that we were hippies, too.

After about five miles, Johnny started bopping up and down in his seat and asked, "Do you partake of the herb?"

Adriana and I both nodded, and Jane lit up a joint the size of a cigar and handed it to Johnny, who passed it back to Adriana, smiling. "We call it the breakfast sacrament. Man, if you want to know the truth, we've been on the road for days. And we need a break. But we're not stopping now. So, the point is, why not go to outer space?"

Adriana was wide-eyed. "Cool."

Jane chimed in, "Amen."

"Getting stoned is my cross to bear." Johnny laughed. "But my cross is more of an armature than a weapon of mass destruction. This old van is just a costume, dressed up to look bad, but not so bad that the state police would trouble themselves to pull us over. You know, harass us, and put me in the pokey because my hair's too long. Man, this is a rocket ship."

Jane picked up a paperback copy of Ursula Le Guin's *The Left Hand of Darkness* that was lodged between the seats. "Let's start with the beginning of the beginning," she said softly, "since that's where it all began. Genly Ai is an envoy from this galaxy to Winter, a planet lost in a solar system we didn't know existed. His mission is to connect this planet with our evolving galactic civilization, but to do so he must overcome gargantuan obstacles in his struggle to bridge the gulf between his own cultural prejudices and those that he encounters. But on a planet where people are of no gender—or both—his gulf is almost beyond comprehension."

I could tell Adriana was turned off. She closed her eyes, mumbling, "I'm pooped," and I leaned back and watched the stark autumn landscape pass by. The sky was gray, and the trees and grass, in the early morning light, were different shades of brown. At some point, I conked out, but when I opened my eyes, Jane was still reading aloud, though I didn't understand anything she was saying.

"Yeah . . . yeah!" I said, trying to sound engaged, but she wasn't impressed.

"Are you a narc?" she asked sarcastically.

"What?"

"You sure act like one."

"No way," I said as seriously as I could, and Adriana glared at Jane, then me.

Jane turned away and thumbed through her book, pretending nothing had happened. Johnny was humming, and as we neared the exit to Niagara Falls, Johnny said, "Ah, the peace within," and lit up another joint. I was already so stoned I could barely think straight but took another hit anyway. I looked at Adriana, hoping that she could somehow read my mind. But she wasn't focused on me. She gazed at the Falls up ahead with an expression of awe that made me once again turn away from my own thoughts and wonder about hers.

Johnny pulled over. "There you go! The seventh wonder of the world."

"Far out!" I mused, reeling inside. "I didn't think you'd drop us off so close. Wow!"

"The pleasure is all ours," Johnny replied.

Adriana perked up. "Yeah, thank you so much."

Jane smiled. "Amen."

I helped Adriana out of the van, and she giggled. "Oh... free at last."

"Yes, indeed. Yes, indeed," I said, and we headed toward the entrance to the park. The sun broke through the clouds and the asphalt in front of us came to life as frost evaporated in a soft haze, masking what Adriana and I could see but not what we heard. The crashing of the water over the cliffs into the river was like a peal of thunder that never stopped.

The ticket booth was empty, so we just walked through the entry gate into a large expanse. We took the elevator to the base of the Falls, and when the doors opened, we were amazed to find that no one else was there. The morning sun ignited the fog with a soft glow, revealing a landscape we never could have imagined. Cliffs glazed with ice and snow towered above us, and the sheer intensity of the Falls drew us toward its vortex. But the spray from the frigid water pushed us back, giving us goose bumps of joy mixed with flashes of terror. If we got too close, I thought, the dense mist might consume us. But somehow it didn't matter. We were both giddy with the majesty of the Falls and the infinite beauty of everything we felt so privileged to be experiencing. Both of us inhaled deeply, sucking in the fresh air as if we had never breathed before.

By the time we left, we were euphoric, cresting on the waves of a supernatural high. In the elevator back to the visitor center, I was beaming, and Adriana kneaded her fingertips into my shoulders with a passion that radiated deep within me.

Outside, the sidewalk was slick. The soles of Adriana's boots didn't have much traction, and she inched along toward the Rainbow Bridge, worried that she was going to slip.

I reached for her hand to give her a little extra support. But she brushed my hand away.

At the entrance to the bridge, I squeezed our duffle bag through the turnstile and pulled it forward. We pressed into a strong headwind.

Adriana grimaced and I held tightly to her hand.

Once on the bridge we wrapped our scarves tighter around our necks to fend off the bitter cold, but when we got to the apex, the view of Niagara Falls was so spectacular that we were totally transfixed. We hugged each other and French-kissed until the cars whizzing by started to honk.

At the customs booth, a Canadian Mountie looked at us disapprovingly, and when he took our driver's licenses, he checked them carefully against his watch list.

"You're clear," he said finally, scraping his throat. "What are you carrying in that duffle bag?"

"Clothes."

"Any drugs?"

I shook my head no and muttered, "We're not that stupid" under my breath, as the Mountie waved us on. But out of the corner of my eye, I could see that he was gawking at Adriana's braced leg. I wanted to scream at him to stop staring, but knew if I did, I was going to piss him off, embarrass Adriana, and make a fool out of myself.

RIDE #6
NOVEMBER 2, 1970
11:30 A.M.

WE FOLLOWED THE SIGNS FOR QUEEN ELIZABETH WAY and trudged along Falls Avenue toward the entrance ramp to Ontario-420 West. I stuck out my thumb and the third car stopped—a red Volvo station wagon with snow tires.

The driver said his name was Sai, but everyone called him George. He insisted that Adriana sit in the front seat, and me in the back. He recognized the kind of leg brace that Adriana was wearing and said, "My auntie in Delhi has one just like it."

Adriana smiled politely.

"Oh, my... listen to me," George said. "There I go. I'm a mechanical engineer and love figuring out how things work." Then he changed the subject to the Rainbow Bridge and its sweeping arch.

George steadied the steering wheel with his left hand while his right danced around in the air as he spoke in a kind of choreographed movement that reminded me of the jerky steps of someone imitating a robot.

I wasn't sure why George felt compelled to act as our tour guide, but it wasn't long before his monologue lulled me into a nap. Adriana curled up in the front seat, leaning against the passenger door. Both of us were exhausted, and the adrenaline rush of Niagara Falls was wearing off.

After about half an hour, I saw Adriana twisting around, trying to make herself more comfortable. I wondered what it was that made her love me. Just being with her made me feel so good. She saw something in me that others didn't.

Adriana glanced up and somehow seemed to sense that I was thinking about her.

"Time to come back to Earth," she said in a soothing voice.

I leaned forward and she stretched back, easing her lips onto mine.

George watched us out of the corner of his eye, acting as if he wasn't distracted. "Toronto," he explained, "is about to go through some major changes—it's a city poised for growth. There's talk about building the tallest building in the world here, and to tell you the truth, we need something like that. When Air Canada 621 crashed just northwest of the city back in July, it was the worst plane crash in our history. Ignominious, I must say.

"You guys headed to Yorkville? It's the hippie scene you're after, I can tell. Now, I don't want to disappoint you, but most of the real hippies left town a couple of years ago. Of course, we still got our share of wannabes, long hairs with headbands, patchwork skirts with beads and baubles, kids sort of like you."

George was poking fun at Adriana and me, but we didn't respond. I was excited to be in Toronto, and I didn't want anything George said to get in the way.

George weaved through the late afternoon traffic and stopped in front of a place called Gandalf's Head Shop, with a marijuana leaf in the middle of its sign and paste-on psychedelic flowers on its front window. I was ready to get out of the car, happy we had reached a destination I knew something about, when Adriana tugged at my jacket.

"This place gives me the creeps," Adriana said. "I don't want to hang around here."

I didn't understand why Adriana's mood had changed so suddenly.

"It just doesn't seem to make sense," Adriana said. "I know you want to explore Yorkville, but hey, we've seen enough... for now. The sky is changing fast, Aaron. I mean, all this is kind of cool, but I think we might want to move on."

"You got a point," George chimed in. "I heard a big storm is moving this way. And if you are only going to spend the afternoon... well, this may not be the right day. So, I'll tell you what I'm going to do. I'm going to take you back to an on-ramp to the Queen Elizabeth Way, where you can pick up a ride back to Buffalo before you get socked in."

Adriana was pleased and gave me a bright, expectant look.

I sighed and turned away from her. "Look, we've come this far. Can we just stay a little while longer?"

"What's the big deal?" Adriana asked impatiently.

"I mean... according to *Evergreen Review*, Yorkville has the best bookstores, with more out-of-print poetry books and underground newspapers than anyplace in the Western hemisphere."

Adriana wasn't buying it. She rolled her eyes, and George did the same.

Thanks a lot, Mr. Tour Guide. I shrugged and stared out the window.

"Why are you pouting?" Adriana asked.

I shrugged again. "I really wanted to at least get out of the car and explore just a little."

"Next time."

"Ha!" I was disappointed.

"Something to look forward to, Aaron. You know, plan for. Maybe we'll even get married on the Rainbow Bridge."

Just hearing the word "married" made me squirm. Not in a bad way.

When George finally let us out, Adriana looked relieved and shimmied up behind me, pressing her boobs into my back as she massaged my neck and shoulders. I turned around, and she playfully pulled away, blowing me a kiss across her palm, and raised her thumb in the air, hoping to get a quick ride.

RIDE #7
NOVEMBER 2, 1970
1:15 P.M.

DENSE CLOUDS BLANKETED THE LANDSCAPE. The temperature was dropping. The north wind bristled against our backs. We donned ski hats and waited for about forty-five minutes. It was rush hour, and cars, trucks, and buses stacked up bumper to bumper along the highway. Finally, a Ford pickup truck pulled over. I threw our duffle bag into the bed of the truck, and we crowded into the cab. The driver explained he was only going about forty miles but that he was glad to help us get out of the city. It all sounded good, and we zoomed along, listening to a Rolling Stones special on the radio. Adriana was nuts about the Stones and hummed and sang along. The driver turned up the volume.

"*Let it Bleed* might be the best rock album ever made," Adriana gushed. "'You Can't Always Get What You Want' knocks me out every time I hear it."

I liked the Stones, but not as much as Adriana. There was something about the music that grated on me. Maybe it was Mick Jagger's brashness or the drugged-out arrogance of Keith Richards. Or maybe it was just the way Adriana acted when she listened to the Stones: detached and zoned out in a world that didn't include me.

As the pickup slowed to a stop, my mood changed. But I could tell Adriana was a little miffed that I wasn't as enthusiastic about the Stones as she was. Being outside energized me, even though we were in the middle of nowhere. Adriana stood beside me, looking around and rubbing her hands together, trying to stay warm but not saying anything. Then she moved closer, sliding her hand under my arm, leaning into my shoulder. "It's okay that you don't like the Stones," Adriana said, "It's just that . . . I know this might come out wrong . . . but if really love me, then you need to love that part of me, too."

"Yeah . . . and we can . . . uh . . . agree to disagree, sometimes," I said softly.

"I guess," Adriana sighed. "But I'm not so sure what that means. You know, how does it play out and how far does it go?"

My body tensed up. "Enough . . . please."

"Fine for me," Adriana said. "Point taken."

It started to rain—icy rain mixed with snow. Adriana pulled an umbrella from the duffle bag, and we huddled together. There weren't many cars, but I kept telling myself that one would eventually show up. Adriana was shivering and mumbled something about the realignment of the stars.

"Look," I said. "Over there, there's a motel across the freeway. We can spend the night there."

"No way," Adriana insisted. "We got to get out of here!"

"Why? I don't get it."

"Aaron, look at the ground. It's getting soppy and it won't be long before it ices over. If I just stand still, I'm going to get less wet. I can wrap my leg, brace, shoe, and all with the plastic wrap I brought along, just in case. If I get soaked, I'm in big trouble. My brace could freeze onto my leg."

I swallowed hard. "I am so sorry. I really am."

"It's okay. We're going to get out of here. Someone will stop. I just know it."

RIDE #16
MARCH 21, 1971
12:15 P.M.

TIME AND PLACE MELT INTO MEMORIES. Standing on the side of the road, hoping for someone to stop, it's like I'm watching the rough-cut of a film whose title I can't remember, jumping from past to present, desperate to re-edit what happened. But I can't.

I have a stabbing pain in my gut. I hunch over. I'm grieving for what could have been.

About five miles north of Lebanon, Ohio, there are no cars in sight. I read the historical marker in front of me pointing me to what was once a settlement called Union Village:

> Union Village, the first and largest Shaker (United Society of Believers) community west of the Allegheny Mountains, was established in 1805. Nearly 4,000 Shakers lived in Union Village, the last living here until 1920. They owned 4,500 acres of land with more than 100 buildings. Union Village was parent to other communities in Ohio, Kentucky, Indiana, and Georgia. Shakers were among the most successful religious communal societies in the United States. Belief in equality of men and women, separation of sexes, confession, communal ownership of property, and celibacy helped define their society.

Standing in front of that marker, I'm shivering inside. I stop reading. I can't get past the word celibacy. Could I ever do this?

The sweet sound of Sister Ethel's voice floats between my ears as I look out across the rolling farmland in front of me:

> Gentle words, kindly spoken
> Often soothe the troubled mind
> While links of love are broken
> By words that are unkind.

The wind picks up, the cold cramping my back. I lower my duffle bag to the ground and struggle to straighten up.

When a car finally stops, my head is swirling.

The driver is a teenaged boy with scraggly brown hair who looks younger than me. He seems harmless enough, but I can't tell if he's a hippie wannabe or just a redneck farm boy. But when he starts talking, he has a German-sounding accent.

"I was raised Amish," he says, "but I quit. Well, they chased me away for screwing our neighbor's daughter. And she was shunned and sent to some kind of reeducation program. Me, I was too far gone. I'm moving to Cincinnati, and that's where I'm headed. How about you?"

I pull a handkerchief from my back pocket and mop some of the perspiration from the back of my neck. The kid keeps pressing me with his questions, and the more he talks, the more I distrust him. Finally, I just blurt out that I'm worried that he isn't old enough to own the car he's driving.

He's furious. "You got it all wrong. I earned this car. My daddy made me work them fields since I was eight. And he promised it to me. You want out?"

I squirm in my seat, thinking I should shut up. I need this kid right now.

The car swerves into the right lane, and the kid says he can drop me at the next exit, or I can wait in the rain, if that's what I really want to do.

I lean forward and rub my right eye with my index finger. There's some gunk, or maybe just an eyelash, but it's making my eye water.

"You crying?" he asks in a snarky tone.

"No way," I stammer, "I just want out," and ask him to please drop me off at the Denny's restaurant near the exit ramp.

The car jerks to a stop. I open the door, and as I reach for my duffle bag on the back seat, the kid shouts, "Stupid! I was going to do something nice just for you. But you'll never know. You'll never know."

I slam the door and trudge off, wondering what on earth he could ever do for me, other than making my life more miserable than it already is.

When I'm about fifty feet from the Denny's, the rain lets up, and the wind dies down.

I need a break. Inside, all the tables are full but one. And when I sit down, the waitress ambles over to me and says, "Man, looks like you need a place to dry off. You want a coffee on me?"

I'm confused. Her kindness is so unexpected.

"Folks call me Heidi."

"Well, I'm just Aaron."

"That's not all bad."

Heidi looks at me as if I'm a Martian, then puts her hands on her hips, acting cute, but making it very clear that she can take care of herself. Her hair is dirty blond and floppy-cut, slung over her shoulder in a ponytail.

I nod. Thank you.

She smiles. Her teeth are kind of yellow, but glowing nonetheless.

Heidi scurries off and brings me a cup of coffee and a menu. Nothing seems to make sense. It isn't that I can't read the words, it's just that my mind is someplace else. I order two eggs over easy, hash browns, biscuits. Heidi seems happy. And I just sit there, looking at the empty table, waiting for something to happen.

"You okay?" Heidi is talking to me, but I feel like I'm only hearing every other word. "You look so pale. You gonna to faint? You need a doctor?"

I glance up at her and can tell she's genuinely concerned.

Heidi sits down in the chair next to me. "I've just ended my shift, and well... honey, I have a little time to listen, if you'd like to talk. You seem like a good man going through hard times."

I can't believe she called me "honey" in that southern drawl. Wow. As much as I appreciate her concern, I can't tell her what's really going on in my head. My eyes well up.

"I understand. Sometimes it's tough," she says. "You live around here?"

I do my best to explain that I'm hitchhiking to Nashville because I have to get my head together. Recenter myself. I don't feel like I'm making a whole lot of sense, but she seems okay with it.

"I see," she says, her green eyes brightening. "Well, I can give you a ride part of the way south. I live in Hamilton County, just outside Cincinnati, in the country."

"Really?"

"I just gotta tidy up a bit. Gwen, who owns the place, asked me to stay late, help in the kitchen. Jeffrey, the dishwasher, went home sick. And the dishes in the sink are sky high. But it shouldn't take long."

I straighten up. "Yeah. Whatever works for you."

After she walks away, I lean back in my chair against the back wall and fold my arms in front of my chest.

Somehow, I feel Adriana next to me. I start talking to her as if she's there, knowing of course she isn't, hoping she'll say something, but she doesn't.

"Why did we press on?" I ask, but she won't answer.

I can still see the motel in the distance, an easy walk from the Queen Elizabeth Way.

My memories of what happened in Canada ice over parts of my brain that I never knew existed. I can hardly move, even though I'm going through the motions of eating, and thanking Heidi each time she refills my cup with coffee when it's empty.

RIDE #8
NOVEMBER 2, 1970
3:30 P.M.

A POWDER BLUE CHEVY IMPALA SLOWED DOWN alongside where Adriana and I were standing on the Queen Elizabeth Way. The man in the passenger seat rolled down his window and asked, "You kids need a ride? There's a heck of a storm heading this way. A real doozy. Twelve to fifteen inches. You ready for that?"

I wasn't sure what to say. There was something about the tone of his voice that didn't seem right. It was like he was acting nice but had something else in mind.

His eyes focused on mine, but he quickly shifted his attention to Adriana.

"Pleased to meet you, little lady."

Then he pointed at my duffle bag and smirked, "Too bad, kid, the trunk don't open. Think you can jam that sucker between your legs?"

Adriana and I squeezed into the back seat, and I shimmied the duffle bag onto my lap, stuffing it as best I could between my thighs onto the floorboard.

Once we're settled, the driver said, "My God-given name's Rafael, but everyone calls me Ralph or Ralphie, and over here is Nicky."

Ralph steered with one hand and sipped from a bottle of Canadian Club whiskey he gripped in the other. After a while he handed the bottle to Nicky, who took a big swig and then passed it back to him.

When Ralph asked for my name, I stuttered.

"Give the kid a drink, Nicky. Go ahead. Sounds like he needs it."

I took a small sip, and Ralph slurred, "You hold onto it for a while. Go ahead, take your time. Nurse it. Share it with your girlfriend."

Ralph was drunk, and the highway was slippery. When a semi in front of him slowed down, he jammed on the brakes and skidded onto the shoulder.

"Porco cane!" Ralph roared, slamming on the brakes, and making a sharp turn onto the exit ramp. He swerved down the access road and finally stopped in the parking lot of a curling rink. There was a huge, midnight-blue neon sign advertising a big tournament scheduled for the following week. I'd never seen a curling rink and wanted to go inside, just to get a quick glimpse of what it was like, but there wasn't enough time. From the outside, it looked like a warehouse made of corrugated steel and cement blocks, but I imagined that inside there were giant moose heads mounted on the walls and Canadian flags hanging from rugged wooden beams.

"We need to change cars," Ralph barked. "I'm not driving this hunk of shit anymore."

Nicky shook his head, disapproving.

Then they started arguing in Italian. I wanted out of the car, but Adriana whispered, "It's okay. I can sort of understand what they're saying. They're a little tipsy, but they're okay. Just riffing, you know, with a bravado that some . . . uh . . . Italian businessmen think makes them sound more important. In a weird way, they remind me of my father."

Ralph jerked his head around, muttering something I didn't understand to Adriana, who was quick to reply in Italian, and he calmed down, answering her quips in long sentences. Their conversation in Italian only lasted about five minutes and was punctuated by hand gestures.

Adriana giggled. But when she said, "Ricorda solo che mi chiamo Adriana Rosario Santa Maria Romano," the car went silent.

Ralph glared at me, and Adriana turned toward me and said, "Believe it or not, Aaron. That's my full name. I know it's a mouthful. Lots of lineage there."

Adriana seemed as amused by Ralph and Nicky as they were with her. It was creepy, but I knew one thing for sure. Whatever they were saying didn't include me, or maybe it did. Maybe they were making fun of me.

When Ralph decided to change cars, Nicky opened Adriana's door and helped her out, escorting her to a black Ford Galaxie about ten feet away. Adriana leaned on his forearm for support. Nicky looked at her braced leg, but never asked her about it.

I walked alongside Ralph, who was shorter than I had thought sitting behind him in the back seat, looking at his thick neck and slicked-back black hair. But Ralph was husky with square shoulders and big arms, and when he glowered at me, I didn't want to make eye contact with him.

We all got into the Galaxie as quickly as we could, and Ralph careened out of the parking lot and got back onto the Queen Elizabeth Way. But the snow was worse, and the wind gusts made it almost impossible for Ralph to control the car. After about half an hour, the fan motor started rattling and the defroster quit working. The windows in the car steamed up fast.

Ralph was pissed off. "We can't go on! Did you hear me, Nicky? We ain't gonna to make it to Batavia today."

Nicky leaned forward, "So, what are we going to do with these kids?"

Ralph jerked one of his arms over his seat and jabbed his index finger at me in the back seat. "I oughta kick your ass! How you going to take care of your girlfriend now?"

I swallowed hard.

"Gone deaf?" Ralph bellowed.

Nicky tugged on Ralph's sleeve and shouted, "You're going to get us all killed if you don't put that hand back on the steering wheel."

"Okay, okay . . . but you better keep me away from that puny kid in the back seat."

I reached for Adriana's hand, but she pulled back.

Ralph was seething, and as his breathing evened out, his driving seemed to improve, but after about ten miles, he exited the Queen Elizabeth Way and turned quickly onto a small street full of empty lots off the access road. A motel sign with green and yellow flashing lights was visible in the distance, and before long, we were there. The motel was painted forest green with brown trim that reminded me in a strange way of the Shaker village where Sister Ethel lived.

I felt myself retreating deeper into myself. I didn't want to hear his insults, but they were starting to feel like poison darts. My hands were clammy. I wanted him to stop the car so we could get out and not be too far from the Queen Elizabeth Way, but Adriana seemed okay with him and acted like she understood him in ways I didn't.

Ralph parked the car in front of the office and then swiveled around in his seat. "So, how much money you got in those bell-bottom jeans?"

I was embarrassed.

"Look, kid, I'm not going to ask you again."

"Fifteen bucks!" I stammered, knowing that if I told Ralph I had more, he'd probably take it.

"Guess you're going to sleep in the snow," Ralph said with an exaggerated grin, and then lurched out of the car, slamming the door behind him. No one uttered a word. Nicky didn't even turn his head. He pulled a cigarillo out of his front pocket and twirled it with his thumb and index finger. Adriana repositioned her braced leg and avoided eye contact. I sank deeper into my seat and stared straight ahead.

When Ralph returned, he was chuckling. "So, it's all taken care of. I got us a couple rooms. We'll spend the night here, and I'll run you both into Buffalo in the morning. But there's one catch, you little twerp. You got to strip the beds and clean the bathrooms before we go. That's the deal. Any questions? I ain't all bad, kid. Look, I got kids myself . . .

yeah, I got a wife and two boys, both of them teenagers, a few years younger than you. I get it, yeah, I get it, but you got to take better care of your sweetheart."

I nodded. "I'm doing the best I can. Yeah. No need to worry about us. We can take care of ourselves."

"Fat chance," Ralph said, his voice tinged with disgust.

I sucked in my gut. I was hurting but knew I couldn't show it.

"Don't get me started," Ralph scoffed.

I knew we were trapped. We had to go along with them, like it or not.

"I . . . I mean . . . we appreciate your help."

Ralph's breathing slowed. "Okay, then. Get your stuff together and I'm going to do you a favor. I'm gonna buy you both a little dinner before we turn in."

I yanked the duffle bag out of the car and followed Ralph, Nicky, and Adriana inside. The restaurant was empty, but there was a table set. A waitress with stringy white hair brought us water, an ice bucket, and another bottle of Canadian Club.

Ralph and Nicky chatted between themselves, not paying much attention to Adriana or me.

Adriana gave me a pointed stare.

My eyes widened, and she just shook her head, exasperated.

When the waitress brought the menus, Ralph grabbed them all out of her hands before she could pass them around. "I tell you what," he said in a pompous tone, "we're going do it family style. Just bring a tray of antipasti—a little of this, a little of that. And a platter of the tagliatelle with sausage and peppers, enough to feed the four of us. Okay? Anyone got any objections to that, speak your piece."

Nicky laughed, and Ralph poured shots of Canadian Club, and toasted, "L'Chaim for our Jew boy, Cin Cin to the rest of us . . . okay?"

Jew boy? I gritted my teeth.

When the food came, Ralph exclaimed, "Amen!"

And while we were eating, Ralph talked about hockey—the Toronto Maple Leafs and their chances for winning the Stanley Cup, but no one, not even Nicky, had an opinion. But it didn't keep Ralph from chattering away. Adriana and I never looked up or at each other. But just as we were finishing, Adriana reached for my hand under the table, and I held her hand in mine, sensing that she could tell I was really worried.

We got up slowly, and Ralph handed us our room key. "Don't mind if we join you, do you? You know . . . let's have a little night cap."

I shook my head, "No, thank you," but Ralph grabbed me by the arm and tugged me along, twisting my wrist and laughing.

Inside the room, there were two double beds covered in red and green plaid spreads. The furnishings were tattered. The cheap wood veneer on the desk was chipped, and the paintings above the beds—of evergreen trees along a mountain ridge—were peeling out of their frames. Nicky sat down next to Adriana on one of the beds, and I sat on the other beside Ralph, who demanded that I keep pace with his drinking to prove that I wasn't a wimp. Every time he took a swig, he handed me the bottle and expected me to do the same. I could barely sit up straight. I was drunk and was even starting to relax until Ralph elbowed me in the side and asked, "What would you do if I told you I want to sleep with your girlfriend?"

I turned my head toward his, dumbstruck.

And Ralph cackled, "Cat got your tongue?"

"I can't hear you, kid," Ralph barked. "I asked you if I could sleep with your girlfriend. I was trying so hard to be nice. So, what if I told you now, you don't have a choice?"

I couldn't process what he was saying. I tried to talk but the words were stuck in my throat.

Ralph chuckled. "That's what I hate about stutterers. Never know what they're really trying to say. Well, let me tell you something once more, loud and clear. You don't have a choice. It's my destiny, and nothing is going to stop me now."

Adriana was speechless. She glared at me, waiting impatiently for me to respond.

"Destiny," Ralph said, "I'm a man of destiny. You know what that means?"

I could barely answer. "Uh... not exactly." My voice was trembling.

"Well, kid, I'll tell you what it means; I take whatever the hell I want. Either you let me screw your girlfriend, or I put bullets in both your heads and dump you in the Niagara River."

I felt sick to my stomach.

"Do you have any idea what it's like to kill somebody? Do you?"

I couldn't answer. I was queasy. My head was reeling.

"Do you?!!" Ralph was shouting, flecks of spit spraying out his mouth. "To stand at close range and fire a bullet into the back of somebody's head when they're on their knees, begging you not to do it? Well, the first time it haunts you, gnaws at you, but each time after that it gets a little easier, and finally after you've done it so many times you lose count, it means nothing. All in a day's work."

Nicky stood up and scanned the room. He brushed the front of his trousers with his hands and then rubbed his palms together. "Ralphie, Ralphie," he said. "Leave the kids alone. They're nothing but trouble."

Ralph scraped his throat and spit a huge wad of phlegm onto the carpet. "Don't tell me what I can and can't do."

"Ralphie, we've been partners for ten years and I ain't never seen you like this. Look, the girl's crippled. Leave her be," Nicky pleaded.

"This is destiny, Nicky. My destiny, and there's no turning back." Ralph's voice was calm, as if he were simply talking about the weather. "So, kid, have you made up your mind? What's it's going to be? A little sex, or a sexy bullet in your brain? Huh?"

It was as if he was pounding my head with a huge hammer, and I couldn't think or talk.

Ralph slapped my face with the back of his hand.

"You animal!" Adriana shrieked.

"Ooh! Ooh! Your little bitch is trying to protect you, candy-ass!" Ralph cawed and gulped a big swig of whiskey.

"I'm going to tell you something, Ralph," Nicky said, "and I'm only going to say it once. If you go through with this, I'm not sticking around. I'm not going to this party, and I might not come back to get you when you're done having your fun."

Ralph yanked the car keys out of his pocket and hurled them onto the carpet. "Go ahead, be my guest," Ralph said, smiling. "You're going to miss out on all the good times."

Adriana grasped the sleeve of Nicky's jacket as he reached over to pick up his keys, pleading with him to help us.

Nicky pulled free and didn't say another word. He walked to the door, turned the knob slowly, and left.

Adriana straightened her leg brace and stood up, locking it in place. I clenched my fist, and Ralph elbowed me in the mouth. I crumpled onto the floor. Adriana charged at Ralph, flailing her arms, but he just brushed her to the side, and she nearly toppled over.

Ralph slapped one hand on his hip and poked the other in his pocket, as if he was reaching for a gun. "Let me give you a little advice. Back off! Otherwise, I'm going to put bullets in your heads right now. You let me do my business, and I'll leave you alone, send you on your way."

Adriana and I looked at each other in disbelief. If we tried to fight Ralph, we were only going to lose.

Adriana buried her face in her palms and started blubbering.

Ralph glared at me. "Now, take off your clothes, you little twerp. Strip all the way down, and march into the bathroom like a good boy."

Ralph seemed to enjoy every second of my misery, and when I was stark naked, he clamped my shoulder in a painful grip and pushed me into the bathroom.

"Go ahead, you puny son of a bitch," he ordered. "Take a seat. It's all yours. Then he twisted the doorknob until something inside snapped, disabling the lock. "Just a little insurance that you won't get too creative and try to barricade yourself inside. I'm going to jam this desk chair against the outside of the door. That way the only way to you is through me."

RIDE #17
MARCH 21, 1971
2:30 P.M.

HEIDI IS SHAKING MY ARM.

"You really conked out, darlin'," she says as compassionately as she can, "time to head out. Done finished my chores."

I stretch backwards and stand up, steadying myself with my hands on the table. Heidi helps me with my duffle bag, and I sling it over my shoulder, following her out the door.

"Just throw that thing into the bed of the truck. It'll be fine," she says with a little giggle.

I look at her pickup, a rusty white Ford 150, hesitating before opening the door.

"You sure you're okay?"

"Yeah, yeah. I'm sorry. I was really out of it."

I open the door and plop down on the front seat.

"Oh!" Heidi laughs. "This is my daddy's truck, the one he uses when he's picking apples. Got a small orchard on my great great grandpa's forty acres, a little parcel of farmland that they say was given to him after the Civil War. That's right. A lot of history in these parts. My car's in the shop. A Karmann Ghia convertible with a little more than a hundred thousand miles on her. I say it's a her because she's mine."

I don't know what to say. Heidi is so giving, and yet seems so not needy at the same time. It's like she understands me in a way Adriana didn't. But I know I can't tell her that, or anything about Adriana, or what's replaying in my head every time I close my eyes. Heidi turns on the radio—and we listen to a mix of the Beatles, Bob Dylan, and Merle Haggard. Heidi taps to the beat on the steering wheel with a big grin on her face. The landscape drifts by. The trees along the roadside are budding. Heidi points to three billboards in front of us and slows down. "Number one, we have; number two, a treat; number three, for you. You know what they're advertising?"

"No idea."

"A motel that was torn down three years ago."

Heidi snickers and speeds up.

I smile, still hurting inside. Heidi cranks up the volume on the radio. Bob Dylan's voice is buoyant, singing "Peggy Day." *Nashville Skyline*. Track 5, and I space out.

NOVEMBER 2, 1970
8:45 P.M.

I STEADIED MYSELF AGAINST THE MOTEL DOORJAMB then staggered over to the bathroom sink. I was shaking and could barely prop myself up with both hands, staring hard in the mirror in the cold fluorescent light.

My skin was blanched, my eyes sagging and welling up as I tried to figure out what I was going to do.

My saliva dried up in my mouth; my throat felt like sandpaper. I turned the faucet on and gulped as much water as I could, but it didn't help. My head was spinning, and I sank down into the corner.

The bathroom tile was freezing. I huddled over and pulled my knees up against my chest, shivering. I started scratching the wall closest to me with my fingertips, picking at cracks in the paint, prying off little chips, lifting them up one by one, studying them in fits and starts, stacking them into a pile that kept falling over.

The silence was deafening, but then I heard a drip of water. I stood up and checked the sink and the tub, the toilet bowl, but I couldn't find any leaks.

Then, something crashed in the other room. It sounded like a lamp knocked off a bedside table, or a chair thrown against the wall.

Adriana was screaming.

I started pounding on the bathroom door.

"Aaron! Aaron!" Adriana shrieked.

And I yelled, "Adriana! Adriana!"

No answer.

I lifted up the toilet tank lid. It was heavy and unwieldy and as I charged forward to ram the door; I slipped and bumped my head against the side of the sink. I started sobbing. What can I do? What can I do?

I could hear Adriana whimpering in pain. Ralph was laughing. I wondered if I was unconscious. My vision was blurry.

Then I heard something strange. Was it just in my head, or was it real?

And then it dawned on me. It was a crow cawing outside the tiny bathroom window.

It didn't make any sense. A crow in the dead of winter.

My legs buckled under me, and I fell to my knees. I rocked back and forth. I could feel Sister Ethel singing.

Please, God
Keep me safe, keep me still
Always open to thy will
The words hovered over me.
Keep me safe, keep me still
Always open to thy will

I could barely keep my eyes open, and before long, I slumped over.

Was I a coward? Was I giving up hope?

My breathing slowed down, and a new logic took hold. I heard a voice inside me, telling me that if I stayed passive, it would be impossible for Ralph to kill Adriana and me. To do anything now could only make everything worse.

Was this sacrificial love? Or was it love sacrificed?

Ralph flung open the door.

"What the hell are you doing in here?" he said, scowling at me.

I looked Ralph squarely in the eyes but said nothing. I expected to stare down the barrel of his gun, but instead Ralph held out a hand and helped me up.

"Can't you see your girlfriend needs you?" he asked, his jaw hanging open, exaggerating his sarcasm.

Adriana was sitting up in bed, holding a blanket with both hands under her chin. I could barely see her face in the shadows. Her brace was splayed open on the floor, bent at the knee, the leather straps unbuckled, as if they were waiting impatiently for her leg.

I got unsteadily to my feet. Ralph stepped to the side and shoved me toward her. I almost fell over but regained my balance, grabbing the foot of the bed. I reached out to hug Adriana, and she pulled me into her bosom. I could feel her trembling in my arms.

Ralph moved in behind me. His breath was heavy and stank of stale booze.

"Tell you what," Ralph said with a scratchy smirk in his voice, "I'm going to let you kids have a little fun. Go ahead, kid, get in that bed. Pull back the covers. I just want to watch."

I hugged Adriana more tightly, but she jerked herself away. Then curled up on her side in a tight, fetal position, sobbing.

Ralph chortled. "Destiny, kid. That's right. I'm a man of destiny. And don't you ever forget it."

I felt my head whirling. If I hadn't been sitting on the bed beside Adriana, I would have toppled over.

Ralph reached over and tickled the bottom of Adriana's foot. She recoiled and wrapped herself even tighter in her blanket, gasping for breath.

"Come on, little lady," Ralph said. "You got to make this right. You got to show your man ... er ... boy ... that you still love him, and he's got to make it very clear that he ... uh ... forgives you. That's it. And I ain't going nowhere until I see it with my own eyes."

Adriana was groaning. I looked at her and then at Ralph, but quickly turned away.

"Not ready, huh? You kids are ingrates. Here I go and save your butts from freezing in the snow, and all you can do is act like a couple of pissants."

Ralph grabbed my arm and yanked me from the bed; I tumbled to the floor, naked, covering myself with my hands.

I stood up slowly. My stomach turned inside out. And I could hardly breathe.

Ralph backhanded me across the face. "Back to the hole!" he shouted, pointing at the bathroom door.

I shuffled toward the bathroom. Ralph stuck a foot into the small of my back and gave me a shove. I collapsed forward, barely able to break the fall with my hands and keep my face from crashing into the bathroom doorframe.

"That's right. I want to see you crawl. Hey, little lady, don't you want to watch your mutt-faced boyfriend crawl like a dog?"

I heard Adriana moving around in the bed, but I didn't dare turn around.

I inched my way forward onto the icy bathroom tile and slipped, gasping for air. The door slammed shut behind me.

RIDE #17
MARCH 21, 1971
4:00 P.M.

I TAKE A DEEP BREATH. "I'm sorry, Heidi, I'm wiped out. And the weirdest thing is I keep hearing this crow cawing in the distance. Reminding me of everything I can't forget."
"Maybe if you talk about it, Aaron, you can."
"But the crow won't leave me alone. And the more I try to chase it away, the louder it gets."
Heidi's eyes invite me into the kindness of hers. "Crows have a special meaning. They're messengers. Representations of the divine."
I force a little grin. "The last thing I feel is divine."
Heidi's eyes open wider, get brighter.
Just looking at her makes me nervous. I don't want to disappoint her.
"To be honest, Heidi, I don't know where to start. What happened is locked up inside me, and I don't have a key." I rock back in my seat. "Enough about me. I want to know more about you."
"Well, to tell you the truth, I'm not doing so good either. I had a big blow-up with my boss this morning before work, and on top of that, I broke up with my boyfriend. So, there. The short of it is, spending time with you helps. I hope you understand. I like helping folks in need. It's just part of my nature. Gets my mind off everything that's messed up inside me."
Heidi looks away, distracted, but then focuses her attention on me.
I crane my neck to look out the window. "Do you see the crow?"
Heidi shakes her head no, and asks softly, "Were you humming a Shaker song? Or was I just daydreaming?"

I clear my throat. "Not that I'm aware of . . . Well, I . . . uh . . . yeah . . . how did you know it was a Shaker song?"

"Long story, Aaron . . . but, I guess, not much time to tell."

"Can I ask you a question? I mean, it's kind of random."

Heidi grins. "I'm all ears, at least for a few more minutes anyway."

"Have you ever heard of Sister Ethel?"

Heidi brightens up. "You gotta be kidding. Yes, Aaron. Sabbathday Lake. I've been there. With my grandma. She knew one of them old Shaker women—they were friends when they were little kids in southeast Ohio, and she moved away, and they hadn't seen each other in nearly sixty years. And I'd heard so much about her that I said, 'Granny, I'm going to take you to Maine. Now that I've got a driver's license. It's my high school graduation present to you.' See, Grandma took care of me a lot, when Mama was in and out of the hospital. Had to get her stomach removed. Cancer."

"Sorry to hear about your mama. Did she die?"

"Yep. When I was fourteen."

I feel the sadness in her voice, and quickly change the subject, sensing Heidi doesn't want to talk more about her mama, or say much else about her personal life. "So, what'd you think of Sabbathday Lake?"

"A little strange," Heidi says. "But beautiful. Being there made me realize that I needed more direction in my life. Helped me to understand some of the boys chasing after me were up to no good. I think a lot of girls, maybe boys, too, became Shakers because they'd been beaten up, molested, or raped, or sadly, all of the above."

"Really?"

"Shakers did what they could to survive. Why is a deeply personal question."

"That's the truth. "

"Knowing that the Shakers came together the way they did gives me hope. They took care of people in need. They were all about peace. They loved to sing and dance. They believed in the equality of men and women. They lived together and shared everything they owned. They grew their own food and raised their own animals. They were into herbal medicine. They built their own houses and made their own furniture. Utility, simplicity and craftsmanship. Gentle curves and clean lines. I could on and on."

"You're amazing, Heidi. You really are."

"Sort of ... but I still got a lot to learn. Shakers welcomed anyone and everyone, so long as they worked hard and openly confessed their sins, They separated themselves from the outside world and stopped having sex."

I feel myself blushing. "I . . . I . . . uh . . . understand, but I don't know if I could ever, you know, be that way."

And Heidi says, "Don't know what's got into me. Being with you, Aaron, I'm a motormouth, when mostly I'm just a country girl."

"I can't believe you've been to Sabbathday Lake," I said, changing the subject. "I've been there, too, when I was a Cub Scout."

Heidi smiles. "You were a Cub Scout?"

"Yeah, for a couple of years."

"Well, I was a Brownie, but never made it to Girl Scouts. Another long story. Anyway, I have a copy of the only album Sister Ethel ever made. One of a thousand ever released."

"You do? Well, so do I."

"Cool. I found it in a second-hand store in Cincinnati."

"I got mine from Sister Ethel."

"You knew Sister Ethel?"

"Not exactly. I was a on a Cub Scout trip and the bus got a flat tire. And a few of the Shakers at Sabbathday Lake helped us get it fixed. And Sister Ethel was there. And I heard her sing, and before we left, she gave me a shrink-wrapped copy of her album. I was the only one in my troop who got one."

"Wow!"

"To be honest, I wasn't sure if I should take it. But I did, and all the other kids made fun of me. Well, I just stuffed it in my knapsack and hid it under my bed when I got home. It was my secret."

"Something wrong, Aaron? You sound so jittery."

"I'm okay. Really. It's just that . . . Sister Ethel has been my secret for most of my life. And I can't believe I just told you about her without ever thinking twice."

Heidi inches closer to me. "I want to hear your heartbeat."

"Well, it's not going anywhere," I say, laughing.

I wrap my arm gently around Heidi's shoulders, and we share a moment, gazing into each other's eyes. But then Heidi pulls away.

"Oh my, it's later than I thought. It's been so good to meet you, Aaron. But I need to get back. I live with a bunch of friends, and it's my turn to cook tonight."

"You live in a commune?"

"Well . . . sort of . . . in fact, we're kind of like Shakers, just kind of . . . if you know what I mean. But . . . uh . . . that's my exit up ahead. I wish I had more time to talk. I really do. But right now, I can't. And I'm kicking myself inside. Aaron, you're . . . I can't even say it in words . . ."

Heidi gently busses my cheek with hers. "You want off on the Interstate or near the on-ramp?"

"Neither."

"How so?"

"I wanna spend more time with you. But . . ."

Heidi quickly jots down the telephone number of the café where she works on a scrap of paper.

"This is the best way to reach me. Where I live, they . . . er . . . we don't have telephones."

"Uh . . . okay . . . I get it." I want to know more but know I have to let go.

The sun streaks through the clouds, but the feeder road alongside the freeway doesn't seem very promising for a ride. There are no buildings, not even a gas station or restaurant in view.

"Not much around here," Heidi says. "Probably you'll be better off on the south side of the on-ramp. That way, folks getting onto the interstate have a place to stop before they speed up, and the oncoming cars might be able to slow down in the right lane. You gonna to be okay?"

"I think so," I say, knowing how tough it's going to be.

Heidi slows down and eases onto the shoulder. "You know, I'd offer you a place to stay, but I don't... uh... really have a guest room."

"I'll be fine." I grin, trying to sound reassuring, and Heidi beams. "Remember if you're ever passing through, come see me. You never know..."

I step out of the truck without looking back and grab my duffle bag. I look deep into the horizon, determined more than ever to get to Nashville. But as time passes, every car that zooms by reminds me of everything that's gone wrong in my life, and my memories of Canada suck me back into a dark cave in my head that makes me claustrophobic, even though I'm standing outside. I see a cluster of rocks in a drainage ditch about ten feet away where I can sit and rest a while.

NOVEMBER 2, 1970
10:00 P.M.

I WAS SUFFOCATING, TRAPPED IN A LIVING HELL, as if a filthy rag had been crammed down my throat. What had I done to deserve this? Why me? Why Adriana?

I felt the bile rising in my throat.

Ralph yanked the bathroom door open. "Get your lazy ass up off the floor!"

I struggled to prop myself up, and Ralph reached over and grabbed my hands, pulling me onto my feet.

"I'm going give you one more chance, kid. You got to show me what you can do. If you really love your girlfriend, prove it."

When I went into the room, Adriana was face down with her face buried in a pillow. I knelt on the edge of the bed and massaged her back through the blankets, but she didn't respond. I pulled back the covers and awkwardly lowered my body onto the mattress. My guts churning; my legs cramping up. As much as I want to hold Adriana, I couldn't take my eyes off Ralph, who sat in the desk chair across from the bed and swiveled around as if nothing was out of the ordinary for him.

"Don't pay me no mind," he said, chuckling. "You kids, just have yourselves a good ole time."

I snuggled close to Adriana, and she turned over on her side. Her cheeks were streaked with dried tears.

I kissed her lips lightly, and her eyes welled up. She reached across the bed, and I gently smoothed my fingers across her thighs.

Ralph started laughing. "You are so pitiful. I knew all along there was something . . . uh . . . wrong with you."

Ralph grabbed my arm, and I stumbled out of the bed.

"You had your chance, pansy boy," Ralph cawed, yanking me toward him. "Now you're mine. All mine." He grabbed my ears with both of his hands and slammed me to the ground. All I could hear was my knees screaming as a crow flew straight at me and crammed itself into my mouth. I blacked out.

When I came to, I was twisted up on the floor near the toilet bowl. Another crow was perched on the edge of the sink, scolding me with shrieking sounds, but when our eyes met, it receded into the musty air and disappeared. My head was swimming, and my body throbbed. The door to the bathroom was closed. I heard nothing in the next room and wondered if I was dead.

I propped myself up against the wall and started picking at the paint around the bathroom doorknob. The chips peeled off in strips that looked like feathers that had been ripped from the wings of the crow that had attacked me. Feathers with an oily purple and blue sheen shimmering in the icy fluorescence of the bathroom floor. Feathers piecing together into the skyline of a city I had never seen before.

My body ached for daylight.

Stuck in a prison where Adriana and I were the only prisoners.

A jail cell without a key.

Knowing for certain that if I tried to fight Ralph, he was going to kill both of us. But who would he murder first? Adriana or me?

I felt so stupid inside. Completely ashamed of myself. I felt so dirty that the smell of my own body was making me sick.

I replayed everything that had happened, everything that had been said. But there was a blank spot. A black hole that was sucking me in. What did Adriana and Ralph say to each other in Italian? What did he say to her, and her to him? And why? Did she goad him on?

Time expanded and contracted—there were more questions than answers, eating away at my guts.

I was desperate. I inventoried in my head everything I could think of on the other side of the door—the furniture, the table lamps, the light fixtures, the bedspreads, the sheets, the pillows, the telephone, and each piece of clothing Adriana and I had taken off in the motel room. I could visualize Ralph's overcoat hanging in the closet, his shirt and pants stretched across the back of the desk chair.

In which pocket did Ralph keep his gun? Did he really have one? I hadn't seen it. But could I take that chance? If I went for Ralph's pants and the gun was in his coat, we were dead. And even if I were to get to the gun before Ralph, would I be able to pull the trigger?

What if Ralph didn't have a gun? What would I do? Could I grab the desk lamp and smash it over his head? Or yank the electrical cord from its base and strangle him?

I turned on the hot water in the shower and the bathroom steamed up. I closed my eyes and imagined Ralph charging through the door, slipping and toppling over, whacking his face against the edge of the sink, knocking himself unconscious, or maybe even killing himself.

The sound of the rushing water helped me calm down, but at the same time knowing I could never overpower Ralph tortured me. I needed a different strategy. I turned the water off. Maybe I could outsmart him.

RIDE #18
MARCH 21, 1971
4:02 P.M.

I HEAR A CAR HONKING, ITS HIGH BEAMS FLASHING ON and off. I straighten up, worried that it might be the police or some redneck looking for a fight. But then I hear a woman's voice, calling out to me. "Aaron! Aaron! It's Heidi."

I walk toward her, squinting in disbelief. But she isn't in her pickup truck. She's driving her red Karmann Ghia.

"I was so happy when I got to daddy's house and saw my car parked in the driveway. Somehow, it got fixed sooner than expected. Course, I don't think it was because of me. I think daddy needed his truck back, and the mechanic in the repair shop knew that if he did him a favor, he probably was going to get a bushel of free apples."

"Ha! I thought I'd never see you again."

"Me too. But one of my roommates left me a note on the kitchen table that he and a couple of other guys in our little community had go to Dayton for a big HVAC job, and I didn't have to cook after all. So I thought, well, maybe you hadn't gotten a ride yet, and you know, I could take you closer to Cincinnati, where it might be easier to get a ride to Nashville. You want to be a country music star?"

I laugh. "No. I'm just a college kid obsessed with seeing the skyline."

"You gotta be kidding. It's not much."

"It's the lodestone for me. I'm a pilgrim on a mission."

"That's crazy!"

"Gee, thanks."

"It's okay. I'm into crystals, too. It's all about belief, and believe me, there's a lot to believe."

"Talk about crazy."

"I never said I wasn't."

"Gee, thanks. That makes me feel a lot better."

"So, you want a ride? Or would you rather sit there pretending you're meditating when you just look miserable?"

Heidi pops open the latch on the Karmann Ghia trunk, and I push my duffle bag inside. I lower myself into the Karmann Ghia. The seats are close together, and the engine is loud, but it doesn't go very fast.

Heidi is in her element. She'd changed out of her waitress uniform into baggy jeans and a flowery crop top. Once we're back on the highway, she settles into her seat and says, "So, in twenty-five words or less, tell me about yourself. Who you are, who you want to be?"

"I'm looking for Nirvana. Salvation."

"You really are on a spirit quest."

"All joking aside. I am on a spirit quest. I need to save myself from myself. I don't really know who I am, but I know I'm becoming someone else."

"Good try, but you failed. I'm 19, going on 21, though some days, after waitressing all day, I feel like I'm going on 30 or 40. I want to go to college and be an art major. I like to draw and paint, and maybe I could even be a sculptor. But I need a little time off to get my act together."

"Yeah, I know what you mean."

"Are you an artist?"

"I wish. I mean . . . Yeah. A wannabe."

Heidi pokes me in the side. "Is something wrong?"

"No, no. Just . . . uh . . . a little preoccupied."

"I get it. I really do. Something is really bumming you out and you need to work through it without talking about it. So, if you gotta space out, go ahead. I know that's what you need. I'm not insulted, because sometimes I get that way myself. Know that with me you're safe, and you can truly rest. Don't worry. I know how to get you up if I need to."

I apologize and reposition myself in my seat. It's like a hundred-pound weight is strapped to my ankle, dragging me back into the nightmare that never seems to end. But my eyes are wide open. And as much as I want to tell Heidi what's clogging up my brain, I can't.

NOVEMBER 3, 1970
1:00 A.M.

I STRAINED MY EARS TO LISTEN. Ralph was yammering on to somebody, someone other than Adriana, but I couldn't understand the words.

The crow was back, squawking, hungry for food. And even though I couldn't see it, I knew it was out there hovering above the motel.

I had to do something. I stood up and started flapping the toilet seat up and down, trying to scare off the crow. Then I plugged the sink drain and turned on the water. The basin filled, and water sloshed onto the floor.

Ralph pushed open the door.

I glared at him, struggling to contain the vengeance surging within me. I wanted to kill him, but I didn't know how.

Ralph was now completely dressed. His blue striped shirt was wrinkled, but his grey slacks were neatly creased, and his black Stacy Adams shoes were buffed to a shine.

"Are you out of your mind?" he yelled. "Stop the faucet right now! Pull that effin plug in the sink to let the water drain out."

Ralph kneed me in the groin, and I keeled over. The floor was slippery, and I couldn't keep my balance. I broke my fall by reaching for the sink with both hands, and once I steadied myself, I turned the faucets off.

Ralph grabbed me by the arm and jerked me out of the bathroom. He flung me onto the bed opposite Adriana, who lay face down, groaning into her pillow.

Nicky was back. I couldn't believe it. And Ralph was goading him on.

Nicky dropped his pants to his ankles, and slowly mounted Adriana, thrusting into her, restraining her wrists with his hands. She was writhing to break free but face down there was little she could do other than gasp for air.

Everything was a blur. It's like I was looking through a window smeared with mud. Something had happened to my glasses. I had no idea where they were. I could barely catch my breath. "How can you do this to us? You even have your own kids. What would they say if they knew?"

Ralph jabbed his index finger in my face. "You know what they'd say? They'd say, 'Daddy, we're so proud of you. You didn't just shoot the little Jew boy and get on with your day.' It's destiny, kid. How many times do I have to tell you? At this moment, it's not my destiny to put bullets in your head, but that doesn't mean it's not going to change. You kids ought to get some rest, and I'll come back and get you in the morning."

Adriana was moaning. She rolled onto her side, and I saw a trickle of blood seeping from between her legs onto the sheet.

Ralph yanked the telephone cord out of the wall. "Feel better? Now no one can interrupt your beauty sleep. No telephone calls. The only one who can wake you up is me."

Adriana was sobbing, mumbling words I couldn't understand.

"Okay, little lady," Ralph said. "Okay. I tell you what Uncle Ralph is going to do. He's going to pick you kids up in the morning and take you to get married. That'll fix things. I might even drive you into Buffalo, after all."

I glowered at Ralph, but knew if I said anything to him, it was only going to get worse.

"Now, that's not a very nice way to tell me 'thank you.' I'm only trying to help you stupid kids make good! You don't seem to get it.

Destiny moves in mysterious ways. Sometimes it's simply out of control. But I get it. I know I hurt your feelings, but hey, you'll get over it."

Ralph picked up my jeans from the carpet and pulled my wallet out of the back pocket.

"See, kid, I'm going to remember you. I'm going to take your driver's license, and if you ever tell any living soul about what happened tonight . . . well . . . guess it's morning by now . . . I'm going to come get you. Maybe not personally, but let's say, an associate—a colleague, that's what you college kids say, right? And that goes for you too, little lady. I've already gone through your purse. Don't worry. I know all about the Romano family. Let me assure you. You're safe now. But I need a drink, and I'll be back."

Adriana scowled. "What do you know about my family?"

I was totally confused. I looked at Adriana and she shut down, wiping her eyes, and covering her face with her hands.

Ralph spit onto the carpet. Then he opened the door and strutted outside, whistling a shrill sound that seemed to delight him but haunted me.

I rushed to Adriana's side and pulled the bed covers up over her back. I lay down in the bed next to her and ran my hand lightly over the back of her thighs, trying to soothe the pain I could feel pulsing through her body.

"Don't touch me. Not now, Aaron. I need some time. I need to rest."

"I'm so sorry."

Adriana muttered something under her breath.

My eyes were stinging with tears. "I feel so . . . terrible . . . I . . . I . . . Is there anything I can do?"

Adriana breathed deeply but said nothing. My stomach hurt; my forehead throbbed. I had to get up. I had to pee.

"We've got to get out of here," I pleaded.

"I know, Aaron. I know. But I just need a little time to pull myself back together. It's the middle of the night and we've got no place to go. If we leave this room now, we'll freeze to death on the side of the road."

I kissed Adriana on the back of her neck and went to the bathroom. The floor was slick and cold from the water that had overflowed onto the tile. I reached for a towel and mopped up the floor as best I could. I wanted to use the other towel, but I knew I needed to save it for Adriana.

My nose was drippy. I tore off a piece of toilet paper and blotted my nostrils. And then my mouth began to hurt. It was like my fillings were falling out.

By the time I got back to Adriana, I was a wreck. I lowered myself onto the edge of the bed. She was shaking, holding the top sheet and blanket up over her nose, just under her eyes.

I was in a panic.

I sprung up and shoved the dresser against the door as a barricade.

Adriana looked at me and said nothing, nodding slowly.

I glanced at the clock on the bedside table. "It's almost 4:30. We've got to try to get a little sleep. If you want, I can move over to the other bed."

"No . . . please, Aaron . . . I want you with me, beside me . . . but not touching."

Once I was in the bed, Adriana changed her mind. We embraced face-to-face, and she rested her cheek on my chest. I could feel her hurting as I massaged her shoulder lightly with my hand.

Half awake, half conked out, half alert, half numb, I saw the crow that I thought was following me around in plain sight for the first time. It was perched in a tree that had somehow pushed its roots through the motel room floor. The crow was cawing, but when I turned toward it everything that was happening stopped. And it didn't move or make another sound until I woke up.

A dismal gray light edged the window blinds. It was nearly 8:30 and I was in a panic, expecting Ralph to barge in the door at any moment. Adriana was breathing heavily, deep in another world. I shook her shoulder gently, and she mumbled something that I didn't understand. I jarred her a little more vigorously, and she snapped alert, pulling her right hand up to her breasts and flicking her wrist. "Che peso! Mi sta qua! You don't have clue! You have no idea what I'm feeling! I can't stand this anymore!"

"Please, Adriana. Ralph's coming back, probably soon. We've got to get up now."

Adriana began moving, but ever so slowly.

"He's probably just setting another trap," Adriana said, her eyes boring into mine. "He wants to give himself a reason to come back and stick his ugly cock in me again. And it's not like you're going to do anything about it."

I could feel the blood draining out of my face, my heart plummeting into my gut.

I turned away from her and pried myself out of the bed, not wanting her to see how hurt I was. I was sobbing inside but said nothing.

Adriana struggled to get up. I wiped my face on the back of my hand and went to her side. She leaned on me for support, her left leg dangling at her side, her right leg hopping forward a few inches at a time.

"I'm sorry, Aaron. I shouldn't have said what I did. I know there was nothing you could do."

I shrugged, not really wanting to talk about it, but then blurted out, "If I had tried to stop Ralph, he would have killed us both."

"I know that . . . believe me, I do. "

I took Adriana's hand, interlocking my fingers with hers, and she eased her lips onto mine in a soft kiss, then pulled away. "I need to get ready. We gotta get out of here."

"What can I do?" I asked, picking up her brace from the carpet and handing it to her.

"Please, Aaron, I can do it myself."

I wanted to do something to make it easier for her, but no matter how much I tried, it felt as if it wasn't making much of a difference.

"Do you need me to help you get dressed?"

"This is so humiliating," Adriana said, starting to cry again.

"Yes... if you could... I mean... my panties. It hurts to bend over... and my jeans."

I reached for her panties and carefully slid them over her feet. Once I pulled them past her knees, I gasped when I saw the bruises on her thighs. Adriana lifted my hands away from the panties and eased them up over her crotch and bottom. I handed Adriana her leg brace and she opened it on the bed by her side so she could lift her leg into place and buckle the leather straps. Then she pushed her feet into her jeans one by one and stood to pull them up and lock her brace. She put on her bra and shimmied into her orange and blue sweater.

I dressed quickly in my jeans, flannel shirt, and beat-up cowboy boots, then walked over to the window and carefully pulled back the edge of the blinds to peer outside.

"No sign of them, Adriana. We have a chance to get out of here, we have to take it."

We put on our jackets, and I slung the duffle bag over my shoulder. I opened the door cautiously, and when we saw that no one was around, we rushed toward the highway.

The north wind slapped us in the face. It had stopped snowing, but it was more frigid. The road was iced over, and there were no cars in sight. In the distance, we heard the morning traffic on the Queen Elizabeth Way, but we weren't sure how to get there. We trudged forward, though everything seemed to be moving in slow motion. With every step, I watched Adriana wincing in pain, but she didn't complain.

"We better cut across that field," I said, pointing to an expanse of tall grass poking through the snowdrifts. "I don't think it's very deep, and it will give us a head start if Ralph shows up and finds us missing."

"Aaron, I can't do that." Adriana's voice was shaking. "If I get my brace wet, the straps will take forever to dry."

I stepped into the snow and sank down to my knees.

"Don't do it. Please. We'll be soaked in no time. We're going to get frostbite."

I stopped in my tracks. "You're right. We can't."

RIDE #8
NOVEMBER 3, 1970
9:38 A.M.

WE BACKED UP AND WORKED OUR WAY ALONG THE ROAD. Walking was tough. The gravel on the shoulder was slippery and caked with ice. After about a hundred yards, we heard a car approaching us from behind. Neither of us moved. We looked at each other, terrified that it might be Ralph and Nicky.

I turned around slowly and stuck out my thumb, holding my breath.

The driver pulled up alongside us and rolled down the passenger-side window. He had a scruffy beard. His eyes were watery, and his nostrils looked irritated and red. He said he had a bad cold but was probably no longer contagious.

I climbed in first, sliding into the middle of the bench seat, and Adriana scooted in next to me. The driver watched as Adriana pulled herself up, but when he saw she had a leg brace, he looked away, as if he didn't want her to feel self-conscious.

"I'm a dairy farmer from up the road. The name's Mack," he said. "Where you folks coming from? Kind of rare to see hitchhikers at all in these parts, let alone after a blizzard."

"We were, um, we're coming from Toronto," I answered, scrambling for words. "I thought we could make it back to Buffalo before the storm hit."

"Wishful thinking, I guess. You got a long way to go. Closest town around here is Grimsby. We're about eighty-some kilometers from where you're headed."

Adriana nestled herself closer to my side and rested her head on my shoulder.

"Didn't get to that motel until late," I said, struggling to give some context to why and when we were where he picked us up.

"Surprised the old lady let you in. She can be pretty particular, and late ain't in her vocabulary."

Adriana sighed, and I said, "We're just glad to be out of that cold."

"Yes siree, I like company, especially in the winter," Mack said. "I gotta pick up some feed in St. Catharines and this old drive can be long and lonely."

I was running out of things to say, but I didn't want to be rude, and as I warmed up, I could barely keep my eyes open.

"Well, I suppose you need a little rest. Go ahead; lean on back—that is, if you can find a spot that's comfortable; that middle seat's a bear. No worries. I'll take you south on the Queen Elizabeth Way to St. Catharines. From there, you get on Ontario-405 East toward Queenston-Lewiston, USA. I'll make sure I leave you in a place where there are a lot of cars. No problem getting a lift, not in this weather."

Mack turned on the radio and dialed in what sounded like a farm radio station, complete with crop prices and school news. The announcer's voice droned on and on. Scenes from the horror Adriana and I had experienced flashed on and off in my head.

Mack started whistling a tune that I'd heard before but couldn't think of its name.

I looked over at Adriana. She was sound asleep, leaning back in a twisted-up position with her head lodged between the edge of the seat and the passenger door. I noticed the lock button was up and reached over her to press it down. She stirred and opened her eyes.

"Almost to St. Catharines," Mack said. "You kids think you're ready for that icy road again?"

Mack turned up the radio. Stephen Stills was singing "For What It's Worth" with Buffalo Springfield. The lyrics "There's battle lines being drawn/Nobody's right if everybody's wrong" made me cringe.

I was against the Vietnam War, but the reality of what Adriana and I had somehow survived weighed me down. If I'd had a gun, it would have been different. I was kicking myself for not trying to grab Ralph's. Rationalizing to myself that Ralph might not have had one was BS. I felt like a coward. Plain and simple. Ashamed of myself.

But what if I had shot Ralph and Nicky, could I have lived with myself, knowing I'd killed two people? Did anyone deserve to be murdered? Even in self-defense?

"It's a mess you got in the States, with Vietnam and all," Mack said. "Got a lot of kids your age coming this way. What about you? You after some kind of asylum?"

I straightened up in my seat. "Not yet. But who knows? That could change. I'm a draft resister."

"On what grounds? If you don't mind me askin.'"

"Moral. Ethical. The war in Vietnam is wrong. Too many innocent people are dying, too many being maimed. For what? I'm all about love and peace. And love doesn't kill."

"I hear you. Don't mean to meddle in your affairs; no need to jump all over me. I'm on your team. I'm a veteran of World War II. I volunteered. But when it comes to Vietnam, I'm sympathetic to boys like you. Fact is, I was only asking because I was thinking I might be able to do something to make a move to this country a little easier. I'm always needing help around the farm."

"I don't really know much about farming. I'm a city kid."

I sensed Adriana tensing up beside me. "Peace is best. That's the truth," she said adamantly. "Too bad someone has to fight for it. My cousin Jerry did two tours of duty in Vietnam, and two weeks before he was headed stateside, a buddy of his stepped on a land mine, and it turned him into a double amputee. But Jerry survived with shrapnel in his legs. Thank God he can still walk."

"Right on!" Mack said, and I nodded, not wanting to get into an argument. I needed to change the subject.

Mack sensed the tension between Adriana and me and started whistling "Oh, Susanna."

It was so bad that even he laughed after the second verse. Adriana rolled her eyes, and I did the same.

We drove along in silence for a while. I watched the mile markers on the side of the road, counting them off one by one in my head.

"I'm going to be getting off at the next exit," Mack said, "and I'll let you off at the on-ramp to the QEW. That'll take you up over the Peace Bridge, and you should get to Buffalo by midday."

"Thanks so much. We truly appreciate your help," Adriana replied. "You're a gem."

As Mack exited the freeway, the music on the radio was interrupted by a special bulletin. Two hitchhikers, a man and a woman, had been found dead in the snow on the Queen Elizabeth Way, both killed execution style with bullets in their heads.

Adriana and I stared at each other, unable to speak.

"You okay?" Mack asked. "I know that's not the news you wanted to hear before getting back on the road. Be careful."

Mack stopped his pickup, and we thanked him again. I grabbed our duffle bag from the bed of the truck. Mack waved. "Stay warm, if you can." He eased back onto the highway and disappeared into the distance.

The last thing we wanted to do was hitchhike, but we didn't have a choice.

RIDE #19
MARCH 21, 1971
5:35 P.M.

HEIDI POKES ME IN THE SIDE, JARRING ME AWAKE; I'm disoriented. I was so zonked out. I think I'm in her pickup truck, but then realize I'm in her Karmann Ghia and don't recognize her voice.
She says I was talking in my sleep. I take a deep breath, not really wanting her to tell me what I was saying, but she does anyway.
"You kept groaning the name Adriana over and over. And I figured, oh, well, she must be your girlfriend."
"Well... not exactly."
"I understand. If you don't want to talk about her, Aaron, that's okay. The last thing I want to talk about is old boyfriends."
I sit up not knowing what to say. "Er... yeah. Adriana was my girlfriend. The first."
"That so?"
"Yeah, she was once upon a time, the one and only. And to be honest, it didn't work out. And that wasn't so long ago."
Heidi smiles. "Now, I've taken you a little further down the road than I thought I was going to."
The landscape doesn't seem much different than it did when Heidi picked me up. The fields of winter wheat. The Silver Maples, the Cottonwoods, and Sycamores. But the more closely I look around, I see I'm someplace I've never been before.
A flock of crows swoops down, and my eyes follow them through the sky.
"Aaron, are you okay?"
"Yeah, yeah. I just have never seen so many crows together."

"In these parts, they call that formation a 'murder of crows.' Not that anyone is going to get killed."

I'm confused.

"When you see a murder of crows, it means unexpected changes are coming. You're not alone. You have good people around you, or maybe someone who's dead, someone you loved, is watching over you."

"C'mon..."

"Believe what you will. We're about to cross the Ohio River on the John A. Roebling Suspension Bridge, headed into Covington, Kentucky. It's super cool. When it opened in 1866, it was the longest suspension bridge in the world."

"Check it out!"

"Wow!"

"Inspiring, huh?"

"Yeah. Thanks."

"Thought we'd get a bite to eat at Roebling Point at the foot of the bridge before I leave you at the on-ramp back to the Interstate going south. You ever eat a hot brown?"

"Never," I say, marveling at how upbeat she is.

"Oh, it's the best." Heidi laughs. "It's Kentucky food—sliced turkey on an open-faced white toast sandwich, covered with Mornay sauce, and maybe a sprinkling of pimentos or tomatoes or even parmesan cheese."

"Sounds incredible. Just like you."

"Huh?" Heidi asks in a silly voice, as she turns into a small parking lot behind the Red Clay Bar & Grill.

I follow Heidi into the restaurant. She's swinging her arms back and forth like she's a rag doll. I feel like I'm in the middle of a slapstick movie, the straight guy who doesn't really know what's going on. The hostess greets Heidi with a big "Hey, gal!" and seats us at a great table overlooking the river. Heidi orders two hot browns and two glasses of buttermilk, and then says, "Hope you like buttermilk."

I feel myself blushing.

"Well, it's an acquired taste." Heidi smirks. "Kind of like me."

Every second with Heidi is more than I could have ever hoped for. And by the time we finish eating, I don't want to leave. The buttermilk is a little weird, but if I could have ordered another glass, I would have, just to spend more time with Heidi. But she says she has to make a phone call. I pay for the hot browns and step outside.

I sit down on a bench across from the front door of the restaurant and lean back in the afternoon sun, watching the cumulus clouds hover overhead, listening to the comings and goings on the street.

RIDE #9
NOVEMBER 3, 1970
11:03 A.M.

ADRIANA TURNED AWAY FROM THE ONCOMING TRAFFIC and muttered, "Stop! Please stop!"

I took her hand in mine, desperate to comfort her.

But she pulled back. "I can't look into the windshields of the cars. I'm so afraid. I can barely stand up."

My heart started beating so fast that I worried I was going to keel over. "I can't get those two hitchhikers shot in the head out of my head. Murdered... it could have been us."

"Please, Aaron, I don't want to talk about it."

"I'm sorry... but I have to."

"You want to tell the police? So, they can terrorize us even more? No one is ever going to believe us. No one is ever going to understand what we went through. I can hardly even explain the way I'm feeling to you."

"I know, Adriana, we have to do what we can to go on. It's just that in my gut, I'm worried that we might be making the wrong decision."

"I need closure, and for me that means letting it go, as difficult as that might sound."

"But it's a gaping wound," I pleaded. "We need help. We need to help each other."

"Aaron, I only have the strength to say this once more. Please. Stop!"

I looked down at the icy pavement. I struggled to hold back, but words surged within me. "What if another two or more hitchhikers are killed because we didn't do anything? What are we going to do then?"

The blood seeped from Adriana's face. "I . . . just . . . feel so dizzy."

I reached for her hand, but she didn't want me to touch her. She glared at me, shoving me back with her eyes.

There was a steady stream of cars, as Mack had predicted, but the drivers seemed more aggressive. I worried that one of the cars had Ralph and Nicky inside, not in the Galaxie that had taken us to the motel but in some other vehicle that they had picked up along the way so they could catch us when we least expected them.

Adriana was blubbering. "If I could talk about it, I would. It's like . . . I mean . . . I can't find the words. It hurts so bad to even think, let alone feel. Inside, I'm just numb."

"I'm so sorry."

Adriana pursed her lips together.

My heart sank to new depths. "Me . . . My whole body is throbbing, and it's getting worse."

I stuck my thumb out, and after about fifteen cars passed us by, a red sedan stopped. Inside was a man dressed in a Canadian Mountie uniform. "Where you headed?"

"Buffalo," I said, trying to act as if nothing was wrong.

He wrinkled his brow, suspicious, but acting concerned about our well-being.

"Well, it just so happens, I'm on my way to work at the border crossing," the Mountie said. "I can give you a lift if you want it. Technically, it's illegal to hitchhike on this stretch of the QEW, but since you're going home to the US of A, I presume, I'm going to help you out. Besides, if you stand out there much longer, you might freeze to death, and that, I guess, is a bigger problem, for us and for you."

Once inside the car, I was relieved but jittery. The Mountie kept asking us questions about college, hometown, siblings, and parents. Finally, after about ten minutes, he wanted to know what we were doing in Canada.

"Sightseeing," I said matter-of-factly.

"Is that so? What about you, Miss? What did you want to see in Canada?"

"We'd never been to Toronto," Adriana said. "It really is a beautiful city... at least when the sun's out."

"The weather can turn on a dime." The Mountie laughed, but then in a serious tone, he said, "Just remember, these winter storms can bring out the worst."

"That's the truth," Adriana said.

I was shocked; she sounded so calm. No one could have guessed that moments before, she'd been at the edge of a total breakdown.

"You got that right," the Mountie said. "You're one brave little girl, heading out on the road like this, especially with a bum leg."

Adriana turned away, pretending she wasn't really paying attention to what he was saying.

I sensed that the Mountie was trying to find out if we knew anything about the murdered hitchhikers, but he never asked us straight out, even though his tone of voice made it feel like a strategy.

Adriana was probably right; if we said anything, we'd be detained. They'd call our parents, and we'd only have to suffer more.

Besides, even if the police were ever able to find Ralph and Nicky, would they even arrest them? What happened in that motel room was Adriana's and my word against theirs—two American hippies against two Canadian citizens.

"I'll take you across to the US side," the Mountie said. "Then I can turn around and pony right back. I'm still early for work, and if anything, I'll have to answer fewer questions if I do it this way. I know that might not make sense, but if I take you, my counterparts on the American side will understand that you two are probably okay, that somehow, I've checked you out, and that you're likely not carrying any drugs with you. Um, that is correct, isn't it?"

"Yes, sir," I said, and Adriana added, "Absolutely."

"That's a good thing. You're both a little scruffy, but I've seen a lot worse."

The Mountie drove us across the Peace Bridge. The US Border Patrol agent at the tollbooth recognized him and said, "Hey, hey, Marty! I see you found a couple of live ones." He waved us on. The Mountie parked on the shoulder near the on-ramp to Interstate I-190 south, and said in a stern tone, "Be careful."

"Thanks again," Adriana said, struggling to sound sincere. "We're really grateful."

"No problem," the Mountie replied and drove off.

RIDE #10
NOVEMBER 3, 1970
2:53 P.M.

THE SUN POKED THROUGH THE CLOUDS, illuminating the white birch and cedar trees in the distance with a silvery glow. The ice of the on-ramp was turning to slush from the traffic flow.

The steady stream of vehicles passing us was in one sense reassuring, but also unnerving. Certainly, by now, Ralph and Nicky had discovered that Adriana and I had escaped. It was great to be back in the USA, but everything felt out of whack.

I reached for Adriana's hand, and she massaged her fingers into mine. We were both shivering. We hugged each other tightly. Time froze—it was as if we were stuck in the middle of an avalanche and couldn't move.

A white Dodge slowed as it approached us. The shadowy face of the driver craned to get a better look at us, and when she stopped, she leaned over and rolled down the passenger window, asking in a crackly voice if we wanted a ride. I opened the door and was shocked to see that she was a nun. Adriana stepped back from the car. I could tell that she didn't want to get in. But once again she didn't have a choice.

"My name is Sister Francis," the nun said politely. The tone of her voice was formal but caring. "God's will. God's speed. I'm going only as far as Mentor, Ohio. Going to visit my brother Albert, who, I am sad to say, isn't doing so well."

Sister Francis asked us to sit in the back seat because she said she didn't want to feel crowded, and for the next two and a half hours, she didn't say a word to us. She had rosary beads hanging from the rearview mirror, and every once in a while, she reached for the crucifix dangling in front of her and whispered a short prayer or hummed a hymn. I marveled at her but kept quiet, not wanting to upset Adriana.

We held each other's hands. Adriana seemed to sleep, but I couldn't. Every five or ten minutes, my whole body shuddered, and a cold sweat seeped into my armpits.

I squirmed around in my seat; the cheap, woven upholstery chafed my skin. I couldn't get Ralph and Nicky out of my head. The only reprieve I got was when I gazed at Adriana, whose skin glistened in the afternoon light. But as the sky darkened, her face seemed to knot up and age. I imagined deep furrows between her eyes and brown spots on the backs of her hands. Her body twisted in the seat, and her forehead tensed. Though her eyes stayed closed, her lips twitched, as if she were trying to say something or cry out.

I wanted to tell Sister Francis everything that had happened, hoping that she would absolve of us of our sins and bless us. But that was impossible. What went on in that motel room was a dark secret that Adriana and I were doomed to share.

As we neared Mentor, Sister Francis told us that the next exit was hers, and she asked if we wanted to get out on the freeway or someplace else.

I watched her eyes in the rearview mirror. She sensed something was wrong.

"If you'd like," Sister Francis said, "I can take you to a motel, where maybe you can rest up a bit more before the long journey back to Columbus."

Adriana sat up, suddenly alert, and explained that we could make it to Columbus by eight or nine o'clock.

"But it gets dark so early, and this stretch of freeway doesn't have many lights," Sister Francis said. "You could be stranded. Not a very good idea in this weather."

"We'll manage. We'll be fine," I said, trying to reassure Adriana that I agreed with her.

Sister Francis exited the freeway and stopped at the first gas station she saw.

Adriana and I quickly put on our jackets.

"Thanks for the ride," I said. "It's been very . . . special."

"Please, just stay with me for a few more minutes," Sister Francis insisted. "I need to make a quick telephone call, and lo and behold, the pay phone is right over there."

After a few minutes, Sister Francis returned. She straightened her headscarf as she got back into the car. "So, I talked to my brother, and God be thanked, he's doing much better. He says he only had a twenty-four-hour bug, or something like that. Anyway, he's got a big house, mostly empty. All the children are grown, and sadly, his wife of fifty-three years passed away, why, nearly a year ago, may the Lord bless her soul. Well, I told him about you two, and he's invited you to spend the night in one of the guest rooms. It's no problem, I promise."

Listening to Sister Francis, I appreciated her offer and was about to accept the invitation when Adriana said, "Sister Francis, I don't mean to be rude. I just have to speak to Aaron about, uh, some of my obligations when we get back to campus, and uh . . . what might be best for us to do."

"Certainly, child," Sister Francis replied, "I understand. I only want to be helpful."

"Thank you." Adriana worked her way out of the car and motioned for me to follow her into the convenience store next to the gas station. Inside, she glared at me. "I'm not going to do this. You know how much nuns give me the creeps."

"Okay . . . okay. But what happens if we do get stranded on the freeway? What are we going to do? I only have fifteen bucks left. How much do you have?"

"I'm not staying in some musty old house."

"You didn't answer my question. How much money do you have with you?"

"Well... I've got more than enough for a motel room... about a hundred dollars."

"What!! You do? Why didn't you tell me? Why did you let Ralph pay for that room for us? We could have... Why?"

"Because I didn't think I needed to."

"C'mon... I can't believe... I...."

"Aaron! How can you talk that way? You saw what they did to me."

"It was awful, as awful can ever be. And worse... yeah... but what about me?"

"What about you?"

"You don't have a clue, Adriana. Do have you any idea what I went through? Just thinking about it is ripping my guts apart."

"I might never heal," Adriana cried.

"Me, too," I said, looking deep into her eyes, "I might never heal."

"We just have to move on, Aaron."

"Oh, how I wish I could. But there's something I need to ask you. I know you're not going to like it. But I need to know something. What did you say to Ralph in Italian? Did it have something to do with your father?"

"Not now, Aaron. We're in a convenience store."

"Please, give me something. I need to know what you said to Ralph in Italian."

"It was just small talk, Aaron. Yes, he probably knew something about my father's family. They have a very successful business. But just remember, my parents split up a long time ago. I hardly ever see my father. Now, lower your voice. Everybody is staring at us."

"Okay. Okay," I said, wishing I was some place other than where I was.

"We are not staying with Sister Francis."

I knew Adriana wasn't going to budge. Once she made up her mind, that was it.

"I give up," I said, resigned that I needed to accept whatever she decided we were supposed to do. "So long as you really have enough for a motel room, that is, if we need it. Let's ask her to drop us off near the on-ramp, and if no one comes, we'll do what we have to do."

Adriana nodded. "Cease fire."

When we told Sister Francis our decision, she grimaced. "I'm just so upset. It makes my blood curdle."

Adriana's face hardened.

"Oh, heavenly father," Sister Francis continued. "Please forgive me for putting these two children in harm's way. In Jesus' name, I pray."

Sister Francis made the sign of the cross. "'For just as we share abundantly in the sufferings of Christ, so also our comfort abounds through Christ.' 2 Corinthians 1:15."

Adriana's eyes widened, as if to say, "back off," but Sister Francis continued.

"'Jesus had compassion on them and touched their eyes. Immediately they received their sight and followed him.' Matthew 20:34."

Adriana repositioned herself and scowled at Sister Francis.

"Trust in the Lord with all your heart," Sister Francis pleaded.

Adriana was seething. "Why don't you just shut up!"

Sister Francis was stunned. "'Do not lean on your own understanding! In all your ways, acknowledge the Lord, and He will make straight your paths.' Proverbs 3: 5,6."

Adriana was about to flip Sister Francis the bird, but I pulled her arm back and she nearly fell over. She was sobbing, and as Sister Francis's car lurched forward, Adriana turned on me. "Aaron, please, just leave me alone. She's a witch!"

"She's not a witch," I said. "She was only trying to help us. You scared her, and to be honest, you scared me, too."

"Get away from me!"

"But there's no place to go. We're in the middle of nowhere."

"Then, get us out of here! Just don't talk to me."

The headlights of the oncoming cars were blinding. I closed my eyes, trembling inside, and for an instant, memories of Sister Ethel's humming washed over me, emboldening me. I couldn't see Adriana's face in the darkness, but I knew she was there, watching me.

MARCH 21, 1971
RIDE #20
6:38 P.M.

WALKING ALONGSIDE HEIDI BACK TO HER CAR makes me wonder what Sister Ethel looked like when she recorded the songs for her one and only album. Was she wearing a traditional Shaker dress, or was she more like Heidi? A farm girl with thick braids and a big grin as she entered the studio not knowing what to expect. Her voice, so soft and firm at the same time. Quiet emotions springing forth, more like a stream than a river. A fountain.

"All of a sudden, Aaron," Heidi smiles, "you're acting so dreamy. The dusk must taste good."

"Delicious," I say, taking a deep breath. "It feels great. Spring."

"Everything's budding out kind of slow this year. But it's happening. I know it is, even if we can't see all of it yet." Heidi glances at me and then stretches back her neck ever so slightly and sings a simple Shaker verse:

Tho' the way be rough and cragged
Mountains high and valleys low
Deep the river current rapid
'Tis the pilgrim's path we know.

I squeeze back into Heidi's Karmann Ghia, still savoring the hot brown and buttermilk. And Heidi asks, "Mind if I put the top down? It's gonna be chilly."

I nod. "Sure. But I'm only going to the freeway on-ramp."

"That so? I thought we'd take a spin first, down past Serpentine River Farms in Ryland Heights. Unless, of course, you're in a hurry."

"Not really, but ... I guess ... "

"Don't want to interfere with your spirit quest."

"Believe me, you're not."

The cloth roof of the Karmann Ghia retracts slowly, and when it seems to get stuck midway, Heidi pulls onto the shoulder and gets out to help it along.

"Poor baby," Heidi grins, and I laugh. "You mean me?"

"You wish. You're just a basket case. A loveable one, but hey, you need some work."

The Karmann Ghia chugs along. Heidi loosens her hair and lets it fly behind her in the breeze. Kentucky Highway 9 has lots of twists and turns and eventually straightens out, before winding again in a sweeping arc as dusk settles around us. Heidi flips on her high beams. The road is empty, and every few miles, Heidi points out the different breeds of horses roaming the countryside.

"They all look the same to me," I laugh. "How can you be so sure?"

"The color of their coats, the face markings," Heidi grins.

As much I want to get a closer look, I know I better get back the interstate. Heidi can tell I'm impatient. "I love hearing you talk about horses, but..."

"Guess you're going to have to come back through here, when you're done doing what you got to do."

Heidi leans over and smacks her lips onto mine. "That's a little girl kiss. Playful. Innocent. With nothing else in mind."

The road darkens, and before long, we're on I-275 headed to the juncture with I-71.

I don't know what to say. I feel like I'm caught in a tornado, my thoughts and memories swirling together with my hopes and aspirations in a violent storm that I can't control.

Heidi pokes me in the side. "Now, don't go all pouty on me. We're just getting to know each other. That's all."

"I know. I shouldn't be thinking what I'm thinking. What if we had met when we were kids..."

"Aaron, I get it. You've got a lot of baggage in that head of yours. And so do I. You need to lighten up. Me, too. Shed a few pounds. Never ain't never unless you make it so."

RIDE #11

NOVEMBER 3, 1970

7:15 P.M.

AN EIGHTEEN-WHEELER STOPPED ALONGSIDE Adriana and me, pulling onto the blacktop shoulder of the on-ramp. The driver leaned out the window and dangled his arms over the cab door, tapping a soft drumbeat with his fingertips. He had a long ponytail tied with a big rubber band and was wearing a t-shirt with a peace sign emblazoned across his chest. His arms were brawny and covered with murky tattoos.

"Where you kids going? I got a full load of pickles and brine. I got to be in Columbus by nine tonight. To be honest, I'm running on caffeine and speed. I'm desperate to talk to anyone who can help keep me going."

I was reluctant to get in, but Adriana was already walking toward the cab door.

"Look, buddy, if I didn't have a wife and a two-year-old, I'd be a hippie too. Friends call me Echo, because sometimes folks wonder if I'm really there, or if what they're saying to me is just bouncing back at them," he said, grinning. "Don't worry, kid. I'm harmless. Honest."

I wasn't so sure.

"If you want to stand out there in the cold, be my guest," Echo said. "If you can get another ride from Mentor to Columbus, be my guest. Ain't nothing but a bunch of rednecks in this town."

Adriana lifted her hand to her lips and blew me a kiss.

"Now I get it," Echo said, pointing his index finger at me. "You should forgive her. Whatever she did ain't that bad. Forgiveness, man. That's power."

I felt so manipulated, but I hoisted myself into the cab, anyway. Adriana had trouble pulling herself up, and when Echo saw that there was a brace on her leg, he reached over and extended his hand for her to grab onto. Adriana unlocked her brace and managed to position herself next to Echo, but he motioned for her to get in the back, where there was a mattress, a small battery-powered lamp, and a few magazines.

"Bet that leg of yours gives you hell sometimes," Echo said.

Adriana looked at him but didn't respond. She moved to the back and stretched her leg out on the mattress.

I sat back and tried to enjoy the ride. The front seat had cushiony springs. I'd never been in a big rig like this, and the view of the open road was more expansive than I could have ever imagined.

Echo patted his leg with one hand as he drove, as if he was listening to some song in his head that we couldn't hear.

"Man, I been driving eighteen-wheelers since I was about eighteen. So, what do you think of that? I had a direction early on. A real trajectory. I come out of West Virginia, Beckley, down in the southern mountains, coal mining country. My father and grandfather were miners. Grandpa died of black lung, and Daddy is going the same way. When I turned sixteen, I said, 'Daddy, I ain't going to the mines,' and he ordered me to get out of his house. Mama was bawling but weren't much she could do. I just moved out, stayed with a buddy of mine from high school. His daddy was a crippled veteran of World War II, and his mama died of cancer. Wasn't much more than a shack, but it was perfect for me. I quit school, did handyman jobs wherever I could find them. I contributed my share.

"But then I met an old coot that told me they were always looking for truckers. 'If you stay out of trouble, don't have accidents, you got a job for life.' Well, I don't intend to do this for the rest of my life. But for right now, it's as perfect as it's going to get. Got married last year. I did the right thing, but it took me a while to figure it out. I got her pregnant and she had the baby before I popped the question. Can't believe it took me that long. That little girl of mine is the cutest little thing. Man, I can go on and on.

"Go ahead, pick up that stack of papers in between the seats. I got pictures. Man, do I got pictures. Seems like whenever I'm around, there's a picture, me, and that little girl. She's a sweetheart, and she sure loves her daddy."

I heard Adriana tossing and turning on the mattress in the back of the cab.

"I can't sleep," she said. "Mind if I put on the little light?"

"That's what it's for," Echo said. "Pardon the magazines, you know, the male-oriented ones. I believe a man got to take care of himself, and that don't have to mean having to pay a call girl. Shoot, sometimes I'm out on the road for two, three weeks at a time. Pick up a load in Fresno, drive another to Miami, go to Chicago, Indianapolis, Pittsburgh, and then back again. I've crisscrossed this county two dozen times, or more. Done lost track. Speed does that to you. You ever try a white cross?"

I shook my head, "No. But I've heard kids in the dorm talking about them. I guess they're diet pills."

Echo smirked. "You might want to ask your girlfriend about that. Not that she needs to diet."

I was embarrassed, but when Adriana and Echo laughed, I joined in. Echo reached into the glove box in front of me and pulled out a joint. "This is some pretty good weed. Now, I ain't gonna partake of the herb right now. Man, I'm already kind of fried. But you go ahead. It's actually mighty good."

"Sounds great to me," Adriana said. "Please and thank you again."

"I like your attitude," Echo said, smiling. "Here, light this baby up."

I inhaled deeply and passed the joint back to Adriana.

In a short time, I was drifting around in what I imagined was an ether space, wherever that was. Seconds melted into minutes, minutes into a state of being where the specifics of time seemed irrelevant, ebbing and flowing with the rhythm of whatever was on the radio, whether it was news or the Beatles, Led Zeppelin, or the Rolling Stones. Adriana massaged the back of my neck and then slid back onto the mattress. "This is exactly what I need. True rest." She had a peaceful expression on her face, the first I'd seen in what felt like oh so long.

I leaned back in my seat, but I wasn't sleepy. If anything, I was more alert. "This is kind of strange," I said, a little disoriented. "I'm definitely stoned but it's different. My mind is buzzing with images and thoughts that link together in ways that I can't put into words."

Echo smiled. "Cool. Good time to chill out and stay awake at the same time."

"How's that?" I asked.

"Well, I added something special to that little cigarette. I call it a blend."

"With what? I . . . I . . . I feel like I'm on some bizzarro ride in an amusement park and I can't get off."

"Now, don't get all agitated.. I just ground up one of them white crosses and sprinkled a little bit on top of the weed before I rolled it up. It's good for you. Sure helps keep me going. It's a long way from here to there."

"Aaron, tone it down," Adriana insisted. "I'm trying to get some rest."

I looked at Adriana in disbelief. "How can you sleep? Did you hear what he just said?"

"Don't be so edgy," Echo said. "You have to ride with it."

"I feel like my eyes are darting back and forth. I can't focus on anything long enough for it to make any sense. Maybe it's because my body is so tired, and my mind is so awake."

"Sounds to me like the heebie-jeebies." Adriana snickered.

"Now, don't go paranoid on me," Echo said. "No demons in this truck. Just a boatload of pickles in brine, probably enough cucumbers to feed an entire regiment of the US Army over there in the jungles of Vietnam."

"That's a relief," I smiled. My body was starting to relax. "I'm alright. I'm fine."

"Is that so? You're white as a sheet," Echo said matter-of-factly.

"Do you have any water?"

Echo turned sharply in his seat and pointed Adriana to a compartment in the back of the cab, holding the steering wheel tightly in his other hand. "Open that door. It's a little bitty icebox. And... there you go. Go ahead, grab the thermos. Go ahead. Take a sip and pass it up here."

I reached for the thermos, but it dropped into my lap.

"Man, don't go all high maintenance on me. That's the last thing I need. I got a long night ahead of me."

"I don't... I mean, I'm fine... probably just dehydrated," I said. "I'm usually not so jumpy. Just not used to the speed, I guess."

"Just remember, we're all in this together," Echo replied in a soothing voice. "If you got to pee, let me know. You need a soda, or something to eat, we can grab a burger or something else. I don't got enough time to sit and schmooze over dinner, but I'm a decent guy. And if you can wait, that's even better. I ain't gonna to cause you no harm."

"I love you, Aaron," Adriana said, leaning forward to whisper in my ear. She pecked my cheek with a soft kiss.

I mumbled, "I feel so foolish," and Adriana whispered, "Don't worry. You are."

"You see that sign? Columbus—sixty miles," Echo said. "And we're ahead of schedule. There is a God." Echo turned up the radio and started singing along with Creedence Clearwater Revival's "Proud Mary" as he tapped out the rhythm on the dashboard with his fingertips.

Finally, I was able to close my eyes without them blinking open every few seconds. "Time to check out," I said under my breath and floated off into another world, somewhere between salvation and the land of the cursed, stuck in a purgatory of memory and anticipation. And when Echo asked where we wanted to be let out, I was so mixed up, I didn't know what to say. Adriana sat up on the mattress in the sleeper and told him that we could walk from 17th Street. And even though I knew 17th Street was right; I was still confused.

When Echo pulled the eighteen-wheeler onto the shoulder, the brakes squealed, and I got the chills. But my cheeks were hot. I felt as if I had some kind of virus or flu, but I didn't want to say anything. I pulled myself out of my seat and helped Adriana get out of the cab.

"No way to truly express our gratitude," Adriana said to Echo.

I chimed in, "Yeah. Very... cool."

Echo shouted, "Welcome home! Wish I was there!"

I was lightheaded and struggled to get the duffle bag repositioned over my shoulder. The sky was cloudy, and the air was raw and damp.

"I had a good nap," Adriana said.

"Wish I did," I muttered. "To be honest, I was trapped in a nightmare that took me somewhere I really didn't want to go. But now I can't remember exactly where that was."

"That so?" Adriana asked, wanting to end the conversation with a question instead of an answer.

We headed toward the dorm, walking side by side without talking to each other. I didn't want to tell her that I felt sick. Adriana set a brisk pace, and I could barely keep up with her. Each step was an effort.

In the lobby of the dorm, Adriana was anxious. "Just being back in the dorm makes me feel weird. It was creepy before, but it's creepier now. It's as if they already know what happened. Aaron ... I need more time to myself."

I understood all too well what she was saying. As much as everything in the dorm looked about the same, it felt different to me, too. "Do you want me to come with you to your room, so you can get your stuff out of the duffle bag?"

"Not now, Aaron. I'm going to bed. You should do the same. In the morning, if I still hurt like I do now, I'm going to the health center to get checked out."

"Do you want me to come with you?"

"Don't worry. I'll be okay."

When the elevator arrived, it was crowded with kids coming up from the basement. There was only room for one person. Adriana kissed me lightly and whispered, "Talk to you some time tomorrow. I love you."

I waited for the next elevator. By the time I got to my room, I was even more feverish. I jammed the duffle bag under my bed without unpacking, stripped down, and got under the covers. My teeth were chattering. My head sank into my pillow, and I wrapped myself tighter in my blankets until the trembling inside me stopped.

Sleep came slowly, and when it did, it was erratic. I felt the urge to pee every ten to twenty minutes or so, but when I went into the bathroom, only a little dribbled out. I just gazed into the toilet bowl and shuddered, haunted by my memories of what it was like locked naked in that bathroom in Canada. Then I trudged back to my bed where I conked out until I woke up again and again, on the hour, every hour.

NOVEMBER 4, 1970

MY THROAT WAS PARCHED. I could barely move. Time swelled, and time shrunk. Around 6:15 a.m. I stumbled out of bed to get some water. My eyes were half-open, and I didn't see my roommate Randy standing in front of me until I almost walked into him.

Randy Dorne was a big, burly jock with green eyes, stringy blond hair, and a squared-off chin. He was loud and boisterous, always bragging about his hockey scholarship to Ohio State and the cheerleaders he had at his beck and call. He grew up in Youngstown, Ohio, where his father and uncles worked in a steel mill, and his mother was a school nurse. The details of his life were so different than mine, it was as if we'd grown up in different countries and were barely speaking the same language.

As much as I tried to avoid Randy, I couldn't. Whenever Randy was around, he was always in my face, taunting me, insulting me, calling me "hippie dippie" or "Tinker Bell." Randy was a bully who made it clear to everyone in my dorm suite that he was the head honcho, meaning if he said clean the rug after he or his hockey pals puked from too much booze, you got down on your knees and scrubbed away or you suffered the consequences. Randy would go out of his way to buy a gallon can of peas just so he could dump it under the covers of your bed. But worst of all, he might give you a swirlie, grabbing you when you least expected it and dragging you into the bathroom, pinning you down and dunking the back of your head into the toilet bowl as he flushed it over and over again.

At a freshmen party in the dorm lobby, about two weeks before Adriana and I left for Canada, Randy was carrying on, making fun of me, and I couldn't take it anymore. He was slobbering drunk and trying to pick a fight. And I planted my feet and clenched my fists, and Randy just started laughing. "You're such a puny kid; I'd be ashamed of myself if I punched you out." Still, from that day on, he was different: not exactly friendly, but less of a bully to me. It was as if he understood that I could speak the same body language as him, even though we both knew he could beat me up anytime he wanted.

Randy was glaring at me. He was wearing a scarlet and gray tank top that showed off his huge biceps, and when he folded his arms across his chest, he looked like a gladiator from ancient Rome. "You been in a fight, Aaron?" he asked, as if he already knew the answer. "Somebody whupped you good."

"I don't want to talk about it now. Maybe never," I said, coughing. "I just need to get a drink of water."

"As you wish, Aaron, my boy," Randy said. "Only trying to help—that is, if you need help. I know you're scrappy."

I put fifty cents in the vending machine in the hallway and got a can of Pepsi. Randy had followed me out, and after my first sip, he elbowed me in the side.

"That's right. You look like a piece of shit." Randy smirked, but then he looked at me with more concern. "Seriously, Aaron, what happened?"

"I was hitchhiking with my girlfriend, and some idiot skidded to a stop, got out of his car, and screamed that just looking at me made him sick, that I was a filthy hippie. And I spit in his face, and he grabbed me and threw me onto the ground ... and just started kicking me."

"Is that so?" Randy shrugged his shoulders in disbelief.

"So, I did my best to defend myself, and after I, uh, after he kneed me in the nuts, he left."

"What'd he do to your girlfriend?"

"Nothing."

"Man alive. Now that's a whopper. What really happened?"

I headed back into our dorm room and set the bottle of water on my desk.

"Come on, Aaron. You're about the only person in this godforsaken place I can talk to," Randy said. He came inside and shut the door. "Everyone else just steers away when they see me coming, but you always got something to say, even if it is bullshit."

I flipped Randy the bird, and he laughed, a sneer pasted on his face.

The telephone rang and I picked up the receiver.

"Aaron, we need to talk," Adriana said. "Can you meet me downstairs?"

"Okay, okay," I said reluctantly. I was still so tired. "But I need to shower . . . and get dressed. How about in about thirty minutes?"

She sighed loudly.

"What's wrong? Are you alright?"

"I don't want to talk about it on the phone, Aaron. Please. Hurry."

"What can I do?" I mumbled and hung up. I hung up the phone. I reached for a towel on the shelf behind me and rushed toward the bathroom.

Randy yanked the towel out of my hand and popped me on the butt. I scowled and he just stood there, proud of himself, laughing. "Go ahead, you need a shower, man. You're a mess!"

When I got downstairs, I saw Adriana sitting on a couch in the lobby. She was wearing a loose-fitting, cream-colored dress and was leafing through a magazine that she dropped to her side as I approached her. She'd been crying.

Adriana straightened her braced leg, extending it forward as she steadied herself and stood up. I grasped her hands in mine and looked deep into the sadness of her eyes. I wanted to say something to console her, but I wasn't sure how. An uneasy silence settled between us.

"I couldn't sleep, Aaron. I was dizzy, and I was hurting so bad, I went to the health center and got checked out."

"What? Did you tell them what happened?"

"I didn't have to. It's obvious." Her voice was quivering. "They wanted to know where and when all this happened, but I wouldn't tell them the details. They were upset that we didn't report the crime. They wanted to give me what they called a rape kit exam to check me out and take smears from my vagina. Then they wanted to call the police, but I said no."

I grasped Adriana's hand tightly in mine, and she jerked back. "After it all sunk in, I realized I could be pregnant."

"Pregnant?" The word slammed around in my head.

Tears oozed from the corners of her eyes. "If it's true, you know, it could be your baby."

"But we've only made love a couple of times, and you said it was safe . . . that it wasn't that time of the month."

Her voice hardened. "Yes, Aaron, that's right."

"But w-wha-what, what about Ralph?" I stuttered.

She turned away. "So, what about Ralph? Or Nicky, for that matter. I don't know what to do." When she turned back, her eyes bored directly into mine. "Either way, you or them, if I'm pregnant, should I get an abortion?"

I looked at her in disbelief. "What do you mean? Either way? Me or them?"

Adriana covered her face with her hands and sobbed.

I pulled her closer. "I'm so . . . so . . . sorry," I said. "What can I do?"

"Not much. Not now," Adriana answered, pulling away. "We just need to wait. If my period stops, then I'll get myself checked again."

Adriana leaned down and unlocked her brace, lowering herself onto the couch. "Do you want me to get an abortion?"

I swallowed hard as I slowly sank down beside her. "To be honest, I've never really thought about it, other than in the abstract. I'm not against it, I don't think. But now, it hits hard. And yes, it could be mine. And as much as a part of me might want a baby, it seems kind of impossible. We're only eighteen years old. But that said, it's not . . . I mean, I guess we could. All I know right now is that I want to help you in any way I can."

"I know that," Adriana said. "I know. I've already said too much. I just wish we could be together tonight. I feel like the girls in my suite are staring at me, and they're making fun of me."

I leaned into Adriana, and she cuddled up next to me. "Well, I can't exactly take you back to my room, even though no one's there right now, except Randy Dorne, and my other roommates will be back. I have no idea where they are—must be some party I wasn't invited to."

"As if you want to go to a party looking like that," Adriana said, teasing a little smile. "I know that I can't go to your room, and I certainly don't want to go to a motel. Could we just stay here in the lobby?"

"The security guards aren't going to let us sleep all night on these couches, are they?"

"If we get our books and spread out some papers, maybe we could just happen to doze off. Can we try? Can we?" Adriana was trying to keep her emotions in check, but panic lurked in her voice.

"All right. Sure. I'll go get my books. I do have some homework I should do. I'll go up and get my stuff, and let's meet back here in about ten minutes."

"Okay, but I really don't want to talk to my roommates. All my books are up in the room."

"Couldn't you just run in, grab a couple of books, and leave?"

"It's so hard for me to walk right now. My body is so sore. If I see anyone I know, I might burst into tears."

I reached for Adriana's hand and led her to the elevator, but she stopped short.

"I can't do this. I can't!"

"Okay, okay. I'll just get my books, and they'll be enough for both of us."

"Thank you, Aaron. I know . . . I . . . "

"It's all right; I understand. I'll meet you back at our couch."

Pregnant... abortion... Mine? Ralph's? The words swirled in my brain as I rode the elevator up to my floor. My head was spinning, and when the doors opened, I bolted for the bathroom. I got down on my hands and knees in front of the toilet. I retched, but nothing came up.

I splashed some cold water on my face, then slogged back to my desk and scrounged around for my history book and the journal that I had started for English class. Randy and a couple of his hockey buddies were sprawled out on the chairs in the sitting room, glued to a football game on TV.

When I got back downstairs, Adriana was squirming on the couch, trying to make herself comfortable. "I've got chills," she said. "I don't know what to do."

Adriana reached for my hand, and I nearly lost my balance as she pulled me toward her. She nestled her head on my chest and then reached over to loosen the thigh straps of her brace.

"Aaron, will you rub my leg... here... gently?"

She guided my hand to a pressure point on the back of her thigh. Even though her skin was covered by her dress, her leg felt cold. I pressed my fingertips lightly on the atrophied muscle of her thigh and slowly massaged the tissues and bone.

"That feels so good, I mean, even though I don't have much feeling in my left leg, your touch makes me warmer." Adriana's breathing relaxed, and after about ten minutes, she rolled over onto the cushions and closed her eyes.

With Adriana beside me, I felt as if I was keeping some sort of vigil. I gazed across the lobby, watching the kids in the dorm come and go. To me, they looked like the walking dead, waiting for the vultures to descend.

I leaned back on the couch and felt my mind sinking, descending to somewhere deep inside me. I began writing in the journal I was keeping for my English class, watching my hand move across the page as if it belonged to someone else.

> Before me I am a rational man
> I am righteous, and I am wise
> Strip me to the waist if that is what you wish
> Tear from me my pants if you desire more
> In the mirror I maintain my youth
> In every artery and every vein
> Even as you attack my brain

The words came fast but stopped abruptly. I didn't know what to write next. It sounded stupid. I was exhausted.

At some point, I must have conked out. Around five o'clock in the morning, a security guard poked me in the side with his nightstick.

I rubbed my eyes with the palms of my hands. My neck was twisted and aching; I did my best to relieve it, swiveling my head from side to side. I looked with bleary eyes at the security guard, feeling wooly headed and disoriented.

"You need to see a doctor? Your girlfriend sick?" The security guard had both hands on his hips. His thick leather belt had a holster for his nightstick and slots for what looked to be cans of mace. "She a cripple?"

"No!" I said, my resentment burning through the haze of my fatigue.

"Hey, man," he said, backing off. "I don't mean anything bad. I wish I had a cute girl like that." And he walked away.

Adriana rolled over and smiled at me. "Thank you, Aaron." She tightened the straps on her brace and pushed gently on my back for me to stand up. She stood and faced me, then gave me a hug, pulling me closer to her, easing her lips onto mine in a tender kiss.

MARCH 21, 1971
RIDE #21
6:56 P.M.

WHEN HEIDI GETS TO THE JUNCTURE OF I-275 AND I-71, she exits onto a feeder ramp. "This is the perfect place for you to get your next ride. Here, cars are coming from two directions," she says with a certainty that makes me feel that I have little to worry about. But I'm not totally focused on what she's saying. I'm gazing at her lips. I want to kiss her. But as I lean toward her, she shimmies back, tickling me in the side. She's giggling but there's an edge in her voice.

"Everybody's probably getting home about now," Heidi says, "And, once again, they're no doubt wondering what I'm up to. Not that they don't trust me. It's just that sometimes they can be kind of persnickety. The truth is everyone in my little community has love in their hearts."

I straighten up. It's time to say goodbye.

Heidi takes my hand in hers and says, "Oh, Aaron, I really like you. I do."

"Back at you," I say with a deep sigh, and her eyes brighten up.

She slides over onto my seat, carefully lifting her legs over the gear shift, and pulls herself onto my lap, resting her head on my chest, and we snuggle together.

"You're so gentle, Aaron."

Heidi inches herself forward and we kiss in a way that's so different than anything I've ever experienced. Her lips are so soft and full, punctuating her face with a warm glow.

"I . . . I . . . uh . . . haven't made love in so long," I admit. "I'm not sure I still know how."

"Well," Heidi laughs. "Whatever it is poking my thigh, it certainly seems to have a sense of direction."

She unbuttons my shirt. My body pulses with an energy that makes my skin tingle. Then she raises her arms and slides off her peasant top.

Heidi straddles my thighs and presses her body into mine.

I whisper in her ear that I don't have a condom, and she leans over, sensing my embarrassment as I pull away, saying, in the sweetest voice, "We're not ready for that."

"I know. I'm sorry."

"It's okay, Aaron," Heidi says, repositioning herself. "To be honest, Aaron, I shouldn't be doing this. I have a problem, too, that I can't talk about right now. But understand, it's not you. I want to be with you, I really do, but . . . "

"Maybe that's why we're . . . uh . . . so attracted to each other. Two messed up kids."

Heidi laughs, "Wouldn't it be great if we were just kids . . . you know, if only we had a chance to start all over again."

"Not sure it would be any different."

Heidi studies my face. "What's wrong, Aaron? I don't want to sound pushy. But it's so obvious that's something really out of whack."

I roll my tongue over my lower lip. "'I . . . uh . . . don't know how to say it, especially to you, of all people . . . "

Heidi raises her hands and stretches her mouth open with her fingertips. "I can't believe my tongue is bigger than yours. Here, try this. I know a lot of stupid face tricks."

I rock back in my seat. "Wow!"

"Go ahead, try it."

"I can't."

"I'm not letting you out of this car unless you do."

"Okay. Okay."

Heidi swirls both of her index fingers in front of me, and I lift my hands to my face, pulling apart my lips from the sides of my mouth and sticking out my tongue.

"Yuk!" Heidi grimaces. "Good try. But not very funny."

"It's the best I can do."

"I don't think so. I can tell by the look on your face that whatever happened to you was totally awful. Whatever it is, Aaron. I can handle it. Talking about it could help you heal."

"I know. I know. But right now, I can't find the right words to tell you. I better go. At this point I can only focus on what's up ahead."

Heidi perks up. "Man oh man!"

I take her hands in mine, and she hums a Shaker melody. We gaze into each other's eyes. The sound of her breathing ebbs and flows, and she tries to comfort me. "Healing comes slow."

The tension in my body begins to ease up.

"You'll get there, Aaron. I know you will. But maybe you shouldn't be in such a rush.

Would you like to come home with me? Take a little time to center yourself, then do what you must."

"What?"

"The community where I live will welcome you. We've all survived some difficult times. Men and women. We only want to help each other in ways that can help us heal. We don't impose dogma."

"Sounds great . . . but . . . "

Heidi brushes back her hair with her hands. "I'm not surprised." And then nods. "Wish you'd stick around a little longer.

"The Nashville skyline keeps calling me, and it won't let go."

"Well then," Heidi says. "Let's just be grateful for the little bit of time we've had together. You really are on a mission. I love that. Just don't get yourself killed."

"You don't need to worry about me."

Heidi smiles. "As much as I don't want to say goodbye, I guess we need to say 'adieu'—until next time. If I don't get going soon, Aaron, my friends are going to get the highway patrol to come looking for me. They know the artsy part of me is easily distracted. I like hunting for things in the woods—fossils, arrowheads, petrified wood, even rusted railroad spikes. They say it's a bunch of junk, but then again, most of the guys I live with are tool men. They even got a shed that's full of old metal saws, and I'll tell you, when they first bragged on them, I was like ho-hum, but when they brought me over to see them, it was more than I could ever have imagined. So, we have a kind of truce. They got their stuff, and I got mine. I suppose I'm saving it all to make sculptures out of it one day. I think if I can actually use what I've been hoarding all these years, I might stand a chance to be someone other than who I am."

"You are so beautiful, Heidi. In so many ways. You really are . . . I just need to do what I set out to do."

"I understand, Aaron. On your way back, if you want to stop in at the café, I already gave you the number. Tell you what, I'll buy you another cup of coffee."

There's so much more I want to tell her. I inch my way out of the Karmann Ghia and yank my duffle bag out of the trunk. I wave goodbye, and Heidi sputters off, one hand flapping in the wind, the other blowing me a kiss.

The wind picks up. Cirrus clouds streak across the landscape. I hear a murder of crows flocking overhead, but when I look into the sky, none are there.

MARCH 21, 1971
RIDE #22
7:39 P.M.

I PUSH MY THUMB OUT, AND THE FIRST CAR STOPS. It's a Ford station wagon, with a hippie couple in the front seat and two dogs in the back. The woman has a freckled face and a beaded headband, and her rust-colored hair, braided into long, thick strands, hangs loosely over her muslin peasant top.

I look at the dogs and worry about cramming into the back seat with them.

"Don't worry, they're mutts." The woman laughs. "You'll be fine if they don't lick you to death first." Then she motions for me to open the tailgate of the station wagon and put my duffle bag inside.

I get in the back seat, and she's right. The dogs are lickers, and after we pull away, they trample all over me, nuzzling, slopping their tongues on my face and hands.

"That's enough!" the woman shouts. "Their names are Tom and Jerry. And I'm Maggie and that's Bill. Where you headed?"

I tell them that I'm on my way to see the Nashville skyline, and Maggie turns around and rolls her eyes. I try to explain that it's something I need to do, but the more I rationalize why I'm doing what I'm doing, the more they zone out. But when I mention Mammoth Cave, Maggie's face lights up. Bill says, "Awesome, man. We can get you as far as Louisville. And it's a hop, skip, and a big jump on I-65 from there."

I don't have anything else to say. I'm sick of talking, and Tom, the bigger dog, finally leaves me alone, and Jerry plops his chin on my lap and yawns as I pet the back of his neck. Maggie hands me a little paper bag.

"Here, I got a little treat for you. I baked them this morning. They're my very special brownies. High octane."

I reach into the bag and take one. It smells great and tastes even better.

I wish I'd told Heidi about Mammoth Cave. I wanted to say something about it when she started talking about where she lived, but I didn't think it was going to come out right. I didn't want her to think that I was just another spaced-out hippie, desperate to attach significance to something that ultimately might not matter to anyone but me.

I can feel Heidi's hands massaging my neck and shoulders, reassuring me as I stumble through more memories gnawing my gut.

NOVEMBER 14, 1970

ADRIANA WAS BY TURNS PREOCCUPIED AND DISTANT. She said that she loved me but insisted that she needed more time to herself. I did my best to respect her wishes, even though I thought about her all the time and replayed what happened to us over and over. There was no one else I could talk to about what was swimming around in my head, but she was also the last person who wanted to hear about it.

Nagging thoughts of Adriana being pregnant were weighing me down. I tried to get her to tell me what she was feeling, but whenever I brought it up, no matter how carefully, she shut down. She bit her lower lip and usually turned away from me, with a blank look on her face, like she'd buried all her emotions in a sealed urn—one of those cremation urns with nothing inside but ashes.

Most mornings, I followed her into the cafeteria, yearning to hold her hand or hug her, but she made it clear that she wasn't interested. We sat side by side without saying much until it was time to go to class. Sometimes, she warmed up a little and bussed my cheek and asked, "See you later?"

"Okay," I'd say, but never really knew where and when that might happen. Worse, there were mornings when I didn't know if I wanted it to happen.

Still, we managed to find each other, somehow. We knew each other's class schedule and mealtimes, but after a while, Adriana began to not be where I thought she'd be. She started skipping classes and not going to the cafeteria. She told me that she didn't have much of an appetite and that simply looking at food sometimes made her sick. I began to hope that the silence between us might be a good thing, allowing us to be together, but also separate.

One night, I called to ask her if she wanted to go for a walk and she actually agreed.

We met in the lobby and headed out of the dorm. I could tell that Adriana was having second thoughts, but so was I.

It was miserable outside. There was a cold mist in the air. The temperature was hovering around freezing, and the branches on the trees were starting to ice up.

Adriana was ready to turn back, but then, in the tall grass edging the sidewalk, we saw a puppy curled up in a clump of wet leaves.

Adriana released the lock on her leg brace and stooped down, scooping the puppy up. She wrapped her arms around its shivering body, and I peered over her shoulder and ran my hand over its mottled black and white coat.

"Poor baby... poor baby," Adriana crooned. "It looks a cross between a beagle and a Jack Russell terrier. What do you think?"

"I have no idea. I've never had a dog."

"What are we going to do?" Adriana asked, more animated than I'd seen her in a month.

"Well, we can't keep him," I said. "We live in a dormitory."

"Oh, c'mon! Just one night. He can stay in the bathroom. Just put him in one of the toilet stalls and barricade the door with a chair or something."

Adriana placed the puppy carefully in my arms. It had a strange underbite, and I jerked back because I thought it was going to snap at me. Adriana reached over and scratched the back of the puppy's head.

I held the puppy tightly in my hands, and it craned its neck forward to lick my face.

The cold mist turned to hard rain. The wind bristled against my back. My glasses were fogging up, but somehow, holding the warm puppy in my arms, I felt different, as if I was beginning to see myself differently.

"What are we going to call him?" I asked, excited.

"You decide, Aaron. This is your first dog." Adriana wiped the rain from her face with the palms of her hands. "I got to go, Aaron. I'm soaked. You think of a name." She turned and started walking back toward the dorm.

I blurted out, "How about Moron?"

She looked back over her shoulder and rolled her eyes.

"After all . . . he is a mutt . . . a goofy one at that."

"Is that so? Okay. If that's the name you want, fine. I got to go, Aaron!" Adriana steadied her braced leg with her left hand and swung her right arm forward, trying to balance herself.

I asked her if she needed help, scurrying up beside her and reaching for her hand.

"No, no. I'm fine," she said, motioning me away. "It's a good thing I have another brace just like this one in my room. It's going to take days for this one to dry out."

"I'm sorry. And Moron is, too."

I put Moron under my coat, and the puppy squirmed, licking my neck. I laughed, even with the cold rain dripping down on my cheeks. Adriana slowed down, and we held hands all the way back to the dorm.

When I got to my room, my roommates were surprised, but no one seemed to mind. Even Randy gave an approving smirk. "Cute dog, stupid name."

The next day, I woke up knowing I had to get Moron out of the dorm. But having him with me, even for such a short time, gave me a strange sense of purpose. I hid him under my coat and took him with me in the elevator, careful that no one saw what I was doing. Once I was outside, the rain had stopped, and the sun was poking through the high clouds. I was shivering, not because I was cold, but because I didn't want to let him go. But then, I began to think that maybe he was just lost, and that if I brought him back to where we found him, the person who owned him might find him. What Moron needed was a good home. When I let him go free in the leaves, he looked at me with longing eyes. "You'll be okay," I told him, but when I went back to the dorm, I wasn't so sure.

I called Adriana and told her what I did, expecting her to be disappointed, but instead she said that I'd done the right thing. "There's probably some little kid out there," she said, "who cried all night, hoping that Moron would come home. Of course, I'm sure his name isn't Moron. He just went along with it because he wanted out of the rain."

Adriana and I met on the banks of the Olentangy River, near the spot where we went on that first day to have our picnic. The ground was spongy, and when I accidentally stepped in a puddle, Adriana laughed. "I like to see you wiggle." And I turned beet-red, and she laughed even harder. Then she took my hand.

I followed Adriana, not knowing what to expect. I was hoping that maybe she wanted to make love. But she didn't say anything. She just held tightly onto my hand as we walked back into the dorm. And once we were inside the room, Adriana was beaming.

She stepped away and lifted her desk chair, positioning it to barricade the door to her room. Then she inched her way back to me with her arms spread. I felt my love for her surging inside me, and we hugged, rocking back and forth. She unbuttoned her blouse and lifted my hands to her breasts. I massaged her gently, and we started kissing. She shimmied down her jeans, and we fell over onto her bed. Her brace jutted up, and she jerked forward to quickly unbuckle it.

Adriana stretched out on her back, pulling me between her thighs. I was so aroused, but something wasn't right. Adriana could tell. She propped herself up and sighed.

I was worried I'd done something wrong.

"I'm still so sore. It's not you. It's me."

I rolled onto my side.

She looked at me with compassion, but I could see her lower lip quivering.

Adriana lowered herself onto the bed and rested her face on my belly. We both closed our eyes. It was as if we were floating in a giant balloon, but then there was a knock on the door and the balloon burst. I started scrambling for my clothes. It was one of Adriana's roommates. I pulled up my pants as quickly as I could, while Adriana wrapped herself in a blanket.

When the roommate came in, she didn't even look in our direction. And as I moved quietly toward the door, I whispered to Adriana, "See you soon, I hope."

MARCH 21, 1971
RIDE #22
8:48 P.M.

I FEEL LIKE MY EYEBALLS ARE SUSPENDED in front of my face, gawking at me as I lean forward. The car is rocking up and down. The horn is honking, but when I gaze out the window, there's no one there. We're on a dirt road in the middle of nowhere.

"Man, you were tripping out," Maggie says. "You were mumbling and humming. A cross between a horror movie and a Bugs Bunny cartoon. Far out!"

Jerry perks up and Tom is all over me, wanting me to pet him, too, but he can't stop licking my face.

Bill is chuckling, watching me in his rearview mirror. "Maggie sure knows how to bake them brownies just right."

I clear my throat just as Bill says, "Welcome back."

"Where are we? When did you get off the freeway?"

"Well, well, so glad you noticed. As you can see, our plans have changed a bit. We didn't think you'd mind. We decided to make a little detour to New Castle. It's just a twist in the road. I mean, if there are a thousand people living in New Castle, I might be exaggerating. But there's a guy who collects old hillbilly records there who, from what Maggie saw in an ad in the North Kentucky Tribune, is selling off part of his collection. And man, old bluegrass 78s make me weak at the knees."

I can barely think straight, and all this talk about bluegrass and hillbilly records isn't making much sense. Tom and Jerry are squirming around.

I start pleading, "Please, let me go! Let me go!"

Bill eases on the brakes, and Maggie turns around, reaching for my hand, trying to comfort me.

I jerk back. "Don't touch me! Please!"

Bill pulls a joint out of his pocket and Maggie lights it up, inhaling deeply and handing it back to me. But the smell of the marijuana makes me dizzy.

Bill stops the car, and I charge out the door, stumbling, until I keel over. I can hardly stand up. I swivel around and nearly fall over. But Maggie is at my side, helping to steady me.

"We're so sorry, Aaron. I mean . . . when I gave you one of my high-octane brownies, I thought it would, you know, help."

It doesn't make any sense. I don't remember eating a brownie. Maggie leads me back to the car. I struggle to pull away from her, but I don't have the strength. And when I get back to the car, I collapse on the back seat. I can feel the dogs licking me, but I can't hear anything Maggie and Bill are saying.

"We could leave you out here on the interstate. But we just can't. Not with you in this condition. Don't worry. The secret ingredients in the brownie will wear off, and you'll be fine. Course, it might take several hours. But there is another option. There's a cheap motel down the road, probably fifteen bucks a night. You might want to get a room, and we could pick you up in the morning and take you to Louisville. We're beat, and after we spend the hours, looking, listening, sampling two or three thousand records, we're going to need a rest. Fact is, we'll probably stay at the motel ourselves. See, once we buy the records, we got to pack them and ship them. They ain't going to fit in this car, not with these dogs trampling on them."

I know I don't have a choice. There's no way I can get out on the road and hitchhike. Not now. Not until my head clears.

"I'll tell you what, Aaron. We'll pay for your room. Give you a night off. We know you can use the rest. And there's even a burger joint next to the motel. New Castle is just a sleepy little town with friendly folks."

"In a motel? No! Please."

"You'll be okay. Just calm down."

The drive to the motel is short, and when we get there, Bill takes my hand and leads me into the office. At the front desk, the clerk is a hunched over woman with curly salt and pepper hair, granny glasses, and a cane. "Now, sonny, you look beat. We get a lot of one-nighters, guys working in the mines or on the oil rigs outside of town. The rooms are quiet and clean."

She hands me the key. Bill pays for the room, and Maggie says, "Remember, tomorrow's another day."

"Yes, indeed," Bill chimes in.

My head is still so foggy. I step forward but my feet don't feel like they're actually moving.

Maggie smiles. "Don't worry. You're going to be fine. We'll check in on you later. We have a key to your room."

When they leave, I get up and lock the door with the security chain. I don't want them checking in on me. I take some trail mix out of my duffle bag and snack. I stretch out on the bed, and before long, I conk out.

My dreams are helter skelter; it's as if I'm trapped in Sharon Tate's house and am being chased by Charles Manson wielding an ax. Suddenly, I'm running as fast as I can, going uphill into a long, dark corridor that snakes out endlessly in front of me. My heart is pounding so hard that it feels like it might explode in my chest. I'm gasping for breath. The incline is becoming steeper and steeper, and I begin to stumble, falling to my knees.

Before I hit the ground, Ralph yanks my hair, pulling my head violently backward. "Where're you going, you little fag?"

I jerk awake, choking on my own spit, my blanket soaked in the cold sweat of the nightmares that grabbed hold of me and wouldn't let go. Somehow, I manage to get up and shower.

When I step out of my motel room, Bill and Maggie are waiting for me, acting as if nothing had gone wrong. I'm angry. And when I demand to know what was in the brownie Maggie gave me, she shakes her head.

"Not exactly sure. You flipped out. I mean, my recipe was free form. The ingredients were what I had laying around. You know, eggs, flour, chocolate, pecans, some pot, and maybe a few tastes of psilocybin mushrooms."

Bill says, "You think some of that blotter acid got into the mix? I didn't think you could bake it and it would still work. Sorry, man."

I grab Maggie by the arm and gasp, "I could have died."

Maggie starts rambling on about how I was spared by divine intervention.

I can't believe it. They're both so spacey.

"Look, Aaron, we can give you a ride up to the freeway, and we can part ways, friendly like."

I'd had enough. I rush up to Bill, clench my fist, ready to punch him in the face, and he kicks me in the groin.

I curl over and stagger forward.

Bill pushes me to the ground, but as I'm falling, I grab his ankle and he topples over. I pummel him in the chest, and his head rears back and I bloody his nose.

Maggie's shouting. "You're going to kill him!"

I get on my knees and pull myself up. Bill is dazed.

Maggie glares at me, and Bill rolls over, blotting his nose, and wiping his face with a hanky he pulls from the back pocket of his jeans. "Man, my heart was beating so fast. I almost passed out."

I step back, and as much as I'm kind of sorry, part of me feels good.

"Man, you're a psycho," Maggie blurts out. "You know, I picked up on this weird vibe when we picked you up. The way you were talking about looking for the truth. A deeper truth. But I let it go. The brownie was a gift, a very special one, from my hand to yours."

Bill coughs. "You need help, Aaron. Like a shrink, or maybe a Hopi shaman."

"Why do you think you did what you just did?" Maggie asks, her voice softening.

Just the tone of her voice is getting under my skin. But there's nothing more I want to say.

"Well, good luck getting a ride," Bill laughs. "Just and wait see. Believe me, there will be consequences."

Maggie takes Bill's hand and heads for the station wagon. The dogs are already inside, barking. And they speed off.

I stand on the side of the road, squinting into the early morning sun that slices across the barren landscape. The light is so intense that it hurts my eyes, but I don't turn away. I stuff one hand into my jacket pocket and stretch out the other, my arm straight, my thumb high and proud.

MARCH 22, 1971
RIDE #23
9:11 A.M.

FINALLY, AFTER WAITING FOR AN HOUR OR MORE, a grizzly old man in a rusted-out Chevy van stops alongside me. He rolls down the window on the passenger door slowly. "How do? How do? How do you do?"

I open the door, and am about to get in, when I see he's chewing tobacco with a plastic milk jug between his legs for his spittle.

"Ain't nothin' to worry about. That boy down the road asked me to pick you up and run you up to the highway."

I don't get it. "Who?"

"Your friend Bill."

I shake my head. "Bill?"

"Yeah, the boy who just bought all them hillbilly records."

I stare deep into his sagging eyes.

"Bill said you might be dangerous. Psycho."

I step backward and turn to walk away.

"I wouldn't do that!" the man shouts. "Bill's daddy lives up on that ridge over there. Now, Bill and him had a big falling out years ago, when Bill turned hippie and got all tangled up with that flower child Maggie. They say they started screwing at a love-in in San Francisco, and little Bill got hooked. But all of that said, his daddy still looks out for him. And the news you bloodied his nose traveled fast."

It's clear that this guy is nothing but trouble. "How far to the highway?"

"You going to walk? I wouldn't do that if I were you. There are wild dogs on that road."

I stare at him, not wanting to say yes or no. The thought of wild dogs chasing after me terrifies me. But I'm not going to get into that van. No way.

"I'll take my chances."

"Suit yourself."

I start walking toward the highway. But that old coot won't leave me alone. He just shifts his van into first gear and inches along behind me, gritting his teeth with a sarcastic smile and following me all the way to the on-ramp. I have no idea where I am. All I know for sure is that I have to get away from him.

I'm hot, sweaty, and pissed off. I lower my duffle bag to the ground and stomp over to him. I clench my fist and punch the side panel of the van.

The old man leans over and jerks the passenger door into my side. I stumble back and he laughs. I move away from the van, but he gets out and staggers toward me. I drop my duffle bag, ready to do whatever I have to, and he jabs his fist into my gut.

I'm seething. I want to kick him in the balls, but I hold back.

"I could snap you in two," he growls, snapping his fingers. "Just like that."

I lift my duffle bag and swing the strap over my shoulder.

But the old man isn't satisfied. He rushes at me, planting his feet in front of me.

Face to face.

We just stand there, gawking at each other. The cars that pass us are honking their horns. One of them skids up beside us on the gravel shoulder. It's Bill and Maggie.

Bill snarls, "I warned you there'd be consequences. You better watch what you do because this old man is one mean SOB."

Maggie's giggling. "Want another brownie?"

I swivel around, and the old man swipes his foot behind the calf of my right leg. My knee buckles, and he spits a wad of tobacco onto the ground.

"Man, this is too much fun." Bill laughs. "Too bad Maggie and I don't have the time to stick around. Have a nice day."

The old man gets back in his van and putters off. Bill and Maggie watch me through the windshield of their car, as they light up a joint and their dogs yelp in the back seat.

I keep telling myself I'm going to make it to Nashville one way or another.

I walk across the road to a Texaco station. I need to get something to drink, but when I reach into my pocket for my wallet, it isn't there. I can't believe it. Maybe I left in the motel room, where I'd spent the night. But I can't go back there. Not yet. I need to call Heidi first, to see if maybe it fell out of my pocket in her car. I hurry over to the pay phone, but I only have ninety-five cents and that isn't enough. So, I call the operator, hoping that Heidi is at the café, hoping that she'll accept the collect call.

A voice answers that I don't recognize, but she hands the phone to Heidi, who says, "I'm going to get in big trouble for this."

"I'm sorry. I messed up."

"You sure did. But hey, when I saw your wallet on the floorboard of the Ghia, I knew I'd hear from you again, one way or another."

"You mean dead or alive?"

"Well, sort of... You mean a lot to me, Aaron."

"I'm so glad. I really am."

"That's a good thing. I think."

"Meeting you, Heidi, has... uh, well, affected me in ways that... You've touched a part of me that I didn't think was still there."

"That's cool, Aaron. That's cool. But let's get down to basics. Where did you say you are?"

"Outside a Texaco station in, I guess, New Castle. Exit 34."

"Well, that's a hike. But... okay... I can come meet you. My shift ends in about thirty minutes."

"Really?"

"To be honest, it's going to take me about an hour and a half to get there. Do you have some place to wait?"

"I . . . uh . . . yeah. There's a little diner across the road—on US 421. It's called the Red Hook Café. I can't believe you're doing this. Why? I mean . . . "

Heidi giggles. "If you can't figure that one out, then you really are a lost cause. See you sooner than later."

When I hang up the receiver, I'm dizzy. I need something to drink, so I trudge over to the Red Hook Café and sit in a corner booth. And when the waitress comes over to me, I tell her I'm a wreck, and she gets me a glass of water.

Waiting for Heidi is excruciating. I keep watching the clock above the café counter, and as the seconds and minutes tick away, the edgier I become.

DECEMBER 8, 1970

ADRIANA STARTED TELLING ME ONE THING and doing something else. Then, she'd say she was sorry, purring that she wanted to make love again, but it was tough figuring out when or where. Rarely was everyone out of either of our dorm rooms, and when they were, it was usually in the middle of the day. That meant that one of us had to skip class, but we were both already behind. Adriana's grades were crashing. I offered to help with her homework, but she complained she couldn't sleep at night, and if she couldn't sleep, she couldn't think. And she didn't have much of an appetite. Dorm food made her miserable, and when we went to our favorite burger joint on High Street, she wasn't hungry.

The waitress brought my burger and fries, and when she placed it on the table in front of me, my stomach was in knots. But I was starved. I took a bite out of my burger, and Adriana started scooting out of the booth. I pleaded with her not to leave, but she kept resisting.

"Don't let me spoil your dinner."

"You're not. Believe me."

Adriana pulled a Kleenex out of her purse and patted her eyes. She opened a small compact and fixed her makeup. "Why didn't you tell me my lipstick was smeared?"

"Sorry," I said, around a mouthful of burger.

And she smirked. "Aren't you going to eat your fries?"

I wiped my fingers on my napkin. "No, I'm good. They're too greasy."

"Aaron," Adriana said, her voice starting to shake. "I've been putting this off, but I can't hold it in any longer. I'm pregnant."

I glazed over, my lips trembling.

Tears started to track mascara down Adriana's cheeks. "I have to get an abortion. "

"Abortion? What? I mean, what if I'm the father?"

"Aaron, we've talked about this before. We can't have a baby. Not now. And what if Ralph or Nicky is the father? Then what?"

I felt as though the inside of my head was an echo chamber. Pregnant . . . abortion . . . pregnant . . . abortion . . . Ralph . . . Nicky . . .

"Isn't abortion illegal in Ohio?"

"Yes. But in New York it's possible, up until the twenty-fourth week of pregnancy. The law banning abortion was changed this year."

I was stunned. It was clear that Adriana had decided what she was going to do, long before she told me. "So, how much can you chip in?" she asked in a stern voice. "It's going to be expensive."

I straightened up in my seat, stuttering, "I . . . uh . . . I probably only have a few hundred dollars. It's the money my parents gave me to cover expenses for school, and they watch that account balance like hawks. But that said, I'll drain every penny for you."

Adriana started sobbing. "I don't know what to do. I have maybe four or five hundred dollars. But this could cost more, and we have to get there and back."

I gritted my teeth. "Well, we can hitchhike."

Adriana's eyes went wide. "Do what? After all we've just been through? You're crazy!"

I held up my hands, trying to placate her. "We can be more careful; I know we can. In Canada, we made too many mistakes. We're smarter now."

Adriana flung herself out of the booth and stomped toward the door. I felt like the undigested food in my stomach was surging into my throat. I waited for the waitress, paid for the food, and left.

It was late, but I needed to go for a walk to clear my head. The air was cold and raw, reminding me of winter nights when I was a kid. I had to get a job. I had to earn some money fast. But what could I do? I had no training, no qualifications for much other than being a newspaper boy, or maybe a dishwasher in a greasy spoon restaurant, like the one I'd worked at the summer before college.

Just thinking about Adriana getting an abortion made me crash. I saw a little dog sniffing around on the sidewalk in front of me and started thinking about Moron and how much he'd meant to me.

Finally, I made it to a bodega. I went inside and bought two pieces of beef jerky, one for me and one for the little dog that was still pawing around on the sidewalk. I peeled a piece of jerky out of the wrapper and dropped it on the pavement. And the little dog pounced on it, chewing and swallowing his piece in about fifteen seconds. I took a small bite of mine, savoring the jerky taste, anguishing over everything that was wrong with my life.

On my way back to the dorm, I got lost. I took a wrong turn and ended up in a neighborhood of dilapidated Victorian houses and red brick apartment buildings with pock-marked masonry and ragged ivy. The streets were empty, but it seemed that the lights around me were flickering on and off, casting bizarre shadows in front of me. I wasn't sure what was real and what I imagined. By the time I got back to the dorm, I was exhausted. But once in my room, I knew I had to call Adriana.

When she picked up the phone, I asked her if she was awake, trying to keep my voice calm.

She sounded groggy but was willing to talk.

"We need to go to New York right away. I want to help you get done what you—we need to do."

"In the middle of the night?"

"Okay, okay . . . then first thing in the morning."

"How? What? Aaron, please. Goodnight."

Dial tone.

I stared at the phone in my hand for a few seconds, then returned it to its cradle.

My legs ached; my ankles felt swollen. I went into my bedroom, took off my clothes, threw them into a heap on the floor and got under the covers naked.

I fell headfirst into a sleep crazed with dreams of annihilation. Someone handed me a World War II era machine gun, and I charged into a battlefield somewhere in France, somewhere that looked like the TV show Combat. Ralph and Nicky popped up in the landscape, like targets in an arcade shooting game. I gunned them down, but they never died. The harder I tried to kill them, the more menacing they became. They took turns taunting me, threatening me, but as the dream went on, they attacked me one at a time, sneaking up behind me and shooting tiny darts into my ears until I went deaf.

The next thing I knew Randy was jabbing a knee into my back, yelling at me in an angry voice. He jammed the telephone receiver into my hand, but I couldn't understand what he was saying.

I felt like my head was going to explode. I hung up the receiver and rolled over in my bed. But soon Randy was back in my face with the telephone. I recognized Adriana's voice trickling from the receiver. She was calling my name, telling me I had to meet her in the lobby.

When I got downstairs, Adriana was pacing around. Her eyes were red; she'd been crying. "I'm so sorry, Aaron. What have I done?"

I reached for her hands. I wanted to hug her, comfort her, and she brushed me away. "If you want to break up with me, go ahead. I can take care of myself and . . . my abortion. I talked to my cousin Jerry, and once I get to New York, he'll help me."

I tried to swallow. But my tongue felt swollen, making it difficult to talk.

Adriana wiped the back of her hand across her face, smearing tears across her cheek.

"Please, Adriana. We need each other."

Adriana pivoted toward me; her arms folded tightly across her breasts. "I'm scarred for life!"

"Well, so am I! We're both victims. Can we please not argue about who suffered the most?"

Adriana cupped her face in her hands. "We've already said enough. You will never be able to go through what I went through. And I suppose... that's also true for me."

My lips felt numb. "I... I... want to go with you to New York. I want to be with you—to stay with you. I do."

Her hands drooped to her sides. "Are you sure?"

"Yes, of course." I tried to make my voice strong. "But... only if ... I mean... we need to hitchhike to New York. We have to."

Adriana gaped at me. "You are impossible!"

"Please, just hear me out, okay? We have to prove to ourselves that we can do it, that it's like falling off a horse and getting back on. We need to do this, so we won't be afraid for the rest of our lives. I don't want to be bitter."

"You're completely nuts. And you've never even been on a horse. So how could you know what it's like when you fall off?"

"I know. I know. But you understand what I mean. I know you do."

Her shoulders slumped. "Well, I guess we don't have enough money to do much else."

I tried to reposition myself, to act more confident, but it didn't seem to do any good.

Adriana shuddered. "Just thinking about it terrifies me."

"What did you tell your cousin?"

"I just told him I need a loan. A private loan, like. I didn't use the word 'abortion' if that's what you're worried about."

I leaned forward, steadying myself.

"Jerry thinks it's for some kind of VD I've got."

I stared at her. "So, you need money to cure the VD your boyfriend gave you?"

"Don't worry, Aaron. I didn't blame you."

"I suppose that's good . . . I mean . . . But why would we need to go to New York for that? They can treat VD here."

"I don't want it in my school medical records. That's what I told him."

"God, Adriana." I looked out the window and shook my head. "I'm losing it."

"He didn't ask for many details, Aaron. It was obvious to him that I'm in deep trouble, otherwise I wouldn't be asking him."

We stared at each other, the words laying between us.

I mumbled, "You didn't blame me?"

"That's right," she said. "I love you so much that I'm willing to let you go, if that's what I have to do."

I tore my eyes away from her. I shook my head, staring at my feet.

"All right!" Adriana shouted. "I'll hitchhike with you to New York City, so long as we stay at my mother's apartment. But remember, we can't tell her why we're really there. She'd never give her consent, or approval."

"Does she even know I exist?"

"Of course, she does. I love you, Aaron."

"What about your father?"

"Never. I've already told you. They split up when I was in high school."

"Are they divorced?"

"Well, not exactly. They don't live together. But they have some kind of business arrangement. Something about taxes and marital privilege, meaning neither of them can testify against each other in court."

"What?"

"The short of it, Aaron, is that my mother has another man in her life. His name's Harold, and he lives in the city, but spends a lot of time in Queens. And my father lives in Manhattan and has another family, who I don't know very well. My father and I don't talk much.

Except when I need something, like college tuition, he steps up and takes care of it."

"That's good, but...."

"Believe me, once we're in New York, everything will be okay. I promise."

MARCH 22, 1971
RIDE #24
1:11 P.M.

AFTER THREE WATER REFILLS AND A CUP OF COFFEE in the Red Hook Café, the waitress smirks. "That's the limit. You look like a nice boy, but we got a few men over there who'd like your booth."

"Nice boy?" I say to myself, grinning at her as I hand her the change I have in my pocket.

I can feel the stares of the people around me and rush outside. I pace around, kicking the gravel in the parking lot.

When Heidi pulls up, she starts honking her horn, and an elderly couple hobbling out of the café shake their heads. The man is hunched over, and his wife holds tightly onto his forearm.

As I open the door to Heidi's Karmann Ghia, I joke, "Hope that never happens to me."

"It could be a good thing," Heidi says, "to be in love for that many years."

"Is that really possible?"

Heidi is starry-eyed. I'm surprised that she's wearing a white waitress uniform, especially since she didn't have one on when I first met her.

"Oh, if I only had a camera," Heidi giggles. "It's like you've just seen a ghost. I know, I know. The uniform is blinding, especially in the sun. Old George, my boss, decided it was time for a new look."

"Actually," I say, "I like it. More professional. Ha!"

Heidi hands me my wallet and I thank her again for making such a big effort to bring it to me.

Heidi nods and stretches back her shoulders. "So, let's go somewhere."

"Don't you have to get back to work?"

"Not until 5:30 tomorrow morning. I need a break. Where do you want to go?"

"Somewhere I've never been before."

"Sounds dreamy. But... I have an idea, and you may or may not want to do it. But I was wondering if you'd like to meet my friends?"

"In Kentucky?"

"No, no. It is a bit of a hike. In Ohio, about fifteen minutes from the café. You don't have to. I know you turned down my last invite. But I want to try again."

I ask if she means turning around, after driving nearly two hours to pick me up, and she nods. "Not a problem. It just means that you'll have to hitchhike from there back to here and wherever else you're going."

"Okay, I guess."

I scratch my head and focus on the little trinket dangling from the rearview mirror of Heidi's Karmann Ghia.

"Oh, that's my good luck charm," Heidi says. "It's a little dog with short legs. I saw it at a flea market, and it reminded me of Sparky, my dog when I was a kid, who got run over by a car. I was seven, and I cried for days, and as much as it's kind of a bad memory, when I picked up this silly thing, I felt like it had a healing power."

I smile. "Yeah. We do have a lot in common—Sister Ethel. A little dog."

"You had a dog?"

I tell Heidi about finding Moron and keeping him for a night, and she grimaces. "Thank God you brought him back to the spot where you found him. How could you have been so mean to give that innocent creature that name?"

I shrug. "Guess I was the moron."

Heidi's eyes widen. "Maybe so."

"I'm trying to work through it. I am."

"That's a good thing. So, before we get too depressed, you ready?"

"Yeah, sure."

"Now, don't get all gushy on me," Heidi jokes.

I lean back in my seat. Heidi pulls back on the steering wheel. "Hold on!" The acceleration of her Karmann Ghia is slow and deliberate, sounding more like a lawn mower than a sports car. Heidi lowers her window, complaining that there's still some kind of exhaust leak, which was supposed to have been fixed when it was in for an oil change and tune-up.

The whoosh of air into the car makes it difficult to hear everything that we're saying, but it doesn't seem to matter. We're both so excited to be together, but there's something about Heidi's manner that makes me wonder whether she could ever truly get involved in a love relationship with me.

The landscape brightens and the barren farmland and rolling hills glisten with hints of life. Heidi starts talking about the need for crop rotation to solve insect and disease problems in the plants. "Wheat grows best," Heidi says, "when it follows soybeans, that is, if the soil isn't too wet."

I don't know anything about agriculture and listening to Heidi ramble on about the three-year rotation of corn, soybean, and wheat is interesting, but only up to a point. I keep wanting to change the subject, but it's clear she's into it, telling me that when she was growing up, her father put her in charge of seeding the vegetable garden in the backyard of their house.

I don't want to talk about my childhood, so Heidi just goes on and on, but when she senses that I might be bored, she asks, "Did I do the wrong thing? I thought you liked being in the country. I might be a waitress, Aaron, but I'm a country girl at heart."

"I love that. I'm just a kid from the suburbs."

Heidi rolls her eyes. "Different planets. Same solar system," she says and then hums a Shaker song.

"That's beautiful. I feel like I've heard that before."

"You have? I don't remember all the lyrics, but these are the lines that have stuck with me:

Come to contentment lovely guest!

Reign unrival'd in my breast.

Those simple melodies, Aaron, they make my heart smile."

Heidi exits the freeway, following the feeder road for about a mile, and then turns onto a gravel road past a newly painted red barn to a three-story Victorian-looking farmhouse.

"When Jed and Missy founded our community, they answered an ad that read 'Old home for sale cheap' and it was the perfect fixer upper. Built in 1921 by a World War One soldier who came back to this parcel of land where he had grown up, only to find his parents had died from smallpox, He rebuilt the place. It took him fourteen years, and just as he was about to finish, he met the daughter of the minister of a local Methodist church, who had moved back to town to teach elementary school, and a few months later they married and started making babies. But something dreadful happened. One of their kids found a gun in the closet and accidentally killed one of his siblings. And when his mother got the gun away from him, it went off and the bullet shattered two vertebrae in her neck, leaving her paralyzed from the chest down. Well, the family moved away, and the house was sold at auction, and then abandoned for more than two decades before Jed and Missy found it.

"Jed's a Vietnam War vet from the Hocking Hills and Missy is an immigrant from Cambodia. They met in a refugee camp, where Jed was stationed as part of the military police. Jed says it was love at first sight. He didn't know anything about her past. He only saw who she was, kneeling over a friend who had passed out from exhaustion. And it wasn't long before they got together and made those solemn vows."

"Were they married here?"

"In Cambodia. It made it easier for her to leave with him. Man and wife."

Heidi parks in a lot adjoining the house.

"Now, I need to tell you something. Not everyone is into the Shaker thing in the same way I am. Even though we all love the Shaker heritage of this part of Ohio—the songs, the hymns, the furniture. The simple life. Positive energy. Close to nature. We're a family. We help each other and believe in a better world. Fact is, not everyone is a Christian. Not everyone is celibate. It's all a matter of free will and personal choice."

I follow her inside, where we're greeted by a lanky man wearing a plaid flannel shirt, baggy blue jeans, and camo boots. He gives Heidi a quick hug and then extends his hand to me.

"So, you're the guy Heidi's been talking about. I'm Jed."

Heidi motions for me to stay where I am and then heads into the hallway, where I hear her talking to someone, who sounds like she has an African accent. Jed offers me a glass of water from a pitcher on a table in the entry foyer.

"Gee, thanks," I say. "Can't get enough."

"Man, that's the best water I bet you ever tasted. Artesian water from an underground spring. Missy and I'd heard about it, and it took some doing to find it. But when we did, glory be!"

Heidi approaches me slowly, holding hands with the African woman she'd been talking to. "Aaron, this is Aminata. She's our newest resident. From Burkina Faso."

"Pleased to meet you," Aminata says softly.

"You, too," I say, wanting to shake her hand, but she pulls back and glances away.

"Too much, too soon," Heidi whispers in my ear and leads me into a sitting room near a grand wooden staircase. "Aaron, you seem tired. Would you like a nap?"

"Uh... maybe."

"You're welcome to come to my room." Heidi can tell I'm uneasy and says, "Aaron, I have two twin beds."

"That's not what I meant."

"If you'd prefer, Aaron, I can take you back up to the freeway. But, hey, you've come a long way just to say you've been here, done that."

"I can't believe how much I'm messing all this up. I'm here, Heidi, because there's something about you that makes me feel normal again."

"Normal I'm not, Aaron. I have problems, too. Nothing compared to you, I suspect. Me, I just broke up with my boyfriend a few months ago. And well, it was a mess. So, Jed said I could move over here and stay a while. Jed's been like a brother to me since, well, forever, since grade school. Our mothers were friends, and when my mom passed, his mother was like a mother to me. Jed and Missy have a mission. They want to help people who, for whatever reason, don't fit in anywhere else. Everyone has a backstory, and we're all just trying to get by, working out what we can and making the best of what's left."

"That's great."

Heidi clears her throat. "If I didn't feel something special for you, I wouldn't have asked you to come here. I'm better now. I am. But that's not to say that I don't still have problems. To be totally honest, a couple of the guys here have done stuff that I don't even want to know about. I mean, they're on parole for crimes, Jed says, that weren't fairly prosecuted from the get-go. I guess it has something to do with drugs. But they're clean now. And that's all that matters."

I lean forward and lower my head between my knees. I'm a little dizzy.

"Aaron, let me get you another glass of water. You look so pale."

"I'm sorry," I say, doing my best to pretend I'm okay.

"Aaron, you need to stop saying you're sorry so often. Whatever happened to you wasn't necessarily your fault."

"I'm not so sure about that."

"You need to save a little compassion for yourself."

"I guess."

"Take a deep breath."

"To be honest, Heidi, it's not just about me. Being here makes me feel different. Like I'm not alone. But I have so many questions that I'm not sure I should be asking. Why do people come here? What happened to Missy in Cambodia? How did Aminata find out about this place?"

Heidi straightens up. "People who settle in our community have had tough lives. Some have been badly wounded—physically, psychologically. Our community is a safe place."

"I can tell, but . . . "

"That's a good thing. It's hard for me to talk about what others are going through. Missy and Arminata share what they can when they can."

I step up behind Heidi and kiss her lightly on the back of her neck and she says, "Please, Aaron, spend the night. I'll give you a ride up to the freeway in the morning. That way, you can get a fresh start. Have a home-cooked meal with us tonight. The food here is incredible. After dinner, we sometimes sing Shaker songs. You can join in if you want. Me, I'm more of a listener."

Heidi turns toward me and wraps her arms around me in a tender embrace. We gaze deep into each other's eyes.

"I never get tired of looking at you," Heidi says.

"Back at you."

"You can still stay in my room," Heidi says, "even though . . . "

"I understand. Thanks. I know . . . I know we can't . . . you know, have sex."

"To be honest, Aaron, that may be true. But we can still make love."

DECEMBER 11, 1970

WHEN ADRIANA SAW ME IN THE CAFETERIA, she ran toward me and swooped her arms around me. And I did the same, hugging her close, echoing her "I love you".

Adriana looked more disheveled than ever. She was wearing a wrinkled turtleneck sweater with a purple and black weave over washed out jeans with embroidered patches on both knees. Her hair was stringy, and her eyes were puffy.

We went through the cafeteria line quickly, each of us grabbing orange juice, cereal, and coffee.

"I got Froot Loops, Aaron," Adriana said with a little giggle. "I think they're funny. You, on the other hand, are completely boring. How you can eat Wheat Chex every day is beyond me."

I broke open my box of cereal and doused it with a carton of milk.

Adriana scratched the back of her neck with her index finger, cringing at the speed at which I ate. I was so ready to get on the road.

I could tell Adriana was grateful, but she was worried too. She took my hands in hers, her facial expression softening as she spoke. "What made me fall in love with you, Aaron, was that I saw a complement to me in you. But at the same time, a perfect counterpoint to me. Sometimes I don't think you get it. You hardly know who you are. Which, I guess, might be true for me, too."

I gazed down the highway of Adriana's eyes, but I didn't know how to respond.

There was a glint of light flashing in the distance. It was time to get moving.

Adriana pursed her lips, and we went back to our rooms to gather our stuff. I could tell she was disappointed that I didn't have more to say, but I didn't want to upset her by saying the wrong thing.

DECEMBER 11, 1970
RIDE #12
8:55 A.M.

ONCE WE GOT ON THE ROAD, ADRIANA CHEERED UP, singing a few lyrics from Judy Collins' "Both Sides Now," but I was more depressed, feeling a pang of guilt that I was forcing her to hitchhike when she was just as terrified as I was.

We didn't get off to a very good start. Everything took longer than planned, and after about forty minutes of trying to get a ride to the on-ramp for I-70, we decided to just walk there from our dorm. Adriana was limping more than usual. She reached over and repositioned her brace. "I'll be okay. I just can't get it right today, no matter what I do. It's like I'm stuck on a treadmill and can't get off."

I wanted to be kind to Adriana, but I didn't know exactly how. So mostly I kept to myself. I focused on the road in front of us. The weather was good; the sun was strong, and the temperature was supposed to rise into the mid-forties by the afternoon.

Each car that passed us made me flinch, but I did my best not to show any apprehension. Adriana kept to herself, too, and it seemed to me that in the quiet lay a tenuous peace, an acceptance of what we needed to do together.

After about an hour and a half, a green Volvo station wagon stopped. A boy with shaggy blond hair who looked to be about five or six rolled down his window, and said, "Granny wants me to tell you we're going to Pittsburgh, and if you want a ride, you can get in."

The driver popped open the tailgate. We loaded our duffle bag and then climbed into the back seat.

Jack squirmed around in his seat, and after a few minutes, he asked

Adriana, "What's wrong with your leg?"

Adriana smiled. "Uh . . . it was a birth defect."

"What's that, Granny?"

Adriana answered, "Something went wrong before I was born. It's kind of like my leg got sick and the muscles didn't grow right, meaning I can barely move it, and I can't walk without this brace."

"Does it hurt?"

"Sometimes. But I'm alright. It's been this way since I was a baby."

Jack's grandma was wearing a bulky yellow sweater that looked handmade, and her white hair was tied loosely into a bun at the back of her head. "I'm a retired schoolteacher," she said. "My name's Beth, Beth Henshaw, originally from Cincinnati. Jack is my son's boy, and he's just along for the ride. Poor kid, his grade school caught fire a couple of weeks ago. Bad wiring, they say, so he gets an unexpected vacation, which, from his point of view, is not so bad. Course he has to make it all up at the end of the school year."

After about twenty miles of small talk about the weather and how the Ohio State campus had grown beyond recognition, the conversation tapered off, and Adriana and I laid our heads back on our seats.

I couldn't stop thinking about what we were going to do in New York. Was an abortion really the right thing to do? I could tell from what Adriana said—and what she didn't say—that she wasn't sure, either. It was one more thing we could barely talk about—another elephant in the room. There was an invisible barrier separating us, even though we were sitting side by side.

As we neared Pittsburgh, Beth asked where we wanted to be dropped off. "Anywhere along here is good," I said. Adriana reached for my hand and pressed my palm onto the thigh of her braced leg. I could feel a twitching under the straps and tried to comfort her by massaging the atrophied muscle tissue as best I could. Adriana smiled, but when Beth stopped, she pulled away and scooted out onto the gravel, straightening her leg quickly and limping forward.

"Wait just a second," Beth said as I was about to get out of the car. She reached into her purse and took a twenty-dollar bill out of her wallet, then motioned for me to take it from her hand.

"Oh, thanks. But really, that's not necessary."

"I know it's not necessary, but I can tell you both have got a lot on your minds right now. Sometimes Christmas comes early."

"Well, if you're sure . . . thank you very much."

But when Adriana saw Beth give me the money, she poked her head back inside.

"We can't accept that," she said. "It's very kind of you, but."

"No buts about it," Beth said. "I want you to keep it. I guess it's my maternal instinct."

When I looked into Beth's blue eyes, I thought she was probably older than my parents, but her disposition and appearance—her rosy cheeks and the tiny cleft in her chin—all made her seem younger.

"Thanks again," I said enthusiastically. "This is really nice of you."

Adriana backed away.

"How could you take that money, Aaron?" Adriana barked as soon as the car drove away.

"It was a gift. I sure didn't ask for it."

"A gift? It was charity. And I don't take charity."

I shook my head and stepped in front of Adriana, throwing my thumb up in the air without saying another word.

Adriana's mood swings were hard to endure, but I kept telling myself that I had to be patient; I had to be there for her, even if it meant sacrificing a part of myself. She had so much weighing her down: the rape, the pregnancy, the abortion. It was tough for me, too, but it had to be worse for her.

DECEMBER 11, 1970
RIDE #13
11:08 A.M.

THE WAIT FOR OUR NEXT RIDE WASN'T VERY LONG. A shabby Volkswagen Microbus pulled over. It was covered with flower decals, and a big white peace sign covered the side door.

"C'mon in!" the driver shouted. "We got plenty of room."

We pulled open the door and saw there was everything but room inside the van. It was stuffed with stacks of cardboard boxes. Two bicycles, a dresser with chipped veneer, and a tattered mattress were somehow crammed in, too.

"Where you headed?"

"New York City."

"Well, we're moving to Brooklyn, so this is your lucky day."

Adriana and I squeezed into the back of the van and propped ourselves against the boxes. I could tell Adriana's braced leg was bothering her by the way she shifted around. I wanted to help but knew if I said anything, she'd push back.

"I'm Danny, and this here is Shelley," the driver said with a big grin. "The good news is we can take you into the city, but the not-so-good news is that it might take all night. We're having engine problems and going over fifty miles an hour could be dangerous. So, it's slow and steady."

"We love this van because the van loves us," Shelley laughed. "We call it the speckled tortoise."

"Yeah!" Danny chimed in. "Groovy."

Danny and Shelley appeared to be in their late twenties; both were dressed in bellbottom jeans and tie-dyed t-shirts. Shelley had wavy, chestnut-colored hair, and Danny had a big bald spot and two long black braids that dangled from the sides of his scalp down to his shoulders. Danny was a cautious driver, and he pulled off the freeway to rest the tortoise about every hour on the hour, and sometimes sooner when he sensed that the engine was overheating. "We need to stoke up with a little more java," Danny liked to say, and after the fifth or sixth stop, we were all saying it in unison. The coffee stops were long and chatty.

"Got to let the tortoise cool down," Shelley said. And when they did, Danny usually insisted on checking the radiator and the oil.

"We know there's a little leak in the oil pan, but it's hard to gauge," Danny added. "Now, if I just had the time, I could put it all into a mathematical equation and figure it out, but that ain't no fun."

Danny talked about lots of random stuff, but he generally circled back most often to the topic of a spirit quest he was asked to join with some Yaqui Indians in Arizona. Shelley talked about the women's movement and the push to get an equal rights amendment through Congress.

"Women are sick of being treated like chattel," Shelley railed, "sick of being second-class citizens in the most prosperous country on the planet. The battle line's been drawn. Either you're with us or you're against us. There is no middle ground."

Despite their unpredictable, meandering conversation, Danny and Shelley seemed totally together, so much so that I felt closer to Adriana, just from being around them. When Danny and Shelley held hands or kissed each other on the lips when they were sitting across from Adriana and me in a café booth, I had the urge to do the same. And Adriana didn't seem to mind.

"How long have you two been married?" I asked Shelley when we were back on the road.

"We're not," Shelley smiled. "We think that marriage as defined by the courts is out-of-date and ultimately an obstacle to a true union. We only want to stay together if we want to be together."

"True love is liberating, man," Danny said.

The heater in the van made a groaning sound, and we all laughed.

"So, tell me more," Adriana said. "Like, how do you know if you're really liberated, I mean, through love . . . does that make any sense?"

"I remember when I was your age, which wasn't so long ago," Shelley said. "Life was such a mystery. Well, it hasn't really changed. I still don't know all the answers, but I'm picking up a few more clues."

"I think she watches too many detective shows on TV," Danny said. Shelley elbowed him. "But all joking aside, you've got to be willing to let go," he continued. "Love liberates you from within."

"That's right," Shelley said. "We don't even own a TV. We put a high premium on dialogue with each other. TV separates you from the one you're with."

"Well . . . and we also can't afford a TV," Danny said. "But that's beside the point, man. It's not the TV; it's what you as an individual bring to the experience. Marshall McLuhan is right. 'Ads are the cave art of the twentieth century. There are no passengers on spaceship earth. We are all crew. The medium is the message'—but only if you believe it."

I tried to puzzle through the logic of this, but then Shelley was talking again. "My favorite McLuhan quote is 'Diaper spelled backwards is repaid.' Just think about it."

"Time to chill out, man. Let's groove with the Byrds." Danny popped an eight-track into a player mounted under the dashboard of the van and started singing along to their cover of Dylan's "Mr. Tambourine Man."

Shelley pulled out a joint from a little juju bag around her neck. She lit it, took a long toke, and then passed it to Danny, who also pulled in a hit and then handed it back to me.

"Yessirree. Yessiree . . . we're on our way to somewhere, some place in a distant land," Danny said, drumming his hands on the steering wheel like an excited kid.

The pot lifted me into a gentle euphoria. I drifted in and out until I spaced out, and when I woke up a few hours later, Adriana was spreading a moisturizing cream on my lips with her index finger. Her eyes had a pearly hue in the soft morning light, and I felt her love radiating within me.

The George Washington Bridge glowed as the sunrise lifted a dense fog from the sweeping arch of its suspension cables and brought the hazy spires of Manhattan into view.

"Le Corbusier," Adriana said, looking at the bridge. "He described the George Washington Bridge in the 1930s as the most beautiful bridge in the world and wrote that 'it is the only seat of grace in the disordered city.'"

"Wow! It is incredible," I gushed. "I've never seen anything like it."

The traffic across the George Washington Bridge was thick.

"Rush hour, man, rush hour. Let them rush. We can't go very fast."

By the time we got across the bridge, the sun was streaming into the van.

"Do you know your way out of Washington Heights?" Danny asked, looking in the rearview mirror at Adriana. "Where you headed?"

"Forest Hills. That's where my mother lives."

"Easy." Danny smiled. "I'll drop you guys off at 181st and St. Nicholas Avenue. Just take the 1 train to . . . "

"They're going to have go all the way down to Times Square because of line repairs," Shelley interjected. "At 96th Street, you should change to an Express train."

"I know my way from there," Adriana said. "It's the long way around. From Times Square, we take the E train to 71st Avenue. We'll be fine. It's just going to take a while."

Danny smiled. "This girl is in her element. Let her go, man, let her go."

When we got out of the van, Adriana blew a kiss to Danny, and we headed off to the subway. The 181st Avenue station wasn't crowded, and we pushed through the turnstile easily without drawing too much attention to ourselves. But when we were on the platform, a little girl in a plaid parochial school skirt tugged on her mother's wrist and, pointing at Adriana, asked, "What's wrong with her?"

Her mother yanked her daughter away. Adriana looked embarrassed, and I moved in between them, swinging the duffle bag slung over my shoulder from side to side as a buffer and distraction. When the train came, Adriana rushed inside, snagging one of the last remaining seats. I stood in front of her and set the duffle bag down to block people from staring at her.

When we got to 96th Street, we changed to an express train and got to Times Square quickly. The transfer to the E train went much more slowly. Adriana saw that I looked haggard and said, "Here, take my backpack. I'll carry the duffle bag."

"Isn't that duffle bag going to be a little too much to handle with your brace and all?"

"I don't know how many times I have to tell you, I can handle it! I'm not an invalid."

"I know that. I just . . . want to help . . . if you'll ever let me."

"Enough!" She shoved her backpack toward me with one hand and grabbed the duffle bag with the other.

I sat down next to her. And she shrugged, still a little miffed. But then she lifted my hand into hers. Her eyes were tearing up.

"I wonder, Aaron . . . Please don't be angry. But I'm wondering if I should even get an abortion."

I looked at her in disbelief.

"Well . . . What if it's yours?"

I did my best to keep my voice even. "The chances of the baby being mine are slim, very slim."

Adriana sighed. And once again, neither of us knew what more to say until the train finally got to our stop.

As we exited the subway, Adriana said, "I know we're not ready to have a baby. I just don't want you to ever feel that you gave up, you know, the opportunity to have a child."

My throat tightened with emotion. "Well, I appreciate your thoughtfulness. But we both know it's not the right time."

"I know. It's just so hard," Adriana said, trying to console me.

At that moment, I felt so much love for her, but I could hardly speak.

"Are you sure you want to stay with your mother?"

"We have to. If we don't, then when the word gets out that I'm in New York—and it will, no matter what I do—the gossip mill goes into action, and it will be so much worse."

I took the duffle bag back from Adriana and slung it over my shoulder.

As we neared her mother's building, Adriana quickened her pace and smiled as she reached for the doorbell. I was lagging behind, and by the time I caught up to Adriana, her mother was already downstairs. She wrapped Adriana in a big hug, smacking both of her cheeks with loud kisses.

Adriana's mother turned toward me and said, "Aaron! What a fine name. Come! Come on upstairs. Lunch is just about ready. Something very special."

Adriana's mother was stocky and broad-shouldered, with salt-and-pepper hair gathered loosely into a kind of ponytail. She was wearing an off-white housedress with a purple sash that made the whole outfit seem more dressed up.

Adriana and I followed her to the elevator and together we went up to the twenty-fourth floor. The doors opened into a narrow corridor that led around a sharp corner to the apartment.

"Harold's in Manhattan and may not be back here until tomorrow afternoon," Adriana's mother said. "How long are you staying?"

"Probably just a couple of days," Adriana answered. "We don't have much time. We've got to get back for classes. But I needed a dose of New York, and I wanted you to meet Aaron."

"Well, well," her mother said. "The pleasure is all mine."

The apartment sprawled over several large rooms. I sat on the sofa in the living room and marveled at the city view through the large windows. Adriana and her mother made the final preparations for lunch and caught up on the latest family news and gossip. I picked up a copy of the *New Yorker* and read the theater listings and movie mini reviews.

There was a window at the end of the hallway, past the elevator foyer. I looked out at the cityscape, brimming with glass and concrete. I thought about why we were here and wondered how an abortion would change Adriana. Maybe once it was over, we could just move on. Maybe we'd grow closer together. Maybe one day we'd get married and have a baby. And maybe we'd get a dog like Moron to sleep by its crib at night.

Adriana smiled and took my hand, pulling me toward the dining room table. "You're going to love my mother's baked ziti," she giggled. "It's the best, and it's my favorite. Believe me, I've tasted a lot."

Before we sat down, her mother threw her arms around me and kissed me with loud smacks on both cheeks just as she had done earlier with Adriana.

The dining room setting was simple, but elegant: four chairs, white China dishes, antique-looking silverware, wine and water glasses, and a small arrangement of yellow, red, and orange flowers in a low, bulbous vase.

Adriana's mother served the lunch with evident pride, offering us white wine with the grilled calamari salad, and red with the baked ziti. Conversation centered on school. "So, Adriana tells me you're in pre-med."

"Well, sort of. I'm just now taking the core courses, and a couple of electives: English and anthropology."

"We met in history class," Adriana said. "Both of us were bored. The American Revolution really got us down."

"I grew up in Boston," I said. "The Revolution was all over the place. What more could I ever want to know?"

Adriana's mother wasn't impressed. She raised her eyebrows as if to say, "So what?" No matter what I said, she was focused on Adriana and seemed to sense that something wasn't right.

When we finished eating, Adriana helped her mother clear the table. I heard them whispering in the kitchen, and after about ten minutes, Adriana reappeared with a small tray and two cups of espresso.

"Isn't your mother joining us for coffee?"

"No, she's getting a migraine. She went to lie down."

"Does she know why you're really in New York?" I said in a low voice, looking toward the hallway.

"No," Adriana said adamantly, then changed the subject, telling me that what she really wanted to do was get out of the apartment and go into midtown Manhattan and have some fun.

Adriana had her mind made up; I recognized all the signs, and there was no way I was going to stop her.

"C'mon, let's go! I need some air. It's a glorious day. My mother says it's going to go up to fifty degrees. Can you believe that? New York in December?"

DECEMBER 12, 1970
2:15 P.M.

ADRIANA WAS RIGHT; THE WEATHER WAS PERFECT: scattered clouds, a light breeze. The crowds in the subway had thinned out, and our journey into the city went smoothly. After a couple of changes, we got out at Rockefeller Center. Adriana hurried up the stairs to the plaza, not far from the skating rink and the towering Christmas tree that was in place for the holidays. A group of school kids was caroling, weaving in and out of the flags on the perimeter of the plaza. Shoppers and tourists gathered to listen.

Adriana was beaming, and as much as I wanted to share her joy, it was tough. When I was a kid, Christmas was a holiday that didn't exist in my house. Growing up, my family celebrated Hanukkah—I said a couple of prayers and lit candles each night, and my parents gave me Hanukkah gelt: milk chocolate medallions wrapped in gold foil.

The commercialization of Christmas bothered me. I always wished I was someplace else. If I could have hibernated in a cave between Thanksgiving and New Year's, I would have.

Adriana kept reminding me, "Don't be such a Scrooge, Aaron. Christmas is for everyone," and as simple as it sounded, it was tough for me.

Adriana headed off toward Fifth Avenue, walking with purpose. I had to follow.

And as much I didn't want to admit it, Rockefeller Center in December was truly amazing: a colossal Christmas diorama dripping with icing. Gigantic wooden nutcrackers and costumed elves surrounded me; a fifteen-foot Santa held the reins of a dozen reindeer pulling a giant sleigh loaded with enormous boxes wrapped in wild, psychedelic colors. Thousands of glittering lights, shimmering red and green ball ornaments, candy canes, and even dreidels, gold trumpets and Hanukkah menorahs, all tied with garish ribbons and bows that festooned the vast plaza. I felt manipulated by the sensory overload, the spectacle, but the intensity of it all was intoxicating.

Where was Adriana? I lost track of her on Fifth Avenue. I stood in the middle of the pedestrian traffic flow and sucked it all in; the frenetic energy of the street, the throngs of people, the laughing kids, the two guys running a makeshift shell game in front of me, the chestnuts roasting in a street vendor's smoker on the next corner.

My mind floundered around. It was so overwhelming that it was enticing, a fun house with surprises at every turn, but disorienting at the same time.

Suddenly, two arms snaked around me from behind. It was Adriana. "Aaron, are you okay?"

"Well, not exactly. I feel like I've been riding a sugar high, but it's starting to wear off. I just feel kind of zapped."

"I was going to take you into St. Patrick's Cathedral, and then over to the Plaza Hotel and Central Park. But now I think I might need to take you to a nursery school for nap time."

"Come on, Adriana! I don't want to be a tourist. I may as well buy a book of postcards at a souvenir stand in Times Square."

Adriana looked hurt. "Sometimes it's fun to be a tourist, even for me, and I grew up here."

"I'm sorry. I just need a break."

Adriana pursed her lips. "I wish I could believe you. You're trying too hard to control everything around you, especially me. But you can't control New York City."

I shook my head, tired of arguing with her. I turned and walked away, but in the congestion of the crowd, I bumped into a stroller. The baby inside started crying. The mother shoved the stroller into my legs. "Watch where you're going, mister!" I tried to apologize, but she brushed past me without another word.

Adriana came up beside me. "You need to be more careful."

I sidled my way over to the curb and squatted down.

"Please, get up. Fine, we can leave. But do me a favor; stop talking to me until you can compose yourself and act with a little more grace."

"Just go," I said, not looking at her.

"No, I'm not going to leave you here. I'll get you back to my mother's apartment in one piece."

I got up and followed Adriana, embarrassed by my outburst. In the subway, I nestled up to her and apologized.

Adriana shook her head. "Sometimes, you make me feel so inadequate. So incapable of pleasing you. I only want the best for you —for us."

"Well, to be honest, I feel the same way about you."

I stared into the empty space in front of me, looking for words but not finding any that seemed right. And after a few minutes, Adriana turned toward me. She took my hand in hers, holding it tight. We looked deep into each other's eyes, acknowledging that we were both suffering, but not wanting to talk about it.

With each subway stop, I felt a little of our anxiety ebbing away. "I really do want to help," I said softly, and Adriana nodded. "Thanks."

Getting back to the apartment was easy, but when we got there, Adriana's mother wasn't around. There was a note on the dining room table: "Adriana, sweetie. Responsibility calls. Dinner engagement in the city. See you some time tomorrow. Love you so much, Mama."

Adriana's mood brightened up. "Just think, we can have a quiet evening to ourselves, without anyone else around. Aaron, this is a first. Wow!"

I wanted to be happy, but I was still recovering and needed a nap.

Adriana stepped toward me, smiling with half-lidded eyes, and led me into her bedroom. I sat down on the edge of the bed, and her fingers strayed to the buttons on my shirt, unfastening them one at a time.

I swallowed hard, feeling my heartbeat revving up. Adriana stretched back her neck, accentuating its contours. In the light streaming through the window, she was statuesque.

"So, how does it feel to be in my inner sanctum?" she asked in a seductive voice.

"I've never seen so many shades of pink."

Adriana giggled. "More my mother's taste than mine."

I turned around and gazed at all the Barbie dolls arranged in a line on a shelf that extended onto all four walls. I had never seen so many in one place.

Adriana looked a little embarrassed. "I really didn't play with them very much. My mother thought I needed a collection, so every Christmas, I got one from every member of my extended family. When I was five or six, it was wonderful. But as I got older and wanted something else, something I wasn't expecting, it didn't seem to matter. However much I complained, no one ever seemed to hear me, especially my mother."

Adriana forced a little grin. "Let me show you my favorite." She reached up to the shelf and pulled down a Barbie in a bikini; on one of her legs was a brace made from two paperclips and rubber bands.

"You see," Adriana said, "when I was twelve, my mother bought me a bikini that she said I could wear to the beach so long as I wrapped myself in a long towel to cover most of my brace. Well, I didn't like that idea. First of all, I was too embarrassed to put on the bikini, and secondly, I hated the idea of the towel. So, I made a brace for my doll, and that made me feel a little better. I know all this sounds stupid, but that's what I did. And when my mother saw the doll, she broke down and told me that she was sorry."

"That must have been so hard."

"I'm over it." Adriana handed me the doll. "I want to give her to you."

I looked at the doll in my hands, then into Adriana's eyes.

"This Barbie helped me when I needed it most," Adriana said. "Maybe she can do the same for you."

"Thank you," I said, closing my eyes.

"I hope you feel better. It makes me happy to know you're in my room, in my bed, even if I'm not in there with you . . . yet."

"With all of these Barbies staring at me, I'm not sure I'll be able to sleep."

"They're not staring. Actually, I don't think they're very impressed. You're not their type. And the only one that really matters is in your hand."

Adriana pecked my lips with a quick kiss. "Rest up," she whispered and left, shutting the door quietly behind her.

I stripped down to my underwear and crawled under the covers. The pink comforter and sheets were a little creepy, but nonetheless cushy and inviting. I stretched out on my back and started counting the Barbie dolls on the shelves above me, but lost track as my eyelids weighed me down. I held Adriana's special Barbie close to my heart. My mind sank into a dreamy state, somewhere between being awake and falling asleep. And the Barbie doll transformed, reminding me in a strange way of Sister Ethel. She was singing, and all the Barbie dolls on the shelves surrounding the bed joined in:

> Mother has come with her beautiful song
> Ho-ho-tal-la-me-ho
> Ho-ho-tal-la-me-ho
> She's come to bless her children dear
> Ho-ho-tal-la-me-ho
> Ho-ho-tal-la-me-ho

MARCH 22, 1971
3:48 P.M.

IN HEIDI'S BEDROOM, TWO TWIN BEDS ARE SEPARATED by about five feet. Centered on the white wall behind them is a simple wooden cross, also painted white.

"The wall and the cross come together," Heidi explains. "One and the same. But sometimes in very unexpected ways. Faith and life. Life and faith. Questioning each other."

Everything Heidi is saying makes sense ... kind of. I want to be enthusiastic, but I'm not sure I am.

"Did you know there are more than 150 shades of white?" Heidi asks. "And each one of them changes with the light in which they live and breathe. Praise God."

I sit on the Shaker rocking chair in the corner and take off my shoes. Heidi senses that I'm tensing up and points to her bed. "The pink lace tatted on the pillowslip was made by a woman who called herself Sister Margaret. I met her once in Lebanon, not so far from here. She was a clerk in a tourist shop. I was looking for information about the Shaker community that had been there, and she said her great great aunt had been a member. I was shocked. The Shaker community had died out nearly a century earlier. But this old woman had a certain air about her, and she was wearing a white bonnet that framed her face in such a way that she seemed of a different era. She said that technically she wasn't a Shaker and joked that she was just another old maid from a small town in Ohio. Well, after I paid for a little booklet they sold about the Shaker community, I saw her tatting thread next to the register with a strand of lace that was still in progress. And when I asked her about it, she gave it to me."

"What a great story," I say, shuffling over to the the bed next to hers.

"Make yourself comfortable. I'm going to fix some green tea. Dinner is served at six o'clock, leaving enough time for prayer, maybe a little singing, fellowship, communion. There are no rules here. We live in our holy family as brothers and sisters by choice. Inspired by Shaker life. But updated. Modernized. And not necessarily Shakers in practice. A response to the needs in today's world of not just men and women, but boys and girls. All equal. In all rights and privileges. In other words, Aaron, we cut each other lots of slack."

Heidi seems to glide across the floor, singing:

Come life, Shaker life!

Come life, come life eternal!

Shake shake out of me

All that is carnal

I feel a weight lifting off my heart as my eyes close. Heidi leaves the room quietly and I doze off.

DECEMBER 12, 1970

AROUND 6:00 P.M., ADRIANA KNOCKED on the door, but before I could rouse myself, she rushed inside and plopped herself next to me.

"Sorry to wake you." She giggled, looking at her doll in my hand, and then at my face. "I'm so glad you made a new friend. You certainly look comfy."

I rolled over onto Adriana's lap, and she caressed my face with her hand. And everything around me transformed. "You've got great pillows."

"Goose down. My favorite."

"Mine too."

I cuddled up. The muscle tissue of Adriana's strong leg was firm, more of a cushion than a pillow, and it felt just right to me. I massaged her knee and calf with the palm of my hand.

Adriana leaned forward and stroked her fingers through my hair. "Aaron, what's gotten into you?" she whispered. "You're acting so spaced-out."

"I'm still dreamy."

"Well, it's time to get up. My cousin Jerry is in the living room, and he wants to meet you."

I pulled myself upright, staring at Adriana's face.

Adriana got up from the bed and took a few steps toward the door. Then, she straightened her sweater, still not looking at me.

"Something wrong?" I asked nervously.

Adriana came back to the bed and grabbed my hand. "I feel terrible. I can't believe I'm getting an abortion tomorrow."

Adriana hugged me so hard; she was shaking. Tears streamed from her eyes, and from mine. Everything we'd been through surged within us.

Adriana sobbed. "I have to go through with it."

I pulled the comforter up over my face and Adriana stood up. "Aaron, please. Jerry's waiting in the living room. I think it would best if you get dressed and join us. But if you don't want to, it's okay. I can just go somewhere, and come back a little later, or I can just stay here with you and ask Jerry to leave. But he wants to take us to dinner."

"I . . . uh . . . that's great . . . but I'm so out of it. I don't really want to get up. I mean, your bed is amazing."

Adriana wiped her eyes with a Kleenex.

"I don't want to let you down. But I just need a little more time to myself."

"It's okay. We won't be long. Do you want me to bring you something?"

"No, no. I'll be fine."

Adriana left the room, closing the door softly behind her.

Regrets were swirling around me. Every question I asked stacked up like a house of cards. And as each thought went awry, everything toppled over, and I had to try to piece it all back together again.

I dragged myself out of bed. Pulling on my jeans was difficult; I had a painful twinge in my lower back. I must have been sleeping in some twisted up position.

I squatted down and then straightened up, stretching back and then bending forward. Gradually, my muscles loosened up. Leaving the bedroom and walking around the apartment helped, but it was eerie with no one there.

The furniture smacked of the late 1950s and reminded me of my parents. The blue-green slipcovers on the couch and chairs were clean, but a little faded. The coffee table had a walnut finish that didn't match the mahogany stain of the claw-footed end tables. Pink and purple chalkware lamps faced each other from across the room, and the vases on the counter dividing the living room from the kitchen had an enameled, Asian flair. Photographs clustered on the walls, tables, and on tchotchke-cluttered bookshelves lined with decorative frames, showing different periods of Adriana's family life: hand-tinted portraits of her as a baby, Polaroid pictures of her opening presents on Christmas morning surrounded by cousins and grandparents, Easter egg hunts and color snapshots of her getting ready for her senior prom.

I lowered myself onto the sofa and thumbed through the magazines on the coffee table. I was getting bored. It was now past nine o'clock, and I was disappointed that Adriana hadn't called. I went to the bathroom and stared at myself in the mirror. My face looked older, a little more wrinkled. My beard seemed less splotchy, and the nubs of hair sprouting along my chin line were thicker.

I stood at the commode and stared down into the bowl. I couldn't pee. But I flushed anyway—it was something my mother did when I was a kid after I did something wrong. And once I said I was sorry, she'd lead me into the bathroom and flush the toilet as a symbolic gesture that she had forgiven me.

I flushed again and again, wishing I could rid myself of all the horrible things that had ever happened to me. But no matter how much I tried, I couldn't make peace with my past, and I wandered back into Adriana's bedroom. I picked up her doll with the leg brace, and its face seemed to come alive with a beatific glow in my hand, telling me without words that maybe there was still hope.

The front door to the apartment squeaked open. Finally, they were back. I wanted to go in and talk to Adriana and Jerry, to pretend, at least, that I was okay, that there was nothing wrong with me. But my feet felt like they were stuck in cement. I took a deep breath, and somehow the curse holding me back let go. I placed the doll gently on

Adriana's pillow and the light emanating from its face dimmed, but its presence stayed with me as I walked into the living room.

Adriana and Jerry were laughing, standing together as they hung their coats on a rack near the front door. Jerry was shorter than I expected. His face was pudgy, but his features were drawn in clean lines. His broad shoulders accentuated his girth, and he moved with a slight limp in both legs.

Jerry had his arm draped over Adriana's shoulder. Her face was flushed, and she was slurring her words. "Feeling better, Aaron dear?"

Adriana separated herself from Jerry. "Poor baby. Jerry is so sorry about what I . . . I mean, we, have to do."

I recoiled, disappointed that Adriana had apparently told him about the abortion.

"You are so cute, Aaron," Adriana said. "Especially when you're sad."

Jerry plopped on the sofa and crossed his legs.

Adriana asked me if I wanted a "nightcap." Then she wanted me to eat something.

"Ugh. I'm not hungry," I muttered, and she put her hand on her hip.

"Hummph!" Adriana scowled.

"Let me take care of this," Jerry said, standing up. "I'll fix a little . . . uh . . . charcuterie plate. Adriana's mother has a tasty bit of everything, I'm sure."

"Okay, okay," I said, glancing at Adriana.

Jerry opened a bottle of red wine on the counter. Adriana beckoned me to come closer to her. She took my hand and playfully placed it on her breast, pulling me into her bosom and tickling my lips with her tongue. I squirmed, but her kiss was intense; even with Jerry there, I felt myself responding. But I was confused. So many mixed signals. It was as if my body had a mind of its own.

"You know how much I love you?" Adriana asked, her eyes moving purposefully toward me, then to Jerry in the kitchen. "Jerry only means well," she whispered. "I saw the way you were gawking at him.

Just remember what he's been through. He still has shrapnel in his legs that they couldn't remove. It's incredible he's even walking at all. He is such a sweetheart, a unique mix of macho and silk."

Jerry came in, setting down a tray with Italian delicacies on the coffee table. He brought three wine glasses and then poured wine for all of us. He lifted his glass. "Cin cin!" Adriana and I echoed him, and we all drank.

The salami and prosciutto were more delicious than I expected, as was the assortment of cheeses, olives, and cornichons. Before long, I was lightheaded. Adriana was sloshed. She swaggered around the room, rambling on about how photographs in neat, tidy frames didn't reveal the dysfunctional relationships of the people in them.

"But it took us years to figure it out," Adriana said, and Jerry chimed in, "That's the truth."

"I hated it," Adriana added. "Whenever we walked into the living room, the men were mumbling in one corner, and the women were chattering in another, sometimes playing cards, sewing, or just gossiping. But the moment they saw us, everything changed to Italian—the language, the mood, the hand gestures. It made us mad, and we decided to learn to speak Italian on our own."

"Not exactly," Jerry laughed. "My father had a reel-to-reel recorder, and I found some 'Learn Italian' tapes in a junk store in Chinatown."

"And when we finally started to understand what they were saying," Adriana said, "we didn't let them know. We found out what was really going on. We couldn't believe it. Our family was mixed up with businesses that, let's say, weren't on the up and up. Our fathers joked that they were on the management team, working for a boss whose name they never said out loud. Everything they talked about was in a kind of code."

None of what she was saying made any sense. I felt like I was stuck in the middle of an episode of *The Twilight Zone*, but I hadn't seen the beginning and had no idea where and when it was going to end.

Adriana turned to Jerry and gave an exaggerated sigh. "I told you, Jerry. Poor Aaron is such an innocent."

Jerry raised his eyebrows. "Innocent no more."

"Innocent little Aaron! Ding-dong, ding-dong." Adriana could barely keep her balance. She was drunk and careened onto the sofa.

"Girl, you need some rest," Jerry said, wagging his index finger. "Aaron, take her to bed. I can let myself out."

"No, no, no!" Adriana said. "I want more wine, and I want it right now."

"Adriana, my dear, if you don't want to go with your beau, then let me lead you on." Jerry stood behind her and gently pushed her up. "Aaron, please. Take her hand. She needs your help."

"Aaron, you do this and you're sleeping on the sofa." Adriana flung off Jerry's hands and stormed down the hall to her bedroom.

"Leave her be. I'll take care of this," Jerry said, and he headed down the hallway toward Adriana's room.

I grabbed Jerry's arm. "What's really going on here, Jerry? I never seem to be able to get it straight. She's so manic."

"Aaron, breathe a little more deeply. Evenly. Now, please, sit down. It's never been easy for Adriana. Growing up in this family . . . I'm sure she's told you about it."

"Not exactly."

"Okay, look, my father's been indicted by a federal grand jury and is likely to spend the rest of his life in prison. And that's just the tip of the old family iceberg."

"Did she tell you what happened in Canada?"

"Canada?"

"Never mind." I was exhausted. "Tomorrow is going to be a very long day."

Jerry shook his head, giving me an amused smile. "You are impossible. You look smart, but what comes out of your mouth makes me think that you grew up in a goldfish bowl."

"I'm a wreck inside," I admitted, slouching forward.

"That's obvious."

"But..."

"Okay, okay. I understand."

"What about Adriana?"

"She'll be fine. Believe me." Jerry yawned and moved toward the door. "Good night. See you tomorrow. Dinner, maybe?"

"Not so sure about that, Jerry. I've got to see what Adriana's got planned. We might get on the road... It kind of depends..."

"Sure thing. Ciao," Jerry said and let himself out.

I stared at the door. I didn't know what to think. Was Adriana as calculating as Jerry insinuated? Or was she simply afraid, doing whatever she could to survive? Her whole life seemed like an awful balancing act, a tightrope between different kinds of messed-up relationships. I wondered how I could love her the way I did and be so suspicious at the same time.

I went to Adriana's bedroom and tapped on the door, not expecting her to even hear me. But much to my surprise, she let me in. She had already taken off her leg brace but managed to hobble forward, leaning heavily on her right leg in a kind of hopping motion. Her left leg was limp, but it helped her balance as she moved ahead.

Without uttering a word, she unbuttoned my shirt, giggling to herself. I stripped down and followed her into her bed. She laid on her back, breathing heavily in a drunken stupor.

I spooned up to her side and massaged her torso, her breasts, her thighs, but she didn't respond. I laid on my back beside her, staring around at the darkened room. Moonlight edged the window blinds and illuminated the room with a strange glow. Adriana sounded as if she was stuck in a nightmare. As I watched, her head rolled back and forth on her pillow; indecipherable words spilled from her lips. "Help! Help!" she half-screamed, but then sank back into an indistinct mumbling, her eyes still closed.

I wanted to shake her, but the other side of my brain wanted to listen in; maybe I could finally learn what was really going on in her mind. Maybe she'd say something more about the family business. Everything seemed so shady.

My feet were cold, and I reached for my socks, just as Adriana snapped awake.

"Where did you come from? I thought I locked the door."

"You did," I said. "But when I tapped on the door, you got up and let me in."

Adriana propped herself up on her elbows, a sour look on her face. "My head is throbbing."

"Bad hangover?"

"Don't be so smart! What time is it? My appointment is at nine."

"Do you want me to get you some aspirin or something?"

"I can't. Aspirin is a blood thinner, and it will make the bleeding worse. I can't."

"Bleeding?"

"From the abortion, stupid."

I kneaded my fingertips lightly into the small of her back. Adriana sighed, and I continued, gradually increasing the pressure.

"You should try to get a little more rest," I said. "Are you sure you can't leave a little later?"

"I wish I could. But it might take us forty-five minutes or more to get there. It's a clinic, a very private one that Jerry told me about."

"You said you weren't going to tell him. Thanks for filling me in on the details."

"He's a gem. Don't worry."

"Sounds like you two have planned the whole thing."

"Don't be ridiculous. This is the most difficult thing I've ever done. And the way you're talking, it sounds like you're jealous of me talking to anyone other than you about my rape."

My heart sank. "Our rape."

"Yes, Aaron, our rape." Adriana said, changing her tone, trying to be compassionate, and pulled herself out of bed.

I followed her with my eyes and then stretched my legs under the bed covers, drifting into a semi-conscious state, where I mulled over what Adriana said to me about being jealous.

After a while, I heard Adriana calling me.

"I made breakfast. Come and get it. We gotta go soon!"

I pulled myself out of the bed and wrapped myself in the robe that Adriana had left hanging for me on the bedpost. In the kitchen, a little table in the corner was set with toast, orange juice, and a steaming cup of coffee.

Adriana was already dressed, and as I walked toward her, she handed me a plate of scrambled eggs. I sat down, and Adriana joined me, but without a plate for herself.

"I think it's better that I don't eat, not quite yet."

I took a long sip of coffee and Adriana's face tightened up.

Adriana looked edgy. "We've got to leave in about thirty minutes. We're taking the subway and the bus. Jerry will pick us up, after it's done. You'll need to call him when the procedure is over."

The pressure was building. I could barely swallow my food. Adriana had gone to a lot of trouble to prepare it for me, though, so I gulped down as much as I could. Still, I couldn't finish.

I got up and hurried into the bedroom, took a fast shower, and was dressed and ready to go with a few minutes to spare.

Once out on the street, I struggled to keep up with Adriana; she weaved through the crowded sidewalks and hurried down the steps into the subway.

When our train came, there were no seats. Adriana squeezed into the middle of the aisle, and I managed to find a place to stand a few feet away from her. After a few stops, Adriana was able to sandwich herself into a seat between two older women, though she had trouble releasing the lock on her brace. The older women were staring at her, but Adriana was oblivious. She looked so withdrawn, so worried, so anxious. I wanted to comfort her but wasn't sure how.

When we exited the subway, her body language said, "Don't talk to me now." And by the time we got to the abortion clinic, she seemed disoriented, her eyes darting around as if she didn't know where she was or where she was supposed to go.

The clinic was in a nondescript storefront on Avenue D in the East Village in an area that looked bombed out. Buildings on both sides of the clinic were gutted and surrounded by chain link fences; their abandoned interiors were filled with huge piles of rotted wood, steel girders, and broken pieces of gypsum board.

In the clinic, the waiting room was empty, and the stark white walls seemed to buttress the coldness that had settled in between us. We sat next to each other but might as well have been in different time zones. I tried to hold Adriana's hand, but she pulled back. When the nurse at the front desk called her name, she stood up and shook her head.

I tried to get her attention to wish her well, but she kept her face turned away.

Once she was gone, I asked the nurse how long the procedure would take.

"It depends," she said. "Hopefully, not too long."

I couldn't get comfortable in my chair. I stood up and paced back and forth, fidgeting with my wallet and the keys in my pocket. Then I squirmed around in my seat until the chair started to squeeze me again, and the cycle started over.

After about two hours, the nurse called me to the front desk.

"Your, uh, friend is okay. She'll be discharged after the doctor checks her out." The nurse's face and voice were almost void of emotion.

The air in the clinic was tinged with antiseptic, irritating my eyes. By then, the waiting room had filled up with women; all appeared older than Adriana and me. I felt as if everyone was gawking at me.

Their glazed stares reminded me that they were probably all victims, too, just as Adriana and I were. I started wondering whether, in each of these women's lives, some man or other was the perpetrator of their suffering and remorse. I felt a strange urge to hug every one of the women in the waiting room. But that was impossible. More likely, they found my very presence an aide-mémoire of the brutality of someone else's passion, or vengeance. I was probably a pariah in their eyes. And given what had happened to Adriana and me, I understood. All too well.

DECEMBER 13, 1970
12:23 P.M.

ADRIANA'S FACE WAS BLANCHED. I could tell that she was hurting. And so was I. We were both damaged, but once again, we had survived.

"You're incredible," I said, as the nurse helped with her clothes and took her by wheelchair to the exit of the clinic. Adriana insisted that she was fine, that she could walk on her own, but the nurse kept reminding her that the clinic had a specific protocol that needed to be followed. Once we were on the sidewalk, Adriana stood up, grasping my arm, as we moved forward. It was clear she was weaker than she thought, but she was as determined as ever to get on with her life.

I felt connected to her in a very deep way, even though she didn't have much to say. I took her hands and pulled her gently toward me. She hugged me tightly and whispered, "Thank you, Aaron, for all your support."

I nodded and closed my eyes. Adriana did the same, and as we embraced, I had the faint hope that maybe the abortion would bring us closer together.

When Jerry picked us up, he was solemn. "Adriana, my dear, you are blessed. I know you are," he said, as I helped her into the back seat of the car.

Adriana started sobbing. "I want to leave. As soon as we can. I want to go back to Ohio. I can't stay here. Not now. If my mother were to see me, she'd know. She'd see it my eyes. She'd feel it in her bones."

Jerry stopped his car near the entry ramp to the George Washington Bridge. "I kind of thought that's what you going to say. So, I stopped at your mother's apartment before heading over here and packed your things into the duffle bag by your bed. I hope that's okay."

"Jerry, you're a diamond," Adriana gushed.

I reached for Adriana's hand, looking askance at Jerry, and said, "We can spend the night in a motel, if you need to rest up. We passed a lot of them in New Jersey on our way here."

Adriana straightened her posture as best she could. "I'll be fine. They gave me an antibiotic and some high-powered vitamins and some iron supplements."

A freezing wind blew across the Hudson River. The temperature was dropping fast as the sun sank into the winter horizon; incoming clouds cast heavy shadows on the water. The light had a dingy glow, casting the girders and cables of the George Washington Bridge in an eerie sheen.

"I don't think hitchhiking today is such a good idea," I said, as Jerry was about to drive off. "Seriously, we got to find another way to get back to Columbus."

"How many times do I have to tell you? I'm alright," Adriana insisted. "I appreciate your concern, but . . . "

"Let's take a bus, you know, a Greyhound. Hey, it'll be an adventure." I smiled, trying to convince her.

"We don't have enough money. Please, let's go."

Jerry was watching us, his window rolled down. "Adriana, as much as I'd rather not admit it, Aaron is right. You can't do this to yourself, not now. I'll even pay for it."

"Oh, Jerry! What would I do without you?"

"Quite honestly, I don't have a clue." He jabbed a finger in my direction and muttered, "I should make you hitchhike back by yourself, but I won't, this time."

I felt my gut collapsing. "Look, Jerry . . . I . . . we appreciate your help, but please give me a little credit. Taking the bus was my idea in the first place."

"Pardon me," Jerry replied in a surly tone.

Adriana grabbed my arm, "Aaron, what's wrong with you?"

"Maybe Jerry's right; I should hitchhike back to Columbus by myself. It will help me clear my head."

"Don't be ridiculous!" Adriana exclaimed.

"Aaron," Jerry said. "Don't be so touchy. I would have thought that after all your time with Adriana you would have come to a deeper understanding of the Romano way: sarcastic, irreverent—but terribly endearing."

"Enough said," Adriana added, and the car went silent.

The traffic to the bus station was bumper-to-bumper, but when we got there, we lucked out. The bus to Ohio didn't seem to be too crowded, and we were able to sprawl out in seats across the aisle from each other. Clustered together in the back of the bus was a group of noisy high school kids and two cranky chaperones on their way back home from a weekend field trip. As we headed up the Westside Highway to the George Washington Bridge, the driver dimmed the passenger lights. In the darkness, the kids sounded as if they were trapped in a haunted house, hyped up on caffeine and sugar, and no matter how much the chaperones shouted, the goofing around and belly laughs got louder.

The bus driver barked into his microphone: "Please, settle down!"

A man one row in front of me jumped out of his seat, turned toward the back of the bus, and yelled, "Shut up!"

One of the chaperones positioned himself in the aisle and said, "Now, sir, please watch your language. These are minors."

"I don't care if they're still babies on the tit; I said shut up! Is that English enough?"

The high school kids quieted down, and the man returned to his seat. I couldn't see his face, but from his build he looked like a construction worker with bulging biceps and scruffy painter pants. A beat-up Yankees cap was pulled down over his eyes.

Adriana acted as if none of this was bothering her. She folded her jacket and placed it behind her head as a pillow. Somehow, this made me feel even more annoyed, and when the kids in back started up again, I could barely contain my frustration.

The goofing around intensified, and one of the kids started patting his seat in a kind of drum roll. I turned around as a chaperone pulled a ruler from his knapsack and whacked it on the kid's seat.

The kid winced. "I'm bleeding! Geez, you attacked me!"

One of the high school girls chanted, "I'm gonna tell. I'm gonna tell!"

"I need you to stay in your seats and quiet down!" the driver said again over the PA.

The guy in front of me lurched up. "I can't take this anymore!"

His eyes were crystal blue, and his pupils looked dilated.

"What do you want to do?" I asked, hoping to defuse his anger.

"Vigilante justice. Know what I mean?" he said. "You with me?"

"I . . . I don't think . . . I mean . . . that might not be the right approach."

"Look, man, you're either with me or against me!"

The guy's eyes were rolling around in his head like marbles.

"They're just kids. Look, they're bothering me as much as they are you . . . and hey, what about all the other people on the bus?"

"Wimps! That's what they are . . . Man, that's what you are too!"

The guy slammed his fist onto his seat.

"Actually," I said with a shaky voice, "I'm not."

"You really are nuts!"

"Probably so. But if we start a fight, we're the ones that are going to be thrown off the bus, not them."

The guy scowled at me, but then flipped back around, muttering, "They better shut up!" He pulled a small flask from his jacket pocket and took a long sip, grumbling to himself.

I tried to zone out but couldn't. When the kids weren't making a racket, someone else a couple of rows away was snoring.

By the time we crossed the Pennsylvania state line, I was a wreck. Thinking about Adriana's abortion haunted me. What's going to happen to her? To me? To us? How long is it going to take for Adriana to heal? Can we ever make love again?

When thoughts of Adriana weren't gnawing at me, I was worrying about my parents. What were they going to do when they found out I had drained my bank account?

I checked my watch every fifteen or twenty minutes. Fatigue, anxiety, and drifting in and out of sleep jammed me into a place that was somewhere and nowhere at the same time. I was both in the dream and outside of it, watching what transpired but powerless to alter the sequence of events.

Nothing made sense. I was going back in time, stuck in the back seat of an imaginary car, speeding off down a twisting road that unwound inside my head.

By the time we got to Columbus, I was completely frazzled. The high school kids in the back of the bus crowded into the aisle ahead of me, and by the time I got out, Adriana was pacing the sidewalk impatiently. She looked up at me as I stumbled down the steps of the bus.

"I'm wiped out," I said. "I hardly slept at all."

"Me too," Adriana said. "I was already hurting, and during the night, it only got worse."

I hoisted our duffle bag onto my shoulder and reached for her hand, but she brushed me away.

"I need a little space. Don't worry... it's okay." Her voice sounded so sad.

"Do you want to hitchhike to the dorm, or walk?"

"The night air feels good after being in that bus for eight and a half hours."

"I know. I know."

"You look stoned."

"I wish."

Adriana was having trouble walking; each step looked painful.

"Are you sure you want to walk? I have enough cash for a cab."

Adriana forced a little grin. "Okay, I give in. A cab would be nice."

Columbus didn't have many cabs, but there were a few waiting curbside, not far from the entrance to the bus station. I rushed up to the first in line, and the driver nodded. We climbed in quickly, and we got to the dorm in about ten minutes.

While I was paying, Adriana got out and headed up the sidewalk, and by the time I caught up with her, she was already at the elevator. She looked sick; her face was pale.

"They said I might get a low-grade fever."

"Infection?"

"Shhhh... not so loud. I don't want everyone to hear. Remember, they gave me antibiotics. I'll be fine. I just need rest."

"Is there anything I can get for you?"

"We'll meet up tomorrow. I'll call you. Just give me some time to myself. Trust me."

The elevator stopped at Adriana's floor, and she slogged off.

MARCH 22, 1971
6:10 P.M.

HEIDI TIPTOES INTO THE ROOM AND WAVES A FEATHER under my chin. I think I'm dreaming but when I turn over, I can feel her breathing. She's hovering over my face, as if she's going to kiss me, and when I open my eyes, she says, "Surprise!"

I see two mugs of steaming green tea on a tray on the bedside table. Heidi hands me one and parks herself on the edge of my bed.

"You are one of the soundest sleepers I have ever known. Watching you is a real trip. Sometimes you thrash around, but mostly you purr like a kitty. I'm so glad you don't snore."

"What time is it? Aren't we late for dinner?"

Heidi takes a sip of tea. "No, it's okay. We all decided you needed some rest. So, best to wait. Right now, it's time for tea."

I put my lips to the mug, but it's too steamy for me, and I jerk back, the tea sloshing onto my hand.

"You are a mess!" Heidi laughs. "Have you ever thought about what you're going to do once you get out of college?"

"Not really. That's four years from now."

"Have you ever thought about changing schools?"

"My parents would kill me. The only way I got to go to Ohio State was because it was a state school, and I could pay in-state fees."

"How's that?"

"An army buddy of my father's agreed to become my legal guardian."

"Oooh, that's weird."

"Kind of... because to be honest, I've only met him once. He lives in Cleveland. I mean, I know he'd...uh...be there, if I was in trouble, but of course . . . I . . . uh . . . I'm just waking up."

"That's the first step," Heidi says. "The second step is dinner, and we better get going. Everyone's waiting."

I sip on my tea, and then gulp it down. "The temperature's just right. Somewhere between lukewarm and cooled off. Love it. Thanks."

Heidi grimaces. "Sounds kind of yucky to me."

I lace up my hiking boots and follow her downstairs. There's lots of chattering, but when Jed sees us, he and Missy start singing. And one by one everyone joins in.

Welcome, welcome, ev'ry guest,
Welcome to our music feast:
Music is our only cheer,
Fill both soul and ravished ear;
Sacred Nine, teach us the mood,
Sweetest notes to be explored.
Softly swell the trembling air,
To complete our concert fair.

Heidi is beaming and leads me to the table. Everyone introduces themselves and Missy scurries into the kitchen and wheels a serving cart laden with soup bowls and two loaves of fresh-baked bread into the dining room.

"A simple dinner tonight, in your honor, Aaron. Rutabaga and carrot soup."

"And to keep with the carrot theme," Jed adds, "carrot cake with cream cheese and walnut frosting for dessert."

"Oops." Heidi smirks. "I forgot to ask him if he likes rutabagas."

I'm distracted, scanning the faces around the table, wondering who they are and where they came from and how they ever ended up here. Heidi pokes me in the side with her index finger. "Well, do you?"

"Huh?"

"Rutabagas! Do you eat them?"

"I eat just about anything. I'm good."

We all join hands and Jed prays, "To the Jews who believed him, Jesus said, 'If you hold to my teaching, you are really my disciples. Then you will know the truth, and the truth will set you free.' John 8:31-32."

"Yes. Yes!" Missy exclaims.

Jed bows his head. "Blessed are you, O God, for giving us food to sustain our lives and to make our hearts joyful and generous. In Jesus' name, Amen."

Everyone says, "So be it," and Jed serves me a bowl of soup.

"Thanks," I smile but feel myself knotting up.

During dinner, Heidi talks about how she hates wearing uniforms to work and that she needs to find another job. "I have to do something more creative. Maybe I should go back to school. There's a community college about fifteen miles from here. Maybe Daddy will let me pick apples full-time, and I can save up."

"You keep talking about apples," I joke, "but I haven't seen one since I got here."

"Well, they're not in season."

Once we finish eating, everyone disperses in different directions. Part of me wishes they'd stick around so that we can get to know each other better, but deep inside, I worry that I might be getting myself into something I can't get away from.

"Too late to sing tonight, Aaron. Suppose that means you need to come back another time."

"I guess so," I say, looking at Heidi, and she winks.

Heidi takes my hand in hers and we go upstairs. I sit in her Shaker rocking chair and wait while she changes into purple and red pajamas in the bathroom. I'm so attracted to her; I can barely contain myself. I understand the ground rules of my sleepover, and I don't want to do anything to upset her. I wait as patiently as I can while she gets ready for bed, and then I hurry into the bathroom to do the same. I tell her that I don't have any pajamas and that I usually just sleep in my boxer shorts and a t-shirt, and she says, "That's okay, Aaron, so long as you keep your private parts covered."

"I know," I say. But I'm harder than I thought. I try to pee, but nothing comes out. So, I just wrap myself in a towel.

"Aaron, are you blushing?" Heidi muses.

"Not . . . uh . . . exactly," I say, careful not to be dishonest, but at the same time guarded. Part of me feels ridiculous but the need to show respect to Heidi is more important.

Once I settle into my bed, Heidi asks, "Will you pray with me?"

And before I can answer, she closes her eyes and folds her hands in front of her, and then whispers her prayers. I can't make out everything she's saying, but the words "Dear God, God of love, I open my heart to you" are clear, and after a short pause, she prays for me and my safety.

I gaze into Heidi's eyes and say softly, "I hope I'm not disappointing you."

"Not at all. Quite the contrary. Good night, Aaron. Sweet dreams. The truth will set you free."

Heidi closes her eyes, and I do the same.

When Heidi's alarm goes off, I can hardly believe it's morning. I'm looking forward to breakfast, and to spending more time with her, but I'm not so sure about her community.

Everyone is rushing around. And it's only 5:00 a.m.

"Aaron, I'll go make some tea, or if you want coffee I can do that. I'll pop a couple of slices of bread in the toaster. I need to be at work in about thirty minutes. Those truckers start pulling in at around six o'clock."

"I'm fine. I am. Whatever you want is good for me."

"Then tea it is. A gentle way to start the day."

"I don't know how you do it," I say. "Do you ever get tired?"

"It's what I have to do. It's my cross to bear."

I dress quickly and follow Heidi as she rushes downstairs, tying her hair into a ponytail.

I feel Heidi welcoming me into her world. But I'm not ready. I want to please her. But deep down, I worry we're so different that a relationship with her might never work. I want more. I need more, even though I don't know exactly what I'm looking for. Getting out on the freeway again, thumb in the air. I have to do it. I can't back down now.

Heidi hands me a mug of jasmine tea and a piece of toast buttered and slathered with homemade blueberry jam.

"You want to stick around? You know, while I'm at work. Jed says he could use a little help fixing the fence line on the southern edge of the pasture, where his horses like to graze."

"Horses?"

"Well, I guess it's only one horse right now. Old Bessie passed away a couple of weeks ago. And his other mare, Minnie, is going down. Something wrong with her eyes and she has trouble finding her way back to the barn."

"Do you ride? I've always wanted to, or at least, I used to think I did."

"Me, not... uh... not since I was about ten. Daddy used to take me for pony rides when I was a kid."

Jed walks into the kitchen and says, "Hey, Aaron... glad you want to give me a hand. Pays fifty bucks and you get to hang around for another night with the clan."

I'm confused. I glance at Heidi, and she grins, knowing that I hadn't yet said I'd do it, but I guess in her mind it was already a done deal.

I don't know what to say, and neither does Heidi.

Heidi kisses my cheek and rushes out the door.

Jed has a commanding presence. His jaw is more squared-off than I'd noticed, and he has a scar on his forehead that reddens when he knits his brow. "You're not in a hurry, are you?"

"Well, not exactly. I should be back in Columbus for classes on Monday. But it's only English and American history and I'm getting an A in both. So I'll be okay."

"I was always jealous of kids like you, brainy types. Seemed to me if you had that gene, you didn't have to work as hard."

"I wouldn't say that. I study a lot."

"I'm from the school of hard knocks," Jed smiles, "and man, the army was just right for me. Or so I thought, until I got to Vietnam, and it hit me: they were real guns."

Jed moves toward the door, and I follow him outside, across a grassy field and down a gravel path that leads to the pasture.

"Minnie's still resting," Jed says. "These days she's moving pretty slow. Did Heidi tell you she's a rescue horse?"

"She said something about Minnie not being able to see very well."

"Man, that's the least of her problems. She was nearly worked to death by the time I got her."

The fence line that Jed wants to repair is torn apart.

"Think that teenaged boy across the road was drunk out of his head and rammed it with his pickup truck. Course, he didn't own up to it. And when I talked to his old man, I knew it was a waste of time. You know how to cut fence posts? I got some logs over there and an ax."

"To be honest," I admit, "If you put that ax in my hand, I wouldn't know what to do with it."

"Well, I guess I just bought myself a pig in a poke," Jed laughs. "But I already knew that, Aaron. I just wanted to buy a little of your time."

I stuff my hands into the front pockets of my jeans.

"Don't go all sheepish on me," Jed says. "I think you're a fine young man, even though, I must tell you, I'm not a whole lot older than you in years, but because of what I went through in Vietnam, I've got the body of a twenty-eight-year-old and the head of a senior citizen."

Jed points to the branches and logs strewn along the fence line and motions for me to help him pick out the right-sized pieces for him to split into rails and posts. Some of the wood is crusted with mud. Jed pulls a rusted machete form his tool bag and shows me how to scrape it off before dragging it over to him.

I marvel at the precision with which Jed wields his ax, and he jokes that maybe one day he'll give me lessons.

After a few hours, we take a break. Jed stacks a few logs so we can sit and tosses me a bottle of water. It's lukewarm, but it does the trick. I'm thirsty and tired. Getting up at 5:00 a.m. with Heidi was tough.

Jed pulls a paper sack from his tool bag and hands me a thick slice of bread and a chunk of summer sausage.

"That's Missy's hippie bread—wheat flour, oats, flax seeds, sunflower seeds, cracked wheat, honey, molasses, lemon juice, unsweetened apple sauce, and whatever else she might decide to throw in."

I take a bite of the summer sausage and then taste the bread. "That's amazing!"

"What gives the bread a little extra kick is the apple sauce." Jed smiles. "Homemade with apples picked in Heidi's daddy's orchard—a mix of Granny Smith and McIntosh."

"I've never had anything like this."

Jed clears his throat. "Man, this country air is really something."

I look at Jed, wondering what's really on his mind, and he says, "Now, Aaron, if you really want that bad to get back on the road, I'll give you a lift to where I think you oughta be to get a good ride."

I stutter, "I'm alright . . . I'm . . ."

"I want to tell you something, Aaron, and I do hope you can handle it. Heidi has a crush on you."

"She's incredible."

"She certainly is. Very special."

"I know."

"But she's still a little bee-stung, you know, from the boyfriend that went bad."

"What happened?"

"Not my business to tell. She's over it . . . sort of . . ."

I brush back my hair with both hands. "I get it . . . but I'm on my way to Nashville."

"Well, then, guess I don't have to concern myself with you. But just in case, I need to give you a little advance warning. She's like a sister to me, and if anyone tries to hurt her, they're in big trouble."

I rub my hands together and hunch over. I have a weird pain in my gut. I've been plugged up for days. I know it's gas. But I can't let it out. Not now. Jed kneels beside me and helps me back to my feet. I start back to the house.

Jed calls out to me. "Hey, Aaron, wait up!"

I turn around, a little startled.

"Heidi's in love with you. Don't you understand?"

My eyes are burning. "I know."

"Man, I need to tell you something, and I'm not sure if I should. Heidi's still . . . well . . . a virgin."

"She is? I mean . . . "

Jed hurries over to my side and tells me that I should rest up a little, and that he'll take me to the feeder road for the freeway when I'm ready. He even offers to drive me to Nashville, but I refuse.

I'm a wreck, but somehow manage to make it back to house. I rush into the bathroom, and when I exit, Jed is waiting for me.

"Jed," I say as calmly as I can, "I appreciate all your help, but I gotta get on the road."

"I understand, Aaron. I understand," Jed replies, trying to reassure me. "I'll give you a ride up the road a ways."

I go to Heidi's room and grab my duffle bag and follow Jed to his Jeep. Once I'm inside, I calm down. I have nothing more to say, but Jed keeps yammering on, and I zone out.

I thank Jed for his hospitality and pull my duffle bag out of the Jeep. The road is empty, and Jed laughs, "Don't worry. It will all work out."

DECEMBER 15, 1970

SITTING AT MY DESK IN MY DOOR ROOM, staring at the telephone, I felt as if the walls were closing in on me.

"Adriana, why aren't you calling me? Why?"

Every fifteen or twenty minutes, I picked up the receiver and listened to the dial tone, hoping that her voice would miraculously materialize on the line.

"Adriana, please, understand. All I ever wanted was you."

No answer.

"Why do I keep talking to you when you're not even there?"

I wasn't hungry for breakfast.

The air in my dorm room was stale. I had to go to class. I was already falling behind, and I worried that if I didn't show up, I was going to be in big trouble.

A cold front had pushed through overnight, and the humidity had dropped. The air was frigid, and the sky was stark blue. The winter sun cast harsh shadows as the light moved across the campus.

I saw a giant red maple leaf on the sidewalk in front of me. There was something about it that made me stop. The leaf held a quality of form and texture that drew my eye. Its underside, now facing up, was still wet from the previous night's rain.

I bent over and lifted it carefully with my right hand, somehow managing not to tear it. I placed it on the palm of my left hand to examine it, and a strange light radiated from the leaf, reminding me of the glow I saw in the face of Adriana's Barbie doll with the paperclip leg brace.

For an instant, the sunlight saturated the leaf in my palm with a reddish hue that accentuated the intricacies of every vein and capillary in its structure. I was awed by the leaf's infinite beauty and by the deep sense of pleasure I felt, having discovered something that most people would have missed by simply walking by in a hurry. But as I studied the leaf, its color faded, and in seconds it became a brittle mass in my palm. And a gust of wind carried it away.

A crow was cawing in the distance.

Out of nowhere, Randy lurched up behind me and slapped me on the butt. "What do you think you're doing in the middle of the sidewalk? Directing traffic?"

"I was . . . thinking."

"Now that's dangerous."

"I'm on my way to English class."

"Don't matter no-how," Randy said, laughing.

I flipped him the bird and rushed off.

When I got to class, I sat in the back row, not wanting to attract attention from Mrs. Dell. I'd missed a lot of classes. Mrs. Dell started exactly when the bell rang, and for the first thirty minutes, she talked about the structure of the upcoming final exam. I wanted to listen but probably heard only every other word she said. I couldn't stop thinking about the abortion, about the rape, about how miserable I felt. My head began to throb, and by the time the class ended, it hurt just to keep my eyes open. I heard the rest of the class filing out of the room, but I just sat at my desk, hoping to regain some composure before getting up.

Mrs. Dell walked toward me, and I quickly pushed back my chair.

"Aaron, are you alright?"

"Yeah, yeah, I'm fine."

"Well, I've been wanting to talk to you. You started out so strongly in this class, but your performance has dropped considerably."

"I've been . . . uh . . . having . . . girlfriend problems."

"I see," she said as she put her hand on a chair at the desk next to me. "May I join you?"

"Uh... of course." I repositioned myself in my seat.

"What I mean," she said, sitting down, "are you on your way to another class? If so, I'd like to set up a time when we can talk for a bit."

"No, I'm... I do have some things I have to do."

"Well, I won't take too much of your time." Mrs. Dell crossed her legs gracefully. She was wearing a navy blue pantsuit and a starched white blouse. I couldn't tell how old she was, because her clothing was so unlike what the other teaching assistants usually wore.

"I've read through your journal, and overall, I'm impressed by your creativity. Some students never take journal writing very seriously, but it's clear that what you write means a great deal to you. There is, however, one piece that concerned me. It's the poem that begins, 'I am a rational man'... and continues 'Strip me to the waist if that is what you wish/Tear from me my pants if you desire more.' It was one of your most recent entries."

I looked down. "It was, uh, about something that happened to a friend."

"I see. This friend must be very special to you."

"Yes," I said softly. "We're very close."

"I'm concerned," Mrs. Dell continued, brushing back her hair with the palms of her hands, "not so much by the writing, which is quite direct, but by your choice of the first person. You make it sound as if this actually happened to you."

"Well, I guess, I was identifying with what my friend must have gone through." I couldn't look at her and got up.

"I understand, Aaron, and I don't mean to probe, but it's so obviously about something terrible."

I turned away and glanced at my watch. "I need to get back to the dorm. I'm expecting a call that I don't want to miss."

Mrs. Dell wanted to talk more, but I couldn't bear it and left as quickly as I could. It was nearly 5:30. I jogged back toward the dorm.

As I crossed the Oval toward South Campus, I saw a crow pecking the grass. I was thinking it could be the same one I had heard on my way to Mrs. Dell's class, but it wasn't cawing, and another crow was circling overhead.

The sky stretched out in front of me like saltwater taffy, streaked with cirrus clouds that glowed purple and orange. I felt like a runner in a race that I could never win. But I had to keep running, just to prove to myself that I could do it.

By the time I got to back to my room, I was breathing hard. Randy was sitting at his desk, scratching his crotch, and when I came in, he glanced up.

I tried to catch my breath. "Have I gotten any calls?"

"You are so puny!"

"Please, Randy. I need to know. Seriously, dickhead, did my girlfriend call? Yes or no?"

"No. But someone did leave a note for you under the door. It smelled like it had perfume or something on it, so it might be from her, or maybe it was delivered by someone else. Never know with them girls, do you? You see, Aaron, my boy, that's why I got me more than one."

"Where is it?"

"Oh my, what did I do with it?" Randy smacked his forehead in mock dismay. "Golly-gosh, I hope I didn't throw it away!"

"Randy, come on!"

"You are so red in the face, man! I can't believe it. Okay, here you go." He pulled the note from a stack beside him and tossed it onto my side of the desk.

I grabbed the envelope and tore open the flap. I stepped out of the room into the hallway, unfolded the note, and read it.

Dearest Aaron,

Jerry was so worried about me that he told my mother what I did, and she insisted that I come back to New York immediately. She bought me a plane ticket, so I left. I think she's right. I feel awful. I tried to call you this afternoon but couldn't reach you. No one answered your phone. Please understand. Thanks for all you did. I'll be in touch when I can.

Love to you, Adriana

She was gone, just like that.

Randy stuck his head out into the hall. "What are you doing now?"

I shoved past him, back into the dorm room. I grabbed the phone and dialed Adriana's mother; I needed to talk to Adriana.

Her mother was polite, but impatient. "I'm sorry, Aaron. She gets in late."

"Please, have her call me when she gets in."

"That may not be such a good idea. Not now. After all she's been through, and for that matter, all that you've been through."

Adriana's mother was evasive. I could tell she didn't want me to talk to Adriana, and I wasn't sure if she'd even tell her that I called.

"Please, Aaron. Understand. Adriana is going to need some time. Thank you for calling. Goodbye."

I had the chills. My voice was shaking. It was as if I was listening to a radio broadcast that I didn't want to hear, but the volume knob was jammed all the way up and the on/off switch was broken.

"Man, what's going on? You look like you're about to pass out." Randy was standing right behind me.

I slammed the receiver onto the phone, and it cracked the mounting plate on the wall.

"Oh, nice!" Randy said. "We're going to have to pay for that."

I looked at Randy, still unable to speak.

"Come on, dude; spit it out!" Randy shouted. "Are the cops coming for you? Did your girlfriend kill someone with an ax, and now she's running for the border?"

"She left me. She went back to New York."

Randy shook his head and rolled his eyes. "Stupid bitch."

Something about Randy's tone of voice felt right to me. As much as what he was saying hurt, I knew he was probably right. "Yeah. Stupid bitch! How could she do that after all that we've been through together?"

"Been through? What have you been through? Judging from the way you look, she must have been one helluva good lay."

I shook my head. "I don't really want to talk about it."

"You want me to take you drinking? Is that what you're saying, Aaron?"

"Yeah. Maybe so."

Randy raised his eyebrows, and I followed him out of the dorm.

We hit the bar district, near campus. I downed beer after beer, shots of peppermint schnapps, and the buzz shoved the pain of Adriana's abandonment far enough in the background that it was almost bearable.

But a few hours later, in the middle of the night, I barely made it to the toilet in time to keep from puking all over my bed. I stayed in the stall for what seemed like hours until the dry heaves finally passed. And the whole time I was in there, I thought about being locked in the bathroom in Canada. Each time I vomited, the sour, acidic smell singed my nose with memories that kept making me sick.

Curled over the toilet, I begged for forgiveness. Why hadn't I tried harder to fight Ralph? How could I have been such an idiot?

In just three months of being on my own at college, I had managed to destroy my life.

I propped myself up against the sink and did my best to avoid the mirror. I didn't want to see what I looked like; I already knew by the way I felt. My eyes were bloodshot and burning; I doused them with cool water and my vision went blurry. I needed a clean towel but did what I could to blot my eyes with toilet paper.

I could hear my roommates milling around, getting ready to go to class, and stumbled out of the bathroom and got to my desk. I scavenged in my knapsack for a bottle of water that I left in it the day before. My mouth was parched, and my head was pounding. I took a long swig of water and slumped down in the chair at my desk.

It was 7:30, and I needed to be at chemistry class at nine. I jerked open one of my desk drawers, looking for my notes and syllabus. I lifted a stack of paper, and all the pages slipped out of my hand, fluttering in the air like bats swarming out of a cave.

I felt dizzy; I lowered my head between my knees, trying to steady myself. As I straightened up, I saw Randy gawking at me, his arms folded across his burly chest.

"You are one piece of work. You're all quiet and withdrawn, but when you get a couple of drinks in you, you turn into a wild man."

"You should talk. You're the one who's standing around in his underwear."

"I don't know if I can ever go drinking with you again, man. You flipped out. It's a good thing one of my hockey buddies was in the bar. I don't know that I could have gotten you back here by myself, even though you are a wimpy-ass shrimp."

"I'll tell you one thing for sure, I'm no wild man today. I'm sick."

Randy grinned. "Ain't that the truth."

"I have to shower. That is, if I can get out of this chair."

I pulled myself up slowly and staggered back into the bathroom, a towel in hand. The gush of hot water felt good and woke me up somewhat, but after I dried off, I wanted to go back to bed. I felt drained and weak, but I told myself I had to go to class.

I put on jeans and a sweater, and while I was tying my sneakers, Randy said, "Here, take one of these. It will help you get through the day."

He placed a small pill on my desk beside a glass of water.

"What's this?"

"It's a white cross. It will perk you up. It's just a diet pill I got from one of my girlfriends."

"Man, it will probably make me sicker. I don't want it."

"No, seriously. Take it with a couple of vitamins. I got some of them, too. Vitamin C and B-complex. They're kind of a hangover chaser."

"I never want to hear the word 'chaser' again."

"Get a grip, Aaron. I'm only trying to help you."

"I've tried this stuff before. I can't handle it. Adriana, I think, took them all the time, you know, every day."

"Smart girl."

"Kiss my ass."

"Okay, as you wish. But I'm going to leave this here just in case you change your mind. And here, these are the vitamins. You got the whole package now."

Randy walked out of the room whistling, heading off to class. Had all the drinking the night before really had no effect on him?

I scooped up all the papers and books lying on the floor and packed what I needed into my knapsack. I still didn't have much of an appetite but thought that maybe if I got something to eat before I left for class, I would feel a little better.

I stared at the pill on the desk and was about to throw it away when suddenly I changed my mind. What I really needed was to shift my life into a different gear. Too much had gone wrong. I scooped up the pill and went downstairs to the cafeteria.

I slogged through the breakfast line, struggling to decide what I might be able to swallow without immediately throwing it back up. I settled on scrambled eggs and hash browns but had trouble getting it all down. The eggs were watery, and the hash browns were too greasy. I looked at the white cross once more, then swallowed it with one big gulp of water.

To my surprise, by the time I got to class, I actually felt a little better. I was more alert and more receptive to the lecture and discussion than I ever thought possible. The nagging malaise from boozing the night before subsided, and my fingertips tingled as I jotted down notes as quickly as I could. When I saw Randy at the end of the day, I asked him if he could spare any more of the diet pills.

"Actually, I'm kind of conflicted," Randy said. "You know, whether or not I should be doing this." He looked at me for a few seconds before reaching into his desk draw and pulling out an envelope with about a dozen white cross tablets inside.

"Just remember, never take more than one a day," Randy warned, handing me the envelope. "But you are already so pitiful. I suppose these can't make you any worse. It's kind of like my daddy used to say, 'You cain't go to the dance if you ain't got a ticket.' Know what I mean?"

"Not really. Is that supposed to make sense?"

"You'll figure it out," Randy said, grinning. "You'll figure it out."

JANUARY 15, 1971

EVERY TIME I POPPED A WHITE CROSS IN MY MOUTH I thought of Adriana, and sometimes started talking to her, even when she wasn't there.

An hour or so after taking a white cross, my body had an electric buzz that I only noticed when I wasn't doing anything. So long as I was active, whether physically or mentally, I was more engaged with whatever I was doing, and I was more optimistic about the future. Maybe Adriana was still in love with me; maybe, in due time, she would come back to Columbus. I also started to have fantasies that my true calling was to be a poet, even though I didn't know much about poetry, other than what I wrote in my journal. "Before me I am a rational man," was a line that resonated within me, and made Mrs. Dell realize that it was me who had been raped, even though she didn't say it. There was something about writing those words that helped, something about poetry that turned me on. The songs that Sister Ethel sang were poems, simple texts about profound ideas.

Of course, my parents wanted me to have some kind of a profession, and if I ever mentioned anything to do with poetry, they would have thought it was ridiculous. "So you want to be drafted, is that it? Go to Vietnam and get yourself maimed or killed?" How they made a connection between majoring in English and getting killed in Vietnam was both maddening and mystifying to me.

So I was pre-med, which meant having to take a long list of science requirements—chemistry, biology, physics, and then organic chemistry—before graduating and taking the MCAT exam and sweating it out to see if I could ever be admitted to medical school. My interest in all this could scarcely have been lower. But by agreeing to take this path, I was able to broker a kind of compromise with my parents: an independent study major that enabled me to take just about any course I wanted to. When it came time to sign up for courses for the next quarter, I picked the history of the modern poem and cultural anthropology as electives, not having any idea what to expect.

"Sounds cool," Randy said as we talked about our upcoming schedules. "That is, if you're a total nerd."

I flipped him the bird without looking at him.

Randy chuckled. "Aaron, my boy, you have really toughened up."

"Just keep getting me those little white crosses, and I'll be fine."

"You're hooked, dude. And now, this is the part where I tell you that the price is going up. It's all about supply and demand. You see, all the girls I know can only fill their prescriptions once a month, and they only get so many, and for obvious reasons, they want most of them for themselves. Then there's me, and well, you're lucky to get some leftovers. My buddies on the hockey team would probably beat the shit out of me if they knew you were the beneficiary of what might otherwise be available for them. You need to cut down, man. I'm serious."

I knew Randy was right—in his twisted, smart-ass way—and I started skipping the pills for as many days as I could. Most of the time I felt okay, but after a couple of weeks, as the residual effects of the pills left my system, things started to get tougher.

I craved the highs, and I dreaded the lows—the dark doldrums when I worried about everything from Adriana to my parents. And worst of all, I couldn't stop grieving for the innocence I had lost.

More and more of the time, I felt terribly lonely. I had no one to talk to about being raped. I had a gnawing void in my gut, as if parasites were eating the parts of me that had died. Some days I could barely walk; on others, I could hardly move my arms and hands. I had to pull myself out of chairs, and even lifting a fork or spoon hurt. I couldn't eat. I lost my sense of taste. Just looking at food could make me gag. I wanted to call Adriana but knew I shouldn't. I worried that if I did, she might hang up on me, or say something mean.

The white crosses helped. Somehow, when I was on speed, I could accept reality for what it was. My grades improved, and I felt more in tune with my inner self. I became more aware of everything around me: academically, socially, and even politically.

I even decided to run for freshman senate. Randy became my campaign manager. Of course, Randy didn't really do much other than put the word out to his hockey pals and cheerleader friends. I made a handbill that said "Aaron Berg! A Fresh Voice for Freshman Senate." My RA let me mimeograph it on a ream of yellow paper and I distributed about five hundred copies. I woke up early every morning for about a week and left them on tables in the cafeteria so that when kids came down for breakfast, they would see them. On the day of the election, Randy made a crude poster with magic markers and stapled it to a big stick. He paraded around the lobby of the dorm, wearing his hockey jersey and a stupid crown he made from red balloons. The crazy thing was it worked: I won the election by a margin of thirty-eight votes.

In freshman senate, though, I was an oddball. I was the token hippie, even though I didn't really want to be like most of the hippies I saw on campus. I may have looked the part, with my long, frizzy hair and bellbottoms, but I was different. I stopped listening to pop music. I found a classical station, and when no one was around, I listened to some of the most incredible music in the world.

One day, Randy walked into the room while I was listening to Telemann's Trumpet Concerto in D.

"Anyone else catches you listening to this," Randy roared, "I'll have to beat the shit out of you on general principle."

I jumped out of my chair and playfully tried to strangle him, but Randy rocked me back onto his desk with one hand and turned the radio off with the other.

The truth was that for me, pop music no longer had any appeal. The senseless deaths of Jimi Hendrix and Janis Joplin weighed heavily on me; I certainly didn't want to die choking on my own puke. I was convinced that with the white crosses, I'd found a better way to use drugs. Speed was medicine for me, and when Randy couldn't get more white crosses, he gave me a "black beauty."

"Just what the doctor ordered," Randy said. "I ain't joking, if you know what I mean."

"Yeah, I guess so. But what's the difference?"

"Here, try one—free of charge. If you don't like it, wait for the next batch of white crosses to arrive. You're a big boy; you can figure it out. One of these ain't going to hurt you."

I shrugged and put the black beauty into my shirt pocket. "Okay. In the morning."

"Man, you are one strange dude. You're supposed to do speed at night. It doubles your time on this earth—that is, waking time."

"That's the difference between me and you. You're a redneck, and I'm not."

"Well, at least I ain't a Jew boy from New Yawk City."

"I'm from Boston. Totally different world."

"A Bean Town baby!" Randy walked out, still hollering, "A Bean Town baby!"

I had to read Macbeth for English class, but I couldn't focus. I took the black beauty out of my pocket and popped it into my mouth. Then I went into my bedroom and lay down until the speed jolted me.

I went back to my desk, picked up my copy of Macbeth, and didn't put it down until I finished. Then I went into the bathroom and washed my hands. The water rushing on my skin made me grin, thinking that I was succeeding at what Lady Macbeth failed to do, purging myself of the guilt that was eating me up inside. For that moment, I was invincible.

I was jazzed; I had to go somewhere, do something. I walked into the hallway, checking out faces that I had never paid much attention to. A fat kid whom I never met waddled up to me. I was about to laugh when the kid said, "Congratulations, I voted for you. And I'd like to meet with you and talk about some of my concerns about what's going wrong in this dorm."

"I'd like that," I answered, riffing mentally on the random thoughts that were racing between my ears. Then I told him that he'd made my day and asked him for his name and room number, promising that I'd come see him. We shook hands, and he waddled off, and I headed for the elevator.

My vision was a little blurred and I rubbed my eyes. I found myself an empty lounge chair in the corner near the back windows and sat down. I was short-winded, but after about half an hour, the speed settled in and my jittery thoughts eased down.

My sense of time was disintegrating. Had it been a couple of minutes since I took the pill or a few hours? Sitting in the lobby and watching people walk back and forth, I was a flipbook of emotions. I wanted to be around people, but I was also paranoid about getting too close. I had never stayed up all night in the dorm lobby, other than with Adriana when we got back from Canada, and the kids I now watched had faces I'd never seen before.

One girl who called herself Angel was pretending to be a ballerina, whirling around the columns and chairs until she fell over and landed spread-eagle on the carpet in front of me.

"Are you okay?" I asked.

But instead of answering with words, she sprang up and flung her arms around me, and then stepped back with a wild-eyed grin.

"Wanna see? Wanna see?"

I took a deep breath and exhaled slowly.

"Take my hand, take my hand," she whispered.

My voice was coming back, but I couldn't find the words I needed to communicate. My thoughts were skewed. I let her take my hand, and her long coat flew open.

She was completely naked. Her tits were big and supple, and her nipples were erect. Her skin was creamy white, and her pubic hair was dark and bushy, curling out in front of me in stark contrast to her milky white thighs.

I was electrified by what I saw, and as she guided me toward the elevator, all my inhibitions melted away. I was totally turned on, and she shimmied up close to me and massaged my most tender parts with both of her hands. I could barely stand up. I groaned in pleasure as my knees buckled under me. Just as the elevator arrived, I lost my balance.

Angel danced into the elevator and disappeared behind the closing doors. I struggled to pry them apart but couldn't, and by the time the next elevator came, she was gone.

I went back to my room, dejected. For the rest of the night, I lay on my back in bed, my eyes wide open. It was as if my mind and body had separated, and I had to wait for them to come back together before I could do anything else.

In the morning, I was haggard but relieved that I'd made it through the night without going nuts. Tiny bursts of yellow light edged the window across the room, signaling to me in a very strange way that it was safe to get up.

I wanted to find Angel again, but I searched the sea of faces in the cafeteria without success. I waited in the lobby late the next night, and the night after that, but she never reappeared. I started to wonder if Angel was real, or if I was just hallucinating from the black beauty that had sent me soaring.

Angel was gorgeous. And I was so horny.

I started sitting next to girls sitting alone in the cafeteria that I didn't know. I'd pretend I was confused. "Is your name Angel?" And when she said, "No, I'm Jenny or Annie," I apologized for the mistake. "You remind so much of Angel, who I only talked to once in History 101, and I ... uh ... "

And usually whoever I was talking to got up and left. But one time, a girl acted turned on and played along.

"Oh, really?" she asked. "I think you were in my class. And I don't remember anyone named Angel."

I was so embarrassed but did my best not to show it. "Yeah," I said. "You look so familiar. What's your name?"

"Heather."

"Wow! That's cool."

"Are you on drugs?"

"Yeah, speed. I'm zooming."

"I think you're a creep!" she barked and lurched from her seat.

I was miserable and euphoric at the same time.

I began to think a lot about my childhood and how I was always frustrated when my mother wouldn't give me her approval. Even when I got an A on a test or book report, she'd grimace and say, "I keep waiting for you to get an A+."

My thoughts were twisted for days. But I wanted to try another black beauty once the effects of the first one had worn off to see if maybe the second time, I could harness its power.

"Man, are you suicidal?" Randy said.

"No. I know what I'm doing. I have to navigate my path, and for now, that means more speed."

"Sounds like bullshit to me." Randy glared at me. "I've never seen this stuff affect anybody like the way it's done you. I don't want to wake up and find you dead in your bed."

"Come on, man! I mean, the girls who give you this stuff take it every day, right?"

"Yeah, whatever, I guess. Look, I may act like an idiot, but I'm not. I might not have the school smarts that you do, but I can do a lot of things that you can't."

"That's the truth."

"Okay. I'll let you have another black beauty, but you got to tell me the truth if it screws you up."

Looking at me doubtfully, Randy fished around in his desk drawer, brought out a pill, and slapped it into my outstretched hand.

I left the room with the black beauty in my hand and went downstairs to the cafeteria, where I got a glass of ice water. I had to admit, after Randy's little lecture, it was hard to put the pill in my mouth. But I did. After all, it was only a diet pill.

I went into the men's room off the lobby to pee.

Washing my hands, I stared at my face in the mirror for answers, searching for meaning in all the chaos of my life, hoping that something would happen to transform me into someone I actually liked.

MARCH 23, 1971
8:43 P.M.

THE DARKNESS IS BLINDING. The road in front of me is so black that I can't see anything. No cars. No people. My hands are freezing. A car heads my way, speeding past me, but then stops short, spinning around, and edging toward me. I start to run, but I don't have any idea where to go. I've been waiting for more than four hours, and the only car I've seen was a beat-up Lincoln Continental, swerving in my direction, with two rednecks in the front seat who pulled up alongside me and threw empty beer cans at me before peeling off. The car approaching me seems different. The high beams are flashing on and off.

I'm about to run when I hear a voice in the distance. It's Heidi, bellowing, "Jed should have known better!"

I catch my breath. I'm so mad, but seeing Heidi mellows me out. "Guess he wanted to teach me a lesson."

Heidi grins. "Did he tell you about the school of hard knocks?"

"Yeah. I get it."

"He left you out on this deserted road because he wants you to come back, and he knew that I'd know how to come looking for you if that's what I wanted to do. Sorry I had to rush off this morning. I had to cover Beverly's shift. She's come down with something nasty, and it was my turn to fill in."

I sigh. "I'm so glad you found me. I was starting to think I'd better walk somewhere, but I didn't have any sense of where I'd to go, wondering if I should just camp out until tomorrow."

Heidi looks sympathetically into my eyes. "You got a tent in that duffle bag?"

I smile. "Yeah, it's a little pop-up. A one-seater."

Heidi laughs. "Kind of like a motor scooter."

"Not exactly."

Heidi runs her fingers through her hair.

I lean back on my heels and rock forward.

"You look like you're going to fall over, Aaron."

"No, no. It's a stretch I learned once, and it makes feel good when I'm trying to figure out what to do next."

With Heidi I feel so at ease, but I'm not in the mood to see Jed, or the others.

"I can take you up to the Interstate," Heidi says. "Might have an easier time getting a ride there."

"That was what Jed said, but then he left me here."

"It's like I told you, Aaron, he didn't want you to leave. He knows, and I do, too, after whatever it is you went through, you're still suffering. Being around folks like us could help you heal faster than you could ever do on your own."

I kneel down. I feel like I have a kink in my glutes. I well up but don't want Heidi to see.

Heidi reaches for my hand and tries to pull me up, but I stumble, and she falls forward. I catch her in my arms, and she clasps my shoulders. The ground is hard, but it doesn't seem to matter. We roll over and embrace, giving me goosebumps.

"Goosies!" Heidi jokes, and our lips press together in an excited kiss. I look deep into her eyes. "So . . . tell me, have you been healed?"

"That's a big question, Aaron, and the way you're saying it sounds a little weird. Healing is a process. Emotionally, I'm better. But physically, I'm the same. I mean, the plumbing works, but . . . "

Heidi smiles and I cup her cheeks in my hands. "I love you."

"And I love you, too, Aaron. Part of me is overjoyed, but another part is terrified. Did Jed tell you I was a virgin?"

I squirm, but Heidi won't let go.

"Okay... yes... Jed told me."

"It's alright, Aaron. You're not the first boy I liked that he... uh... confided in. He's protective. Overprotective. He's afraid about me getting hurt more than I've already been. Of course, technically, I'm not a virgin."

"I... it doesn't really matter to me. I'm damaged property, if you know what I mean."

Heidi whispers, "I guess saying that I'm a virgin is his way of saying I'm still, in his mind, innocent. Can you forgive him?"

"Of course."

"Amen."

"Can you forgive yourself?"

"Talk about big questions.... What I'm starting to realize is what matters most is who we are right now. The rest is baggage."

"That's good," Heidi adds, "that baggage gets mighty heavy sometimes, weighing us down."

"That's the truth."

I get up slowly and yank my tent out of the duffle bag and spread it flat on the ground as a tarp. Heidi pulls my sleeping bag out and unzips it for us to use as a blanket.

"I only have one foam pillow," I say, a little embarrassed.

Heidi laughs, "I can roll up this old sweatshirt of yours. And well, it's not exactly my kind of pillow. But it's good enough."

I stretch out on the tent tarp and Heidi stoops down and does the same, resting her face on my chest. I gaze up at the sky. The stars are bright, and in my mind's eye, I'm soaring into the universe with Heidi at my side.

FEBRUARY 19, 1971

WHEN I WENT TO CHECK MY MAILBOX, A NEW US ARMY recruitment poster tacked onto the wall of the dorm lobby was staring me in the face. Beneath a group of soldiers huddled together atop a grassy hillside, it read, "Where does the call to be a soldier come from? The same place love of country comes from. Your future, your decision. Choose ARMY!"

I began to think that maybe volunteering for the army was what I needed to do. Maybe then, I could prove to myself that I wasn't a wimp, that I wasn't a coward for not fighting Ralph.

Maybe resisting the draft was just getting in the way.

I knew my parents would try to stop me from enlisting, but what could they really do? I was finally old enough to make up my own mind.

I grabbed my mail from my box and turned around. And about ten feet in front me, I saw Adriana talking to someone at the front desk. I couldn't believe it. It was as if my thoughts had conjured her up. I just stood there and watched, wondering how long it was going to take for her to see me. She was carrying a green canvas overnight bag in one hand and a dark brown leather purse in the other, acting oblivious to everyone around her. But when she finally turned around, she smiled coyly, as if she already knew I was there. Then she reached into her purse to get a tube of lipstick and smoothed a deep rouge color onto her lips. She knew how much that color turned me on and said, "Aaron, I know you weren't expecting to ever see me again, but I had to come back."

I felt myself blushing and asked her if she wanted to go somewhere to get a cup of coffee or tea. And she giggled with an exaggerated New York accent. "I'd love to."

In the morning light, Adriana seemed older. Her high cheekbones were more chiseled, and I could see that a furrow was beginning to form between her eyebrows, which were carefully trimmed and plucked. Overall, she was so groomed that it was clear she had been focusing more on her appearance. Her fingernails were manicured, and she was wearing black slacks and a matching sweater instead of her usual jeans and turtleneck.

"So, what's happening?" Adriana asked, trying to sound like an old friend, back from a long trip.

There was so much to say, but I couldn't figure out how to begin. So I just played along, telling her I was doing great, getting better grades, and how I even got elected to freshman senate.

She acted surprised, but not really impressed. "Wow! You have become quite the college man. Have you decided to pledge a fraternity?"

I laughed nervously.

"Well, it sounds as though you have a new life. Good for you. I have a new life, too. Things have changed . . . for the better. Hey, are you hungry? I need something more than coffee or tea. I'd like to get some lunch. It was a long flight—lots of delays. First, it was weather, then, you know, one thing and another. How about a burger or a salad?"

I tried hard to be upbeat, but just looking at her was a lot to process. She was so different, even though she sounded pretty much the same.

Adriana looked down at her braced leg, as if the alignment wasn't quite right. But she quickly glanced back up at me, not wanting to let on exactly what she was feeling.

As we exited the dorm, Adriana donned a fluffy cashmere hat and wrapped her neck with a thick scarf that inched up past her mouth. We walked across the Oval. I wasn't sure what to think. Her return had knocked me off-center; she had never called while she was in New York, and then suddenly, she just showed up.

"Are you on something, Aaron?"

"Reality, I guess." I didn't want to say that I'd had a black beauty with breakfast. But she could tell.

She rolled her eyes. "Whatever. Let's go to Les Amis. I haven't eaten there since, well, when my mother was in town, you know, around the time I moved into the dorm. It was before I met you."

I felt as if we were walking in separate bubbles; we could hear each other and see each other, but otherwise we were disconnected. At the restaurant the hostess took Adriana's coat, but I decided to keep mine on.

"You look sick. Are you okay?"

"I'm fine."

Adriana ordered a Niçoise salad, and when I asked for a cup of French onion soup, the waiter queried, "Is that all?"

"I'm not very hungry . . . late breakfast," I said matter-of-factly. I couldn't get comfortable. My armpits were itchy, and it was hard for me to scratch myself under my sweater. I took off my jacket and slung it over the back of my chair.

"You seem really jumpy," Adriana said. Finally, she gave me a direct look. "I don't know how to say this, but I have to tell you. I really care for you, but I can't bear it. To imagine us ever getting back to where we started. I'm not there anymore."

I tried to maintain eye contact with her, but she glanced away.

"It's been tough," I said, hoping that she'd see how much I missed her.

"I know I haven't been communicative. I'm sorry about that, but sometimes it's better not to speak if you don't know what to say."

"Why didn't you ever call me back? I mean, I talked to your mother. Did she tell you?"

Adriana looked at me like I was from Mars. Of course, her mother told her. But apparently, it didn't matter to her as much as it did to me.

"I still want to be friends, Aaron. But when I was back home, I met someone. Actually, I've known him for some time. I mean, long before I met you. But we never thought of each other in this way. It just happened. I went to a meeting of NOW and he was there."

"NOW?"

"The National Organization of Women. I wanted to hear Betty Friedan talk about her book *The Feminine Mystique* and the Women's Strike for Equality last summer. Anyway, Jared was there. I mean, he's about ten years older than me, and when he told me that he had just passed his New York bar exam and was working with feminist organizations, it was like wow!"

I was dumbstruck. And when she started telling me about how much they both had in common, I glared at her and said, "Well, I'm a feminist, too."

Adriana snarled, "How can you be so smug?"

"I can't believe the way you're acting. Who went with you when you got your abortion? I always knew it was your decision. Your body. Not mine. I was there to support you. I trusted you. I respected you. I loved you. And I still do."

"Please, this isn't easy for me," Adriana said, "You'll always be important in my life. What happened bound us together forever."

My saliva thickened. I was trembling. "Well, if we're bound together, how can you break up like this?"

Adriana straightened up. "Well, the truth is, Aaron, I've grown. What happened to us was a wake-up call to everything that's wrong with our screwed-up world. I have a mission. And fighting for women's rights is it. But what we shared will always be part of me."

I stared at Adriana, but she wouldn't look in my direction. It was as if she was more focused on what was above and around me, avoiding eye contact.

When the food came, she picked up her fork and started eating without waiting for my order to arrive. The waiter apologized to me for the delay, but if Adriana cared, she didn't show it. When the waiter finally set the steaming cup of soup in front of me, I stood up and gritted my teeth. "No thanks."

The waiter was apologetic.

"It's not you," I said. "Goodbye, Adriana."

Adriana slammed her fork onto the table. "Is that all you can say?"

I was speechless.

"Fine. Goodbye, Aaron, I wish you well."

Outside, the cold air stung my eyes, welling up with angry tears as I strode away. The faster I walked, the quicker my muscles tensed up and began to cramp. I was desperate to slow down but the speed wouldn't let go. I was racing inside. My eyes felt like they were going to pop out of my head.

When I got to the dorm, Randy was just coming back from class. I was gulping water from the fountain near the elevator and saw Randy in my peripheral vision.

"How's it hanging, dipstick?" Randy slapped my back, and the water in my mouth sprayed out.

Randy looked at me more closely. "Okay, okay. I know what you need." He reached into the pocket of his parka and handed me a white paper envelope. "Take this outside. You'll know what to do."

I gawked at him as he walked away.

I closed my eyes and stood still for a moment, then turned around, heading back to the lobby. I exited the dorm, opening the envelope as I walked. It was a joint. I tucked it into the breast pocket of my shirt and hiked down to the banks of the Olentangy River.

Finding a secluded spot, I lit the joint and inhaled deeply. The cannabis smoke filled the air around me with a warm glow. I thought about the day Adriana had turned me on at this very spot. Her memory seemed to rise from the damp grass beneath my feet but vaporized as the insulation around my brain thickened.

It was as if I was in the middle of a jungle on another planet. Vines were growing up around me to protect me from predators, and by the time I finished the joint, I had a head rush. My thoughts were disjointed; at one point, I felt like different voices were arguing inside me—Adriana ranting that I was a wimp for resisting the draft, and me screaming at her that Vietnam was a stupid war that in the end would accomplish nothing other than killing and maiming tens of thousands of people, from American soldiers to Viet Cong to innocent civilians and children with third degree burns from napalm attacks.

I wondered if I was dead. And with the blink of an eye, the landscape transformed into a lotus garden. I was face down, gasping for breath. Snakes wrapped around my ankles, and I was crying for help. And then someone wearing a Richard Nixon mask handed me a gun. A cowboy Colt 45 with a long barrel that made me think of the Lone Ranger. But when it left his hand, it transformed into a German Shepherd, growling at me. I lurched back and lost my balance and tumbled to the ground, hitting my head on a big flat rock. Everything around me stopped.

Polka dots started falling from the sky, and I started singing "Lucy in the Sky with Diamonds" over and over again.

John Lennon appeared. He raised his right hand and flashed me a peace sign, and my body relaxed. The snakes were gone, and the lotus flowers around me were blooming and going to seed at the same time.

I floated back to the dorm. I sat in a lounge chair and relished the sense of peace that John Lennon had bestowed upon me, wandering around in a kind of Nirvana haze that calmed the chaos of my imagination. I lowered my eyelids, and my mind and body returned to a natural rhythm. I leaned back, stretched my legs in front of me, and settled into a deep rest.

In my dreams, I was perched on a ledge overlooking Boston harbor. The dusk settled into a murky haze of pink and gray. The fog blew in fast, and the visibility dropped to zero. The only sounds were that of the waves crashing into the rocks.

The fog was so dense, I lost track of where I was. But I couldn't wake up, not yet. The waves were beckoning me to come closer to the edge of the cliffs, to gaze into the abyss without any knowledge of what was really there.

Then, out of the oblivion around me, Ralph's voice thundered in the clouds. Your girlfriend's a slut, kid. She lied to you. I didn't rape her. She wanted me to screw her, and I did.

My head throbbed. I was dreaming about dreaming, and the layers ran too deep. It was as if I was stuck in a hall of mirrors, and the reflections of myself were endless.

How could you do this to us? I begged Ralph to answer. But the world around me went mute. The sun burned slowly through the fog, and when I woke up, I was sitting on a beach in the middle of nowhere; the air was hot, but a soft breeze blew cool as the tide rolled in.

MARCH 22, 1971
10:35 P.M.

WHEN I ASK HEIDI IF SHE'S COLD, she shakes her head. We untangle our bodies from each other, and Heidi laughs. "The body heat is wearing off fast. Think we oughta make a fire?"
I gulp. "On the side of the road?"
"Yes sir," Heidi says in a silly voice. "Don't think anyone around here is going to mind. Fact is, we haven't seen or heard a car the whole time we've been zonked out."
Heidi walks over to her Karmann Ghia and gets a flashlight and a couple of blankets that are stuffed in the trunk. I pull out a package of beef jerky from my duffle bag and offer her some.
"Great. But I got a box of fresh-baked cupcakes on the seat of the Ghia. Thought I was going home for dinner."
"Do you think they're worried about you?"
"No," Heidi smirks. "I put Jed on notice."
"Was he mad?"
"No way. He only had my best interest at heart. Even though he did warn me that you're a city kid, who barely knows how to carry wood, let alone cut it with an ax."
"Ha!"
Heidi gathers up some rocks and builds a little firepit. Then she picks up as many dried branches she can find and ignites them with a match she has in a cardboard box in her purse. As the flames flare up, Heidi takes my hands and swings me around until we're both dizzy and plop onto the ground. We reach for the blankets and drape them over each other.

Heidi rests her chin on my shoulder and looks at me starry-eyed.

"Aaron, why don't just move in with us for a while?" Heidi says in a seductive voice.

My heart sinks. "I just can't. Not now. I've got to finish what I set out to do."

"I know." Heidi smiles. "I understand . . . but sometimes a change in plans opens a door you never knew was there."

"Yeah. That may be true."

I breathe in the chilly morning air as the sun seeps through the mottled sky overhead. The crow that's been following me around makes a rattling sound. "Meeting you . . . I never expected, or probably ever imagined, that I'd be so blown away."

"That's a good thing," Heidi says, beckoning me to come closer. "C'mon. I need you to cuddle up. Closer." And that's what we do.

FEBRUARY 20, 1971

I NEEDED TO TALK TO ADRIANA. I knew I'd messed up. I shouldn't have left Les Amis the way I did. I took the elevator to my dorm room. Randy was sitting at his desk.

"You're actually doing homework?"

"Not funny," Randy said, "not funny at all. If I don't raise my grade in algebra, Coach is going to have to suspend me from the team. It sucks."

"Sure does. Hey, I don't want to bother you, but thanks. That little doobie did the trick, helped me to get things straight in my head."

Randy nodded.

"I'm just going to make a quick phone call."

"You don't need my permission."

I dialed Adriana's number, and much to my surprise, she answered.

"I'm sorry. I shouldn't have acted the way I did."

"I don't believe you."

"Seriously, I'm very sorry. I don't want to break up this way."

"Well, Aaron, it's over. There's nothing you can do."

"I know. But it's just so hard for me. Can we meet downstairs, just for a little while? My roommate's trying to study, and I can't . . ."

"You're not making much sense. Have you come down from whatever it was that you were on?"

I apologized again.

There was a long pause. "I shouldn't, but okay. I don't have much time; I have an appointment a little later this evening."

"Appointment?"

"That's my business. If you're going to start nagging me with questions, forget it."

"I just need some closure. I want to feel that when we go our separate ways, we . . . I mean, I've thought about what you said. We really are forever bound together by what we went through. Being with you now will help me accept that."

"All right," she said after another pause. "I'll be downstairs in thirty minutes."

I hung up the receiver. I went to my closet and grabbed some clean clothes, then headed into the bathroom for a quick shower. By the time I got downstairs, Adriana was already there, sitting on a folding chair across from the elevator, one often used by one of the security guards.

I fought to keep my tone even, my words measured. "You okay?"

Adriana got up from her chair slowly, as if she was hurting, and I followed her to an empty couch near the entrance to the cafeteria. The lobby was crowded with kids coming in and out of the dorm.

Adriana released the lock on her brace and lowered herself onto a couch. I sat next to her, but not too close. The space between us seemed to ease the tension, but it made me even more self-conscious.

"Aaron, there really isn't much more to say, is there?" Adriana asked, avoiding eye contact. "I know you're sad. Part of me is, too. I'm still grieving."

"Me, too," I said, my voice quivering. "We both lost so much."

Adriana turned toward me. "Not exactly. We're still here. We're alive. We have a lot to be grateful for."

"Yeah. That's right. Except now, there's someone else in your life."

Adriana leaned toward me. "You have to find the strength to go on without me."

I could tell that Adriana wanted to be consoling, but it only added to my despair. I stared at her, pleading with my eyes for her to say something more.

"It just happened," she said. "I didn't plan it. I didn't seek it out. I connected with someone in a new way. But it wasn't out of desperation. It was at a moment when I was starting to feel like myself again."

"Were you thinking of me? At all?"

"Of course I was. When I left Columbus to go back home, you were all I thought about. But as the days passed, I began to realize our relationship wasn't going to work."

"Why? We had so much before it was ripped away."

Adriana went silent. "I only wish you well," she said. But it didn't sound sincere.

Adriana leaned forward as if she were about to get up. She was getting ready to go. She looked at me again and said, "Hurting you is the last thing I ever wanted to do. But I don't know what else I can do. We have to go on with our lives. I promise you; it will get better."

I couldn't find the words to express what I was feeling. My stomach was in knots.

"Aaron, I can tell something's still on your mind, and your unwillingness to say it is grating on me. Now is your chance. I don't know when I'll ever be with you like this again."

I cleared my throat. "Yeah, you're right. There is something that still bothers me."

Adriana stiffened, waiting impatiently for me to continue.

"It's just . . . what haunts me the most about what happened in Canada is what you said to Ralph in Italian before the shit hit the fan."

Her mouth dropped open. "Are you trying to blame me for what they did?" She stood up and locked her brace. "I have to leave. I have an appointment. I have something more important to do than sit here and listen to this."

"So, you're just going to ignore what I'm asking? Don't you get it? Your avoidance speaks volumes."

"Look, I've already told you. It was just small talk."

"But why in Italian? I need an answer."

"I was showing off, okay? How many times do I have to tell you for it sink into your drug-addled head?"

I sucked in my chest and inhaled deeply. "I think it had to do with your family and their crooked business connections. I think you were acting tough and blustery, just like you are right now."

She glared at me, her cheeks reddening. "Okay, I'll tell you. When I told Ralph my full name, 'Ricorda solo che mi chiamo Adriana Rosario Santa Maria Romano,' he said he knew my father."

"What?"

"He was passing judgement. Aaron, the hard reality is that for Ralph and Nicky, it was all about business. Punishing me was their way of attacking him."

I was shivering. "How can you say that? Is it true?"

"That's what he said, but when I talked to my father, he didn't know anything about it. But apparently, they knew about him."

"I don't get it. You told your father what happened?"

"Well . . . I had to. Once my mother found out, there's no way she could keep it from him."

"You mean him and the mob?"

"The mob? Who do you think you are? You don't have a clue."

"It's all starting to make sense. All your cryptic talk about your family's business. Jerry's father being indicted. The puzzle is finally piecing together."

"Look, Aaron, the bottom line is I . . . we . . . were raped . . . and what's going to happen to Ralph and Nicky . . . it's in my father's hands now."

"Your father's hands now? What does that mean?"

"It means that he knows what to do."

"What did he say?"

"He glowered at me, like he usually does. And then he blamed me for letting you put me in harm's way."

"Is that supposed to make me feel better?"

"I have no idea."

"Why didn't you tell me the truth?"

"I didn't see the point. It would only have made things worse."

"We could have gotten away. You had the money for a motel room. We could have gone somewhere else."

"In a blizzard. Fat chance."

I curled over. "You know, it was probably me that got you pregnant. I just know it. You planted that seed in my head. And it's grown into one nasty vine that's strangling me."

I stood up to face her, but I was dizzy. I stumbled forward, steadying myself by placing a hand against the wall in front of me. My eyes connected with hers.

"I'm not going to let you destroy my life," I said. "All of this about wanting to be my friend, about us being somehow joined together forever—it's a bunch of crap."

"You're impossible!" Adriana yelled. "I did what I did with Ralph and Nicky because I had to. I wasn't ready to die. And you did the same! It's not my fault, or yours. Just don't blame me!"

Just about everyone in the lobby turned around and stared. Her face was beet-red, and she spun away and strode toward the exit. Watching her go, I couldn't move. I had a stabbing pain in my chest. I felt lost at sea in a lifeboat without any oars, the waves thrashing around me. I cupped my hands and scooped out the water filling the hull as fast I could. My arms ached, and my wrists cramped. I wasn't going to give up, and somehow, I made it to a distant shore. But I was lost.

FEBRUARY 21, 1971

I TOSSED AND TURNED ALL NIGHT, torturing myself with every detail that I could remember—from my first meeting with Adriana to our first kiss, hitchhiking, making love, the rape, the abortion, and finally breaking up.

I woke up confused and disoriented and looked around my dorm room, searching for something, anything to help bring me back to reality. Randy was snoring in the bed across from me, and while the sound was grating, it brought a strange comfort to the darkness around me, just knowing that someone else was there.

When I went downstairs for breakfast, it seemed like everyone was gawking at me, as if even the furniture in the lobby of the dorm remembered Adriana screaming at me. I could feel the finger pointing, hearing the whispers as I walked by.

I could hardly eat. I looked at the soggy pancakes in front of me and pushed the plate away. I lowered my chin to my chest, squeezing my eyes shut, hoping that when I opened them, everything would be different. I yearned for another high, but the speed I was consuming was beginning to consume me, intensifying whatever I was already feeling. If I tried to work harder, speed seemed to help, but if I was sinking, it just sucked me deeper into the black hole of my own thoughts.

I lost track of time; the cafeteria was nearly empty.

When I looked up, a janitor was wiping the tables around me. He plunged his rag into a red bucket, and soapy water sloshed onto the floor. He grabbed his mop and the sounds of him working straightened me up.

I saw a glint of light in the distance, the sun filtering through a crack in a windowpane, splaying out in an intricate lattice pattern on the stained concrete floor in front of me, speaking to me without words, telling me that I was going to die sooner rather than later if I didn't change the way I lived my life. And as the sun waned and the cafeteria darkened, I made up my mind. I had to stop using speed. Every hit was a double-edged sword.

MARCH 14, 1971

I WAS FRANTIC TO GET OUT OF COLUMBUS. I needed to go anywhere other than where I was.

Someplace where I didn't know anyone. Someplace where I could reinvent myself by introducing myself as someone different.

I longed to hear Sister Ethel singing again. In person. I daydreamed about going back to Maine to find her, knowing full well she would never recognize me. But was she still alive? I bought a road atlas and struggled to find the best route to the Shaker Village at Sabbathday Lake, but it was too complicated. Hitchhiking could take days, maybe weeks.

Deep inside there was a light switch I couldn't turn on. It was stuck in my head, buried in memories I wanted to purge from my brain. But these memories were quicksand, and once I stepped into that past, it was overwhelming. The harder I tried to shovel out, the deeper I got into it, day after day.

But then one morning, I found a beat-up Bob Dylan LP with a photo of the Nashville skyline on the back of the album jacket, and it spoke to me in a language that made perfect sense. It reminded me of all the little things in my life which I had stumbled upon that at first seemed insignificant and ended up meaning so much to me—the wet maple leaf that shriveled up in my hand, the patterning of light and shadow on the cafeteria floor.

This snapshot of the Nashville skyline, as mundane as it was, said it all. And somehow imbued me with a determination I'd never felt before.

I studied the roadmaps to Nashville, and in bold letters in the middle of Kentucky were the words "Mammoth Cave: The World's Longest Known Cave System."

Wow! This was what I was looking for. Mammoth Cave was the ideal place for me to stop on my way to Nashville, to spend one night, to meditate on the grandeur of the place, humbled, repenting for all that I'd done wrong. Praying for forgiveness. Praying to be healed.

There was a campground in the national park. And that was all I needed to know. Mammoth Cave was a metaphor for the journey. Like Orpheus, I had to go deep into the underworld—but there would be no Eurydice to follow me back. I had already lost Adriana, and she, like Eurydice, had already been whisked away. She was gone forever.

When I told Randy, he looked at me like I was nuts. "Orpheus? Eurydice? Why on earth do you want to go to Mammoth Cave? You must have one humongous death wish."

"If I'm ever going to find out who I really am, I have to go there."

Randy tightened the belt on his khaki pants. "You ever been to central Kentucky? You think I'm a redneck, wait till you meet up with some of them toothless idiots."

"I'm going to camp in the national park."

"So, what? You think you're going to be there by yourself?"

"I'll keep to myself. I'll be fine."

"Man, you are so naïve. I can't believe you ever made it out of the third grade."

"I need to push myself."

"Might as well go push yourself off a bridge, dude."

"Come on, Randy. I can handle it. Believe me. I need to prove to myself that I can do it. If I can just do it once, I know that everything will be different—I'll be different."

Randy gritted his teeth. "That is such bullshit. What you need for this trip is a gun."

"A gun?" I shook my head. "No way. You're crazy."

Randy closed his eyes. "As much as I don't want to mess around with the marbles rolling around between your ears, I need to explain something to you that you don't seem to understand. You need to be able to protect yourself. You need the power, man."

I started thinking about Ralph. What would I have done if I had a gun?

"Man, what's wrong with you?" Randy said.

I took a deep breath. "Okay . . . so . . . "

"Look, if you want a gun, I have one that you can borrow. And to tell you the truth, I'll sleep a lot sounder knowing that it's in your duffle bag when you're lost on some stupid-ass back-country road in Kentucky. I'm your roommate, man. I know you're a tripped-out pissant, but I kind of feel responsible for you."

"I've never fired a real gun."

Randy looked askance. "No problem. I've got a six-shot revolver with a two-inch barrel that my daddy gave me just in case I ever needed it. It's simple, easy, with a smooth cylinder action and a quick release."

Randy reached into his desk drawer and pulled out a small metal lockbox, which he opened with a key that he had hidden in a little envelope pasted on the inside cover of the Bible on his bookshelf. Randy lifted the gun from its leather holster and said, "Here, take it."

I was stunned. Somehow it didn't look real. It was so much like the plastic guns I had played with as a kid that part of me wanted to wrench it away from Randy and wave it around, but the gravity of it being a real weapon sank in when he handed it to me.

"It's a detective special, Aaron, an extremely well balanced and quick-pointing pistol."

I grasped it loosely, pointing the barrel at the floor. "Is it loaded?"

"No, dumbass, not yet. Come on, this is serious."

I was surprised at how neatly the grip fit in my hand; it was at once frightening and seductive. Part of me wanted to pull the trigger, just to see what might happen next.

"Now, listen. I'm willing to let you take this with you, but not just yet. You have to go sober—stone-cold sober for a week. You drink nothing, you smoke nothing, you take no pills. And then I give you the gun. It's the only drug you need for this trip."

"But Randy, I just told you, I've never shot a gun. I wouldn't know what to do."

"You ever play war as a kid?"

I felt myself blushing. "Well, yeah, but this is different."

"The only difference, Aaron, is this gun is heavier than a water gun. Trust me; when you flip that safety and pull the trigger, it's quicker than any plastic Colt 45."

I stroked the barrel of the gun with my index finger. "I can't believe it. I can't." But Randy was right; I could feel the power of the gun thrumming in my palm, buzzing up my arm and tickling my brain. It was like a drug. It was power—in the palm of my hand.

Randy's nostrils were flaring. "The thing is, this gun is even more illegal than the speed you've been popping in your mouth," Randy said. "I don't have a license for this, and if, for whatever reason, the police catch you with it, you have to say you just found it on the side of the road and give it to them. Of course, I will then proceed to beat the shit out of you. But at least neither one of us will be in jail."

I stepped back. "Okay. I get it!"

"You still sure you want to make this journey into no-man's land?" Randy asked. "What are you trying to prove, anyway? Is this just because that cunt from New York City dumped you? Aaron, my boy, you can do better than that. Be glad she left you. It was divine intervention."

"I don't want to talk about it. I'm over it."

"Yeah, right. You still got a way to go on that one. You're not over her until you get yourself another girl, and even then, you might have to work on that for a while."

"The voice of experience."

"You got that right!" Randy laughed. "Let's go have a beer."

"No. I'm broke."

"Ain't you always! Why don't you get a job or something? That's what a normal person would do."

"Well, there's not much I can do about it right now. Maybe after my trip."

"Man, I only like you because you're so pitiful. If my daddy were ever introduced to you, he'd pretend it never happened. Okay, come on; I'll buy you a beer."

"I've got to study. Really."

"Whatever," Randy said with a disgusted look and left.

Randy mystified me. He was the quintessential jock: loud and vulgar, the kind of person I'd spent a lifetime avoiding. But every now and then, he made a certain kind of sense; he was like some sort of junkyard Buddha. It was as if Randy had some weird mutation that imbued him with a wacky wisdom, showing me what to do by not doing what he was supposed to.

I hefted the gun into my hand and thought about Mammoth Cave—and Nashville.

MARCH 21, 1971
3:00 A.M.

THE PAST AND THE PRESENT merged together in the darkness.
Opening my eyes, I was alone. In my bed. In my dorm.
Randy's alarm was deafening. But somehow, he didn't hear it.
I was wide awake.

I couldn't wait to leave the dorm, but I couldn't get out on the road in the middle of the night. Who would ever pick up a hitchhiker at 3:00 a.m.? No one I'd ever want to be sitting next to.

My body was sore, not so much from exertion, but more from being tensed up.

Knowing I had Randy's gun put me on edge. Wondering how many times he pulled that trigger. And for what reasons? Target practice? Armed robbery? Threatening someone like me?

Did Randy really think I could use it? Or was he just letting me take it to make me think I can take care of myself?

"What's past is prologue" is a Shakespeare quote Mrs. Dell wrote in chalk on the blackboard in block letters the first week of class. It was her way of telling us to avoid making the same mistakes twice. "Punctuation," Mrs. Dell said, "is half the battle." I didn't really understand what she meant, and now, I suppose, that's the point.

"Live your life with an exclamation mark." That was her advice.

Getting dressed, packing my duffle bag, it starts to make sense.

Mrs. Dell was big on quotes, and every week there was a different one on the blackboard waiting for us. Sometimes it was a game. She'd write the quote on the blackboard, and we had to find where it came from, either in our notes or in our textbook.

"Healthy, free, the world before me/The long brown path before me leading wherever I choose," was a hard one. And when Emily, the girl who sat next me in class, found it in a book of Walt Whitman poems, I wanted to make it mine—the 'Song of the Open Road.' We both raised our hands at the same time, but when Mrs. Dell called on me, I hesitated.

"Cat got your tongue?" Mrs. Dell asked, and memories of Ralph uttering those same words to me surged into my throat. I was speechless. I bowed my head, and Emily took center stage.

After class, Emily thanked me.

"I didn't do much. In fact, I didn't do anything." I smiled. "Other than keep my mouth shut."

Emily laughed and said, "The world before me ... tomorrow."

"Yeah," I agreed. "Tomorrow."

MARCH 24, 1971
5:30 A.M.

I WATCH HEIDI SLEEPING BESIDE ME, flat on my back in the chilly predawn air. Replaying everything Randy told me about the gun, telling myself I had to give up speed. For good.

On the first day without speed, I thought I was fine, but as the hours wore on, I couldn't get the word speed out of my head. It was as if every sentence in my mind ended with the word speed—period.

The withdrawal was excruciating. I couldn't sleep for more than ten or fifteen minutes at a time, and I often woke up in cold sweats, hot sweats, and chills. My body would shake uncontrollably; I grabbed the bedposts and squeezed as hard as I could until my hands ached from exhaustion.

For days, I had virtually no appetite. I dreaded going through the food line in the cafeteria. Orange juice made me nauseated, as did coffee and just about anything else I put into my stomach except for baked potatoes and dry toast. On sometimes, even those foods made me queasy.

I did manage to go to most of my classes and squeaked by with whatever homework I could do. Otherwise, I rarely left the dorm. I went to freshman senate meetings, though the other kids often annoyed me. Everyone had an opinion. I became more and more anxious about the possibility that I might end up in Vietnam. I couldn't believe that I'd actually thought about enlisting. I checked my mailbox at least once a day to see if the draft board had sent me a letter, and every day, even when nothing was there, my spirits drooped a little deeper into the bottomless well of my own despair.

I dreaded calling my parents, but I had to. There was an overdraft notice in my mailbox that was almost a week old. I had ignored it for as long as I could; I knew I had to deal with it. I had drained my checking account, and I was out of money.

My father answered the phone in a gruff voice, angry that I hadn't called home in weeks and hadn't responded to all the messages he had left with Randy. I blurted out a bunch of lies—about how my books were expensive and how much I was studying and how I had to pay for a desk lamp I accidentally broke in my dorm room, but he didn't believe me.

"Where are the receipts?" my father asked in a stern voice.

I was an only child, and his expectations were high.

He met my mother at the hardware store where he was a security guard. She was on her lunch break; she was working as a secretary for the vice president of a lumber company. After I was born, she quit her day job and did the best she could taking care of me. She had slipped in the bathtub when she was pregnant and had two inoperable herniated discs in her back. I always sensed that she wanted to do so much more with her life, other than being a mother, but my father wouldn't let her. He was the breadwinner, and she was the stay-at-home mom, a role she embraced but which made her unduly demanding, insisting that my days begin with chores and end with more chores, from sweeping up crumbs off the kitchen floor every morning after breakfast to scrubbing the toilets before I went to bed. It was always clear that my father was in charge, and that my mother was following orders that were then passed on to me.

Whatever I said to my father usually wasn't enough. I hated myself for stonewalling him and lying, but at the same time, I was just trying to survive the bullies, and the embarrassments of growing up that my parents could never understand and that I could never talk to them about. If I ever told them about what happened in Canada, they probably would have forced me to move back home.

I wanted to scream, but I knew it wouldn't do any good. I'd learned at an early age that the less I fought with them, the less they bugged me. So, I just apologized again and again, and finally they hung up.

Heidi hears me talking to myself but doesn't say anything. She massages my shoulders, and I relax.

We eat trail mix for breakfast, with a red velvet cupcake for dessert. We don't have any coffee, but Heidi says we have time to get some at a truck stop near the on-ramp to the freeway.

Once we're in the car, Heidi is fidgety, and when I ask her if she's okay, she says, "Oh, Aaron, being with you has been so . . . special."

I gaze into her eyes, trying to tell her without words how much she means to me.

Heidi puts her key into the ignition but doesn't start the engine. She nestles her shoulder into mine and whispers, "You like kids?"

I feel the blood draining out of my face.

"Is something wrong?" she asks, concerned.

"Yeah, yeah. Just a little fatigued. Hitchhiking alone is . . . hard."

"Do you ever think about settling down? Having a family?"

"Well . . . yeah . . . at some point."

"Being with Jed, Missy, and everyone else is great, but I want to have a child."

I'm confused. "What do you . . . uh . . . mean?"

"I know it's a lot to talk about right now. But I think about it a lot, and hey, I guess, since we're together, I mean, you know, just . . . I may as well tell you. I want to go to the children's home in Cincinnati with an eye on adopting one of those lonely kids, maybe two."

I well up. Memories of Adriana's abortion flash before me.

Heidi pats my cheeks with her fingertips. "I hope I'm not scaring you."

"No, not really. I just can't stop thinking about what I went through with my girlfriend, not that she's my girlfriend anymore. She left me for another guy."

Heidi's face droops. I hadn't seen her this way before. She always acted so upbeat.

"Oh, Aaron. That's so sad."

"It's more than sad."

Heidi clams up. I sense that I've struck a dark chord, one that brings back memories neither of us want to talk about.

"You need to stop beating yourself up," Heidi says. "Stop blaming yourself."

I want to ask her if she's had an abortion, too, but I know I can't.

I shut down. I don't know what more to say. Heidi sighs.

I don't want to leave, but as daylight breaks over the horizon, I feel the road calling me, and Heidi teases me that the car won't start, but she isn't going to get in the way of me doing what I need to do.

RIDE #25
MARCH 24, 1971
8:43 A.M.

IN HEIDI'S CAR, I'M LOVING EVERY SECOND of being with her. I don't want to open the passenger door, but I know I have to.

Heidi leans over and massages my chest.

"This time, Aaron," Heidi says, "I'm going to leave you in a place where the chances of getting a ride are, I'd say, ninety-five percent."

I place my hand gently over hers and our eyes connect.

"Ninety-five percent... Is that so? How do you calculate that?"

"Intuition, I guess. I've seen a lot of hitchhikers on this stretch when I'm on my way to Sears and they're usually gone when I'm headed in the opposite direction. Either they got picked up . . . or arrested or killed, or both. No telling . . . ."

Heidi smiles.

"Ha! Guess that means there's a five percent chance I'm not going anywhere."

"I don't really want to say goodbye, Aaron. So, I won't," Heidi says, her eyes tearing up. Come back to see me. Okay?"

"I hope so."

"Promise?"

"As best I can."

When Heidi drops me off at the on-ramp to the freeway, I feel so empty.

I wonder what it would be like living with Heidi. Could we ever really make it work? I don't know if I could ever do what she and her community are doing. In the end, I might never really fit in.

Waiting for a ride is unbearable. There's no shortage of cars, as

Heidi had predicted, but not many lookers. It's as if I'm invisible. And after about an hour, I'm sick of standing around, so I pace up and down the ramp until finally a man driving a silver Buick stops a few feet in front of me. He cranks down his window and says in a gravelly voice, "Well, hop on in. Today is your lucky day. I'm going to the racetrack in Louisville, got a bead on a horse that's certain to take first. No ifs. No maybes."

I pull open the rear door and stuff my duffle bag onto the floor, and then get into the passenger seat. The back of the car is cluttered with boxes of yellowed newspapers; tattered magazines are scattered across the back seat. Hanging from the rearview mirror is an old cardboard air sanitizer in the shape of a skunk. If it had ever had a scent, it was long gone.

"The name's Michael—but my friends call me Mickey. And you?"

I'm about to say my name when I stop short. I look at the man in disbelief. He's wearing a plaid sport coat, and he talks with a kind of accent that makes me think of Canada. He's really messing with my head. Nicky? Ralph's partner? Is this really him? I know he told me his name is Mickey, but maybe . . . Mickey is just his alias . . . or maybe, Nicky in Canada was actually Mickey.

Mickey looks straight ahead, his eyes glued to the highway in front of him. "Look, kid, if you don't want to talk, keep to yourself. Just remember, I'm doing you a favor."

I squirm in my seat, trying to get comfortable. I pat my face with my hands, relieved that my beard has filled in. The air in the car thickens with anxiety. Mickey shakes his head. "If I wasn't so tired, I'd get off the highway right now. And teach you a thing or two about politeness and gratitude."

I nod, and Mickey starts chattering about anything and everything that comes into his mind, from baseball to hockey, to Nixon and the Vietnam War. The layers of contradictions pile up in my mind like snow drifting against a brick wall. I feel queasy. Mickey's chattering in his raspy voice about everything and nothing is driving me crazy.

I need the ride, so I don't want to argue. I just sit there, letting his stream of stupid ideas about politics, religion, and life run through my ears like water seeping into a kitchen drain. The landscape is hilly, but the tree limbs are barren. I close my eyes, hoping that I can just zone out. I feel Mickey turning to look at me every so often, but I keep my eyes closed.

I start thinking about Randy's gun. Part of me wants to make Mickey get off the road. To march him into the woods. To force him to tell me the truth, as he begs for mercy with a gun two feet from his head.

But what if this really is just a guy named Mickey? How can I be sure? As much as I try to remember what Nicky looked like, I can't. The only detail that sticks in my head is the plaid sport coat, but is this the same one? In Canada, Nicky didn't say much or stick around, and when I saw him mounted on top of Adriana, I wasn't looking at his face. I was watching his body hump up and down as Adriana writhed in pain.

The afternoon light is waning, and I realize that I probably won't make it to Mammoth Cave before nightfall. I worry that I'm going to get stuck on a dark empty road with nowhere to go. And when I glance at Mickey, I see that he's staring at me. Is he beginning to recognize me?

"Where'd you say you're coming from?" Mickey asks.

"Columbus . . . uh . . . I mean . . . " I caught myself. I couldn't say Ohio State. "I was . . . uh, staying with friends at Buckeye Lake. I'm headed home."

"And where's that?"

"Nashville . . . Nashville."

I cough softly and lean my head back. After a while I hear Mickey whistling a melody that sounds familiar, barely audible above the noise of the tires on the highway pavement. An image of Ralph and Nicky rises in my mind's eye. They're sitting in a truck stop café, drinking coffee from thick porcelain mugs, and laughing about what they did to Adriana and me. I stand outside in the parking lot, watching them through the plate glass window, pulling the gun from my duffle bag. I want to go inside, acting passive and scared. And when they least expect it, I'm going to shoot them both in the face.

I'll shoot Ralph first, and then Nicky.

"Aaron! Aaron!" Mickey is jabbing me in the side.

"Wha . . . what?"

"You're groaning! And it's driving me nuts."

I rub my eyes with my fingertips. "Yeah, yeah. Sorry."

"Well, let me tell you plain and simple. My exit is a mile away. Where you want out?"

"I . . . uh . . . Where's I-65?"

Mickey looks annoyed. "If you hadn't passed out, I could have let you out in a better place."

"I didn't pass out. I'm just tired, okay?"

"Sure thing," Mickey says under his breath. "I'll leave you at the next exit. You figure it out."

"Please, Mickey. I don't know where I am."

Mickey shrugs and pulls the car onto the shoulder. He puts the car in park and looks directly at me for the first time since he'd picked him up. "Watch yourself, kid."

I get out of the car and yank my duffle bag off the floor. Then, I step back from the car slowly, making a mental note of the license plate number.

Mickey glares at me, and our eyes meet for a fiery instant.

RIDE #26
MARCH 24, 1971
5:03 P.M.

ABOUT THREE HUNDRED YARDS ACROSS THE HIGHWAY, I see a café. I need a cup of coffee. Hoisting my duffle bag over my shoulder, I slog toward the entrance as the sky darkens around me. I lean into the door and peer cautiously at the customers, making sure that, by some quirk of fate, Ralph isn't there.

A trucker with leathery skin ambles across the parking lot and pauses beside me. "You going to block the door, or you going to let me pass?"

I move aside. "Sorry. It's been a very long day."

"Tell me about it." The trucker pushes his way through the front door. I follow behind him and take a seat in the corner by the window. While I wait for service, the neon sign outside flickers on.

When the waitress comes to take my order, I have a hard time looking at her. I can't stop thinking about Heidi. I order a cup of coffee and fidget with my spoon as I try to decide what to do next. It's already dark, and it will be even colder by the time I reached Mammoth Cave. I have thirty-eight bucks and change in my pocket, enough for a little bit of food and maybe a night in a cheap motel, but I don't want to spend too much too soon.

I look up. The trucker who had pushed past me when he entered the café is paying the waitress. And as he gets up from his table, I do the same, and follow him outside.

I approach his rig nervously. The trucker turns toward me, and I pull up short.

"Excuse me, sir," I say, trying to sound respectful.

"What's your problem, kid?"

"I was just wondering . . . Are you headed north? I need to get to I-65 South."

"You're asking me for a ride?"

"Yeah . . . I need help."

"What's it worth to you?"

"How about five bucks?"

The trucker laughs. "Enough for a six pack of Pepsi and a couple of bags of Fritos, maybe."

He fishes a Camel cigarette out of the pack jammed in his shirt pocket and takes his time lighting it. He looks at me again and snickers. "Sure. Climb in if you can handle it. I shouldn't be doing this, but I got a son in high school who thinks hitchhiking is God's gift to the unemployed."

The cab is cramped, and I can barely stuff my duffle bag under my feet. The upholstery on the passenger seat is torn, and a couple of broken springs make it hard for me to get comfortable.

The trucker doesn't seem to want to say much. But it doesn't matter to me.

I can't stop looking around the cab. He has all kinds of memorabilia pasted on the door frame: snapshots, movie ticket stubs, business cards, and scraps of paper with indecipherable scribbled notes.

"The name's Ned," the trucker says.

"I'm Aaron, Aaron Berg."

"Berg? Okay, if that's what it is, Mr. Berg. How far you goin' on I-65?"

"Mammoth Cave."

"At this time of year? You're going to freeze your butt off."

"I'm only going to spend the night, then hike around a little before going on to Nashville."

"Well, I guess you're in luck, then. I'm hauling sheet rock and brick to Bowling Green. I can let you out at Mammoth Cave Road, but it's a hike from there, probably ten miles before you get to the entrance of the park. You been there before?"

"Never."

"You're in for a treat." Ned works the clutch and the gears, maneuvering the big rig out of the parking lot and back onto the highway access road. Once he's up to speed, he flicks on the radio and turns up the volume.

Ernest Tubb and Merle Haggard fill the cab with an eerie melancholia, making it hard to talk. But something about the music, rumbling down the freeway in an eighteen-wheeler, makes me feel better.

The sun is barely a dim glow on the horizon; the sky purpling toward night.

"Dusk always makes me think of my mama," Ned says. "It was always the best time of day in my house, just before dinner, when she'd be in the kitchen by herself, stirring a pot, frying some catfish. I'd wander in and kind of lean on the table, or maybe pull up a stool, and she was always so pleased that I had some interest in what she was doing. And we'd talk. I'd tell little bits and pieces about my day. It was special, but it never did last very long. By the time we'd sit at the table for dinner, my daddy would take over, even though he never did much more than grunt something no one around him could really understand. Of course, we knew when he made that sound, you had to shut up. He worked in a steel mill, up at 4:30 every morning, and by dinnertime, he was wiped out from the grit he'd been breathing all day."

There's a silence. I have a feeling Ned's waiting for me to say something, but I'm at a loss.

"You know," Ned says finally, "sometimes life just sucks. My mama toiled away in that kitchen... but Daddy, why, he'd yell at her because the beef stew didn't have enough carrots. It didn't make one bit of sense. Sometimes he'd get up from the table and shake his head in disgust but not say what he was thinking. He'd look like he was going to explode, but the bomb never went off.

"Mama could see it of course... see that fuse burning away in the whites of his eyes. She'd start bawling and he'd storm off up to bed. He'd pass out and be snoring away before she ever got there."

"That sounds... tough," I say, anxious about where our conversation might be headed; it's still a long way to Mammoth Cave.

"I run away from home when I was fourteen, and I never looked back. I'm forty-six now, and I've talked to Mama twice in that many years. I know I oughta call her, but when I pick up that receiver, I can't dial the number. I just can't."

"Why's that?"

"Because I worry she might not be there."

"Yeah. I get it."

"Both your folks alive?"

"As far as I know."

"You got that right," Ned says, "You want to know something? I'm kind of glad I gave you a ride."

"Me, too," I say. "Thank you."

I see the signs for Mammoth Cave, and Ned exits the freeway to let me out, but at the end of the ramp, he doesn't stop. He turns onto Mammoth Cave Road and says, smiling, "I'm going to take you part of the way."

After about ten miles, he pulls into an empty lot. "This is as far I can go. So, bud, this is the entrance to the park." He points through the windshield. "To get to the campground, just follow the signs. You'll get there in about fifteen or twenty minutes, depending on how fast you walk. Likely ain't no rides gonna pick you up along here. And if someone offers you a lift at this time of night, I wouldn't take it, if I was you. Anybody stops for you, tell them you're meeting a group of your friends; that's what I'd do. Morning comes, you should be fine. Somebody'll likely be on their way out of the park, and at least you can see what you might be getting yourself into. You got a tent?"

"A small one. Enough room to sit up and lie down in a sleeping bag."
"Well, all right, then. Good luck to you, bud."

I step down to the ground, handing him a five-dollar bill and thanking him for his generosity, and he shuts the cab door behind me. I sling my bag over my shoulder and hustle along. I hear the truck engine rev behind me as Ned swings the rig around in the parking lot and heads off.

MARCH 24, 1971
6:44 P.M.

THE NIGHT AIR ISN'T AS COLD AS I'D EXPECTED. The road is dark and empty. In the distance I see a few houses, visible only by the lights in the windows. Overhead a sliver of moon shimmers through a thin veil of clouds. As I walk down the blacktop park road, I feel almost as if my feet are hovering over the ground.

When I get to the campground, no one else is there. I pull a flashlight from my duffle bag and gather some twigs and sticks to start a small fire. I haven't done this since I was a Cub Scout, and it takes me several tries to get anything to catch long enough for the flames to build any heat. I scour around for bigger chunks of wood, and once the fire seems self-sustaining, I unpack my sleeping bag and the tent borrowed from Randy. I'd practiced putting it up on the grass outside the dorm, and it had always snapped together easily, but this time it doesn't work. A piece is missing, either broken off or buried in the depths of the duffle bag.

I spread the tent out flat on the ground, knowing I can use it as a tarp, like I did with Heidi, if I have to. I sit cross-legged, and the wave of euphoria I'd felt in the cab of the truck, listening to the lonesome twang of that country music, dissipates.

I dig into my duffle bag and grab a bag of trail mix, thinking the almonds, cashews, dried cranberries, and raisins will give me enough energy to go on. Then, I reach for my water bottle and discover that it's leaked onto the clean socks and underwear at the bottom of the bag.

The fire is guttering. I feed it some dry leaves to keep the flame alive and scavenge for more sticks.

The sounds of the forest close in around me. I hear the trilling hoot of an owl from a nearby treetop; small, scurrying sounds come from the underbrush. Somewhere behind me, a coyote yips and howls. I'm an intruder in a place where I don't belong, and I keep thinking the inhabitants of the forest are probably all plotting against me.

After I finish the trail mix, I empty my duffle bag onto the flattened tent, and finally find the flanges and fasteners that attach the poles together. With these in hand, I'm able to pop the tent together quickly. I hang my duffle bag and my wet clothes on a tree limb to dry overnight, but first I take the gun in its holster and stuff it into the back pocket of my jeans, checking before I do that the safety is still locked. Then I crawl into the tent and refold all my clothes and belongings into a neat pile. I place the gun down within easy reach.

I sit on my sleeping bag in a kind of lotus position, hoping for divine inspiration, but instead have stomach cramps and chills. It's as if every muscle in my gut is frozen in a huge block of ice. I hunch over, breathing deeply, and after a while my anxiety begins to thaw. Outside, embers are all that remain of my fire, and as the cinders become ash, I relax. I zip myself snugly into my sleeping bag and close my eyes, feeling like I'm on a raft in a mountain stream, floating on my back into a deep sleep. I can feel Heidi next to me, her fingers dancing through the hairs on my chest. A waltz. A two-step. A jitterbug. She's dressed in a flowing rainbow-colored robe. In her hand is a magic wand that she's waving above my head, levitating me from my bed into her outstretched arms, whirling me around until I turn into someone I want to be.

I wake up around 7:00 a.m. in a pool of sweat. It doesn't make any sense; it's as if I'm going through some kind of withdrawal from a drug that I didn't even consume. But the more I think about it, the more I crave what I don't have. I'm weighted down by a strange fatigue that makes it nearly impossible for me to concentrate. I wish I had a white cross or black beauty, something, anything to snap me awake.

The early morning air is cold and raw. My clothes are clammy. I roll over onto my side, ready to move on. But I hear an animal sniffing around outside my tent. It doesn't sound very big—a squirrel? A skunk?

It's getting louder, and it sounds bigger and bigger. Now it's pawing the tent, growling. What if it's a guard dog? A German Shepherd or a pit bull? I hold completely still, thinking that if I don't move, it will just leave me alone. But then I hear a voice, an angry man trying to quiet it down, but I can barely make out the words. I ease the gun from its holster and prepare to shoot. My heart is pounding. I unlock the safety. Can I really do this? In the back of my mind, I hear Ralph goading me: Wimp! Pussy!

I point the gun at the place the sound is coming from, outside the tent, My index finger presses lightly on the trigger, when I start having second thoughts. I know I have to do something, but my index finger won't budge. My hands are shaking so hard that I don't know what's real and what's not. Everything around me is disappearing into a blurry vision. I'm lost in a forest in the middle of a thunderstorm, where I can only sense my predators in the gritty clouds drenching the ground around me. I kneel down wrapping my jacket over my head, steadying myself with my hands, when I feel something pecking on my wrist. I pull its squirming body of out of the mud. It's crow, and just as I'm about to pet the back of its neck, it flies off.

Maybe all the speed I'd been taking is exacting its revenge.

My index finger quivers as I jerk back. I stroke the barrel of the gun with my other hand, but it doesn't make me feel any better. It's a game I don't want to play. I'm torturing myself and being tortured at the same time by someone who isn't even there.

Thrusting the barrel forward and back, up, and down, I take aim but have no idea what I'm supposed to be aiming at. The more I strain my eyes, the less I can see. I'm gasping for air.

I point the gun at my face and gaze into the coldness of its construction. In the black, abrupt hole of the barrel I see a mirror reflection of myself; all the sadness of my life stares back at me, taunting me to do something about it. I hear a voice in the distance making fun of me: Either now or never... either now or never.

I lean forward and turn the gun over slowly in my hand. I unlatch the cylinder, and when the cylinder snaps out, I see that four of the bullet chambers are empty.

Two bullets fall into the palm of my hand, and as much as I want to look at them more closely, I know I don't have time. The person outside my tent is a predator, and his dog is barking. I quickly return the bullets, one by one, to the chambers from which they had fallen, and snap the cylinder back in place, knowing that when I pull the trigger, the gun is going to fire.

Why had Randy only given me two bullets? What am I going to do if I miss my target? Am I going to try again to shoot my attacker, or am I going to just give up and shoot myself?

I remember Randy asking me if I was suicidal when I told him I was going to Mammoth Cave. Maybe he was right; maybe I need to muster the strength to finally free myself from the pain stabbing me so deep inside.

A stick pokes the side of the tent, and the man outside asks gruffly, "Anyone in there?"

My finger freezes on the trigger. My heart is beating so fast that I think the blood vessels in my forehead are about to spontaneously combust, terrified that if I fire it, I'll become someone I hate. Someone like Ralph.

My whole body goes limp, and the pistol drops from my hand into the sleeping bag.

"Max!" I hear the man shout, and the dog backs off. I reach forward and unzip the tent.

The man is wearing thick rubber boots with camo pants and a heavy denim jacket.

"Sorry to roust you out of bed," the man says. "I'm a park ranger.

Do you have a permit to camp here?"

"I... uh... got in after dark." I sit up. I feel the blood draining from my face.

"How long you staying?" the ranger asks, propping his hands firmly on his hips.

"I'm leaving this morning." I peel back my sleeping bag and straighten my shirt.

"You a vagrant?"

"Uh... no, sir." I brush back my hair with the palms of my hands.

The ranger seems to be about the age of the National Guard soldiers on the Ohio State campus. And as much as the ranger acts tough, I'm not that sure he really is. He doesn't appear to be armed. Around his waist is a beat-up canvas belt with a water canteen instead of a holster.

"Well, you're still going to have to pay the ten bucks for the permit," the ranger says sternly. "You did spend the night here?"

"Yes... okay. I've got the money."

"That's good, otherwise I'll have to call the sheriff. And the sheriff in this county, he doesn't take too kindly to hippie types like you."

"I understand."

The ranger shifts his weight from one foot to the other. "You been drinking? Your eyes are mighty bloodshot."

I don't want to make eye contact with him, but I know I have to. "No, I just had a long night, I guess. I was so tired, I just conked out."

"That so?"

"Yes! That's so."

"Look, boy, don't raise your voice at me. If you give me any trouble, I'm going to call the sheriff. You understand?"

"Just don't call me a boy," I blurt out. "You're not much older than me."

"But you're in my National Park, and as far as I'm concerned, you're trespassing." The ranger plants his feet more firmly on the ground and wags the index finger of his right hand in front of my face.

"Okay . . . okay." I reach for my wallet and hand the ranger a ten-dollar bill.

"Thank you," the ranger takes the money, and then says in a more friendly voice, "So, you going to explore the Cave?"

"I'd like to, but I . . . uh . . . don't have enough time. And I don't really have any place to store my stuff."

"Tell you what, I'll make an exception and let you stow your stuff in my office, you know, for a couple hours."

"Uh . . . that's okay," I say in a low voice. I don't want the ranger or anyone else rifling through my things and finding the gun.

As much as Mammoth Cave is something I really want to see, I realize, with this ranger gawking at me, I need to let go. Maybe the idea of Mammoth Cave is good enough. Just believing that I can do it, and somehow find my way out.

"What you carrying in that big old duffle bag?" the ranger smirks. "Looks mighty heavy."

I look at the ranger with deadpan eyes. "Just stuff, you know, clothes, extra pair of shoes, probably brought more than I need."

"You carrying a weapon?"

"No," I answer, startled by his question.

"Course you must know that carrying a concealed weapon into a National Park is against the law."

"Yes, sir. I know that." I think about pulling the gun out from my sleeping bag and handing it to him, telling him that I'm so sorry, that it isn't mine. But I know that he won't believe me, that he'll take it away from me and probably take me to the sheriff, who will arrest me.

"I think you need to be on your way." He stares at me as if he knows I'm lying. But maybe he doesn't want to take the chance. Maybe he's afraid, too. Afraid that I might be crazy enough to pull out the gun and shoot him.

The ranger fishes a pouch out of a pants pocket and stuffs a wad of chewing tobacco into his mouth as he turns away. He gazes out into the landscape as the sun breaks over the horizon and begins to burn the low haze off the grass and brush in front of us. He has an angular face with a pointed nose and a squared-off chin. His hair is clipped military-style, but he doesn't act like a soldier.

"So, you got here on foot?" the ranger says, assessing what he's going to do next.

"A trucker dropped me off."

"Hitchhiking?"

I nod, looking down.

The ranger turns and glares at me, while his dog sniffs around my feet. "Tell you what." The ranger grins unexpectedly. "You pack up your things, and I'll give you a ride up the road, drop you off someplace where you might just get yourself a ride. Where you headed?"

"Nashville."

"That so? You like country music?" The ranger chuckles. "I never would have thought a hippie like you could possibly like the kind of music I listen to all the time. They don't take too well to hippies in Nashville."

I think about telling him about Bob Dylan and the rockers who were going to Nashville to record, but I don't see the point. I want to get away, just as much as the ranger wants me to leave the park. I start packing up my sleeping bag, stuffing the gun inside, and taking down the tent, jamming everything into my duffle bag as quickly as I can. I feel the ranger watching my every move, no doubt plotting in his head what he's going to do if I pull out a gun and point it at him.

About ten feet from where I'm standing, I see two crows; one bows and struts forward, spreading its wings and tail, while the other preens its feathers.

"You okay?" the ranger asks.

"Just . . . fine. I mean, this place is amazing. Must be the air."

"You on drugs?"

"No . . . uh . . . no sir."

The crows stretch their necks and their beaks touch.

My knees are wobbly, and I almost topple over.

The ranger grabs my arm.

"I... I'm... okay," I stutter. "Probably just a little dehydrated." The ranger's dog ambles over to me and sniffs the back of my legs.

The ranger hands me his canteen and says, "Here, take a little of this. It's only water."

"I... I..." The words won't form in my mouth.

"Don't worry, I'm not going to poison you, though it's mighty tempting. Don't worry. If a little water don't help, I'm going to drive you to the closest emergency room and get you checked out."

I take the canteen from his hand, lift it to my mouth, and swallow hard.

"You sure you ain't on drugs?"

My mind's drifting around, trying to find a way to focus. I'm in the moment and outside of it at the same time.

"You in some kind of cult?"

"No. No!"

I search the landscape for answers. I look up, swiveling my head, trying to take in everything around me, recognizing the absurdity of what I'm doing, but not knowing exactly what to do about it. "Please, understand, I.... I just can't find the right words."

"Sounds like a mess to me," the ranger says, scratching his head.

"Do you have a gun?" I ask timidly.

"Man, what's your problem? I'm only trying to help you, get you back on that highway you're craving in one piece."

"Seriously. Okay? I know you have a gun, and to be honest, I kind of feel like you're itching to use it."

The ranger stiffens up. "That's right. You nailed it. I know how to defend myself against rodents like you. I have an ankle holster. But do you have any idea which ankle? Ha! Got you there, ass wipe. You want to see my gun? Well, I'm not going to show it to you unless I have to.

And then you're dead meat."

I reach into my duffle bag.

The ranger is on edge. "You need to take that hand of yours out very slowly and show it to me."

I can feel Randy's gun in my hand. My head is swirling. Part of me wants to jerk it out and thrust it into his face.

The ranger is at gawking at me. "I'm a patient man," the ranger says, "but you're pushing me too far."

I take a deep breath and close my eyes.

My hand relaxes and I look up at the ranger. "Am I a coward?"

"What's that? You need to see a doctor?"

"Please, tell me. Am I coward?"

The ranger snickers. "Well, I guess you're going to decide that one for yourself. I know you're all hopped on drugs. And I could shoot you faster than I can snap my fingers. Now, take that hand of yours out of the duffle bag. I'm going to count to three and if I don't see your hand, you're in big trouble."

I let go of the gun, and slowly pull my hand out, and when he sees I'm not armed, he kicks over the duffle bag. His dog starts barking.

"Listen closely," the ranger says, "I'm going to give you one more chance to get out of here, without me having to call the sherriff. To be honest, I don't have time for this shit. If I really thought you had a gun, it would be a lot different."

I stand up, stunned. "Okay, I'll leave."

"I was going to give you a ride, but I done changed my mind. You might contaminate the seat."

I swallow hard, as if I'm in the deep end of a pool and can't swim. I'm thrashing around in my head.

The ranger picks up my duffle bag and pushes it into my chest.

I have nothing to say.

I turn around and start walking away.

The ranger climbs into his pickup truck and slams the door. I glare at him, and he growls, "I don't ever want to see your face around here again."

MARCH 25, 1971
RIDE #27
8:48 A.M.

BY THE TIME I GET TO THE ENTRY RAMP OF THE FREEWAY, the cold morning air warms up.

I hear a crow cawing in the distance, while another circles overhead.

A red pickup swerves toward me and slows down. The driver screams. "Hippies! Better dead than alive!" before he speeds past. Others honk, and one guy wearing a beat-up baseball cap and grimy overalls empties his ashtray from the cab of his tractor as he chugs by on the shoulder of the interstate before turning onto a gravel road. But instead of avoiding eye contact, I look straight at him.

The brightness of the day takes hold.

Crows coming from different directions flock into the sky.

After about an hour, a black Cadillac slows to a stop. The tinted passenger's window hums down to reveal an old Black man. I peer inside; the driver has on a suit that looks like something an undertaker might wear to work. He forces a little grin. "Only going as far as Nashville. About ninety some miles from here."

"Great!" I say, relieved and completely grateful. "That's exactly where I'm headed."

He flips open the trunk and directs me to put my duffle bag inside. The interior of the car is meticulously clean and smells like pine needles.

"Traffic's light," he says, and I smile. We look at each other, not sure exactly what to talk about, but at ease with being together, acknowledging each other with a kind of mutual respect that seems to grow as the miles pass by.

Sitting next to him, I marvel at the strength and determination of his profile, tight wrinkles furrowed across his brow and a little twinkle in his eyes. His radio is tuned to a blues show on WDIA in Memphis. The stinging guitar runs carry me deep into an unknown place within me, where I struggle to reconcile a ceasefire with all the uncertainties in my life. I want to tell him what's going through my head, but the music is so loud that talking is nearly impossible.

The lyrics of B. B. King's "The Thrill is Gone" ring so true, transforming the landscape in front of me. The sun streams through the rear window of the Cadillac as the Nashville skyline comes into view. I want to get out of the car on the freeway so I can meditate on the view, and just as I'm about to ask the driver to stop, I change my mind.

Heidi was right. The Nashville skyline isn't much. But it's just enough. Revealing to me its deepest truth.

In the midday light, forgiveness washes over me. Forgiveness for what's not there. Forgiveness for Adriana. Forgiveness for me.

The old man exits onto a feeder road into downtown and we pass the Greyhound bus station.

"Excuse me, sir. Can I get out here? I'm going to the bus station."

The old man lowers the volume on the radio. "Sure thing, boss. Where'd you say you going?"

"Home."

"Where's that?"

"Columbus, Ohio."

"That so?" The old man scratches his head. "Ain't that north of here? I thought you were coming from the north when I picked you up."

"Yes sir."

"You got a long way to go."

I lean back and smile. My hitchhiking days are over.

Standing on the sidewalk in front of the bus station, I rub my hands together. The temperature is dropping, and I'm cold.

I go inside. The bus ticket to Columbus costs twenty-six dollars, and just when I'm about to pay, I decide to get a ticket to Covington, Kentucky, thinking that when I get there, I'm going to call Heidi to see if she wants to join me for a hot brown.

"That's right, a hot brown," I say aloud, and the sales agent looks at me like I'm crazy. She hands me my ticket and I hurry to catch the next bus.

Once I get into my seat, I push my duffle bag between my feet, and Randy's gun thumps onto the floorboard. I reach down and stuff it deeper into my wadded-up clothes. I know Randy was only trying to help me, but in the end he had it wrong. The gun didn't give me the power to get where I needed to be; it was deciding not to use it that matters the most.

I lean against the window. I'm tired, but I can't sleep. Sister Ethel is singing inside me.

'Tis the gift to be simple, 'tis the gift to be free
'Tis the gift to come down where we ought to be.

Sister Ethel's voice grows faint. Some of the words are muffled. I strain my ears to listen. As she nears the end of the song, she whispers ever so softly for me to join in.

When true simplicity is gained
To bow and to bend we shan't be ashamed.

The bus pulls away from the station, weaving through downtown. Near the on-ramp to the freeway, the driver slows to a stop, yielding to oncoming traffic. I stand up, steadying myself on the handrail above my seat, and step cautiously toward the back window. The Nashville skyline yellow and orange in the distance as the sky clouds over and the buildings on the horizon disappear from view.

I start humming.

To turn, turn will be our delight
Till by turning, turning we come 'round right.

I've made it to the mountaintop. Now, I have to figure out how to get down. Or do I? Maybe I can stay in this place. Forever.

Alan Govenar is an award-winning writer, poet, playwright, photographer, and filmmaker. He is director of Documentary Arts, a nonprofit organization he founded to advance essential perspectives on historical issues and diverse cultures. Govenar is a Guggenheim Fellow and the author of more than forty books, including *Boccaccio in the Berkshires* (2021), *Deep Ellum and Central Track* (coauthored with Jay Brakefield, 2023), and *See That My Grave Is Kept Clean* (coauthored with Kip Lornell, 2023), all from Deep Vellum.